TO THE
ENDS
OF THE
EARTH

"I found *To the Ends of the Earth* so engrossing that I stayed up to the wee hours of the morning to finish reading it in one night. An accurate use of history."

Dr. E. Glenn Hinson
Professor, Church History
Baptist Theological Seminary

"Readers of *The Robe, The Big Fisherman*, and other historical novels by such authors as Taylor Caldwell will thoroughly enjoy *To the Ends of the Earth*. Bunn intricately weaves several sub-plots throughout the novel, thus keeping the interest of the reader."

Christian Retailing

"Bunn skillfully paces action, dialogue, and background, and keeps readers wondering what will happen next. The story has everything that popular Christian fiction should have: adventure, a love story, and characters who mature in Christ."

Bookstore Journal

"The drama accelerates at the pace of a good detective story, with intrigue at every turn. An exciting historical adventure, a vivid story."

A Closer Look

"This compelling novel captured my attention. What a delight it was to enter this gripping and historically accurate story. It gives an excellent understanding of an important period in the development of Christian faith."

Dr. Stan Nelson
Professor of Theology
Golden Gate Seminary

"Peril-filled adventure, romance, injustice, trial, loyalty; *To the Ends of the Earth* is a great choice."

Troy Broadcasting

"What an excellent read. *To the Ends of the Earth* puts flesh on dry bones and brings enlightenment to this period of church history."

Rev. Keith Fraser
Director
Arab World Missions

"*To the Ends of the Earth* was truly exceptional. God has truly blessed Bunn with talent, and is using him mightily to spread His message."

Dr. Paul Garnett
Coordinator of Missionaries to East Germany

"This new historical thriller is an exciting and dramatic read!"

Peterborough Evening Telegraph (UK)

ADVENTURE, ROMANCE, AND THE QUEST FOR WISDOM LEAD THEM...

TO THE ENDS OF THE EARTH

A NOVEL OF THE BYZANTINE EMPIRE

T. DAVIS BUNN

THOMAS NELSON PUBLISHERS
Nashville • Atlanta • London • Vancouver
Printed in the United States of America

This is a work of fiction. Any similarity to real life in the scenes, characters, timing, and events is merely coincidence.

Published in Nashville, Tennessee, by Thomas Nelson, Inc., Publishers, and distributed in Canada by Word Communications, Ltd., Richmond, British Columbia.

Library of Congress Cataloging-in-Publication Data

Bunn, T. Davis, 1952—
    To the ends of the earth : a novel / T. Davis Bunn.
        p.   cm.
    "A Janet Thoma book."
    ISBN 0-7852-7898-2 (hc)
    ISBN 0-7852-7214-3 (tp)
    I. Title.
PS3552.U4718T6   1996
813'.54—dc20   95–34248
                                                            CIP

Printed in the United States of America

2 3 4 5 6 — 01 00 99 98 97 96

For Paul and Ruth McCommon

who teach and shape church history
ever mindful of the Great Commission

Author's Note

In the year A.D. 338, when this story opens, Africa was the name of a Roman province (see map). This wide band of fertile coastland, bordered by the provinces of Egypt and Numidia, makes up what today are segments of Tunisia, Libya, and Algeria. This region was the breadbasket of Rome, a rich and fertile land containing grand estates, thriving cities, and tremendous wealth.

Acknowledgments

Inspired by my interest in Byzantine history, this novel was developed over several years of research and reflection. Its final crafting was made possible through the kind support of Oxford University. A word of explanation about the university system is required before thanking the people involved. Founded over seven hundred years ago, Oxford is made up of a series of colleges, each a semiautonomous body. Most of the university professors and lecturers are members of a particular college's teaching staff. The colleges are each headed by a director, called the Principal. A student enrolls in a college and has his or her studies guided by a personal tutor. These tutors are often the leading authorities in the world on their subjects, and the challenge of working under them is enormous.

My invitation to study at Oxford was arranged by the Reverend Paul Fiddes, Principal of Regent's Park College. Regent's Park is Oxford's Baptist college. My official tutor was Dr. Donald Sykes, Honorary Fellow and former Principal of Mansfield College. Mansfield is affiliated with the United Reformed Church for the training of ordinands.

I am also most grateful to Bishop Kallistos of Pembroke College, who made time during his tenure as President of Oxford

University's Theology Faculty to offer both instruction and guidance.

Dr. Tom Weinandy, OFMCap, of Greyfriars, gave a series of lectures on patristic thought (the teachings of the early church fathers) which was extremely valuable. Dr. Greg Woolf of Brasenose College also assisted mightily with his lectures on economic and social conditions within the late Roman Empire. And Dr. Peter Hinchliff, Regius Professor of Ecclesiastical History at Christ Church, was most helpful with his introduction to the world of the early church.

My wife, Isabella, was completing a Master of Philosophy degree in Christian Ethics at Oxford while I researched and wrote this story. As with all my books, her assistance and loving support were invaluable.

It would not be possible to list all the individuals who assisted with my field trips to the regions covered by this story. I would therefore like to simply offer my heartfelt thanks to all with whom this work brought me into contact.

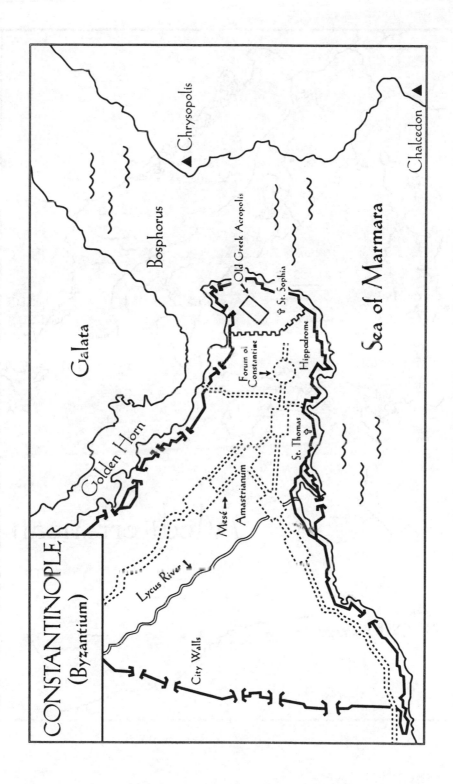

CONSTANTINOPLE
(Byzantium)

City Walls

Lycus River

Mesé

Amastrianum

Golden Horn

Galata

Bosphorus

Chrysopolis

Chalcedon

Old Greek Acropolis

† St. Sophia

Forum of Constantine

Hippodrome

St. Thomas

Sea of Marmara

Adriatic Sea

▲ Rome

GREECE

Ionian
Sea

Carthage
SICILY
▲
Syracuse

Pylos ▲

Mediterranean

AFRICA
PROVINCE

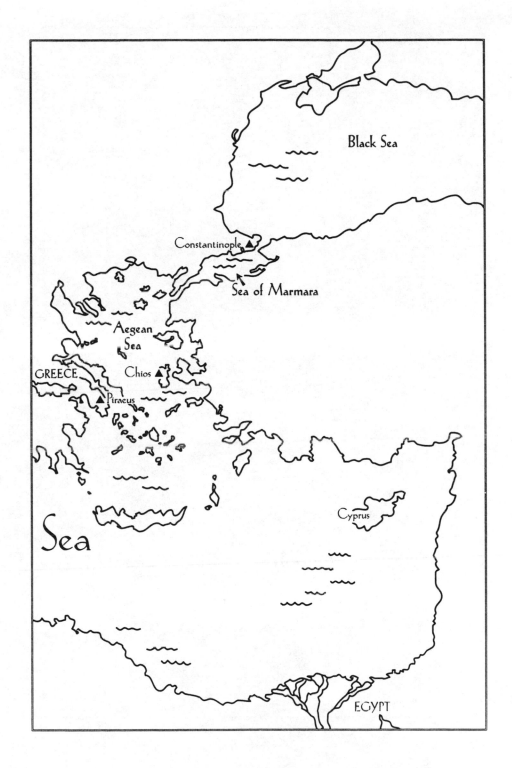

CHAPTER I

The aft hold was fetid with the stink of salted fish and bilge water and sweat. The two bodies grappled in absolute silence, perspiration making their skin as slick as the floor. Their curses were whispered with explosive breaths, their grunts of concentrated effort softer than the creak of the ship's timbers. Feet scrambled and slipped and clenched for tocholds. They wore nothing but the wrestler's coiled loincloth, little more than a thick cotton rope with which each strained to lift the other off balance and slam him down on the hold's floor. Overhead the oars cranked out a continuous rhythm, masking their noise and motions from all those on board.

Travis knew he was outclassed. But there had been little to occupy his idle hours besides studying his opponent's moves. For the eleven days of their voyage, he had spent his bedridden hours holding back, lying as still as he could, drinking in the sun and the good sea air, harboring his strength for this hour of trial, and planning how to win.

The flickering torch transformed their shadows into the writhings of an enraged dragon. Travis felt the boat rise over yet another roller, and timed his groan for the crest. Raffa responded as he had every morning since their training began, slackening his grip, bearing down just enough to keep up the challenge, intent on draining away every last bit of Travis' energy before halting.

Travis kept himself loose, limp. He let the wave carry them down to hit hard at the trough, then leaned his weight upon Raffa. When the hardened warrior slipped off balance, Travis instantly attacked. He rammed forward with all the strength he had left, careening himself and his opponent headlong into the gunnel, hearing the grunt of surprise and feeling the iron-hard muscles lock in angry response.

But Travis was prepared for that as well. While Raffa was still tense and intent on attack, he went limp again, this time totally, allowing the warrior's assault to go unmet. Travis fell back and down, pulling Raffa with him, drawing up his legs to his chest and planting his feet in the man's unyielding belly, hearing Raffa break their silence with a roar of fury, and knowing even before he catapulted Raffa up and over his head that he had won. Travis allowed his own roll to continue, moving so fast he was there to meet the warrior when he landed headfirst on the scummy planking. He planted his imaginary dagger in Raffa's chest, then rolled onto his back and lay there heaving. For the first time in his life, he had won.

"You young scamp," Raffa huffed. "Where did you learn a move like that?"

"I thought it up myself," Travis said, his chest going like bellows.

"Well, it won't work a second time, I can promise you that." Raffa heaved himself over, stood with effort. "Can you make it alone?"

"Yes." Travis rolled over, tried to push himself erect, but felt fatigue rise like a crashing wave. "Perhaps not."

Strong hands gripped and hefted him up. Raffa wrapped one arm about his chest, matched him stride for stride. "You did well today, lad."

Travis nodded and wiped at sweat. Praise from Raffa came so seldom he was unsure how to respond.

"Very well. Tricked me out of my boots, that one."

Travis unleashed the bolt, leaned back as the overhead portal swung down. "Perhaps the worst is over."

"Aye. The healer was right for once." Raffa boosted his young friend into the fresh air. Then he drew himself up, and pulled the portal closed. "'Rest and sweat,' he said, 'with all the water your body can hold. Only way to cleanse the system of poison.'"

Poison. Travis stood gripping the stern railing, his chest still heaving. He heard the oars' rhythmic lapping, felt the eyes on him. Most were friendly, some were not. There were spies on board, there had to be. Poison. The thought had fueled his recovery through those pain-wracked days. That and a desire for vengeance.

A session with Raffa always ended like this, with him sweat-drenched and barely able to stand. Travis watched Raffa lower a bucket overboard, then gasped as Raffa sluiced frigid water over his shoulders. Another bucket, a third, a fourth, and he felt strong enough to make it to his pallet unaided. Travis wrapped the waiting cloth about his shivering form and lay down with a soft groan.

He did not sleep. He felt as though he had spent the entire voyage drifting in and out of unwelcome fever-dreams. He lay and watched the sun rock back and forth through his overhead canopy, the jerky passage timed to the waves' roll, and willed strength back into his shaking limbs.

Their departure had come a scarce two weeks after the poisoning, and he had been carried aboard on a pallet. At first, their daily sessions had been in full display of the men slaving over the oars. Raffa worked each limb in turn, pulling and bending and stretching and massaging, working the poison from the muscles and joints. Travis had dreaded those endless hours, lying there with gritted teeth, sweat streaming and pooling about him. He had finished those sessions more dead than alive, so spent he could not even complain as Raffa's rough hands rolled him about while changing the drenched linens. Shamed by his weakness and his pain, he had wanted to close the tent's curtains, but Raffa had advised otherwise. It was only when Travis saw the men greet him as one of their own that he realized the wisdom of this public display. Now, as he sprawled upon the canopied pallet, there were grins and cheerful queries over who had won. Today he finally had something to report.

As renewed strength gradually wiped away the worst of his exhaustion, Travis thought back to the day before the poisoning. His father had summoned Travis to the rock-lined office, an event so rare he had been left weak-kneed, especially because of the purpose. Travis' twenty-third birthday had just passed. His half-brothers had both been sent away when they had reached the age of eighteen. With each of his own birthdays, Travis had dreaded the summons and the order to depart. The two half-brothers had been sent to centers of the empire, there to cultivate power and wealth, set into place with substantial endowment. But now the estate was no longer powerful, the wealth no longer there to give.

Yet Travis did not want to leave.

Cletus' office was an extension of the main barn, and reflected his military life more than any other part of the estate. The furnishings were austere and uncomfortable, the setting stern. Faded campaign pennants hung from one wall, the same wall that supported a simple soldier's shield and braces and pike. The infamous Roman short-sword hung from a weather-beaten belt beside the door. Travis' half-brothers had loathed that room and all it stood for. Whenever they could, they had made fun of Cletus and his simple beginnings, taking even more delight when they saw how the antics wounded Travis.

The estate was a green and fertile place of cool sea breezes and steady rainfall, located some two weeks' sailing down the African coast from Carthage. The land was not theirs. It belonged to a consul, whose life Cletus had saved during battle. As a reward, the consul had granted Cletus the position of estate manager for life, and on for the life of his son. Travis wanted nothing more than to continue the work there that his father had begun.

The day of his summons, his father had come immediately to the point. "It is your time. Beyond that. I have held you here too long. I want you to travel to Constantinople."

Despite himself, Travis felt a quiver of excitement. Constantinople was at the other end of the Mediterranean, the new capital of the empire. Though a mere dozen years old, the city was already sparking legends of its grandeur, and had come to be known by a second title, New Rome. But the unknown's appeal was not enough. His place was here. He drew himself up and protested, "I don't want to go."

"What you want and do not want is irrelevant," Cletus declared flatly. "Look around you. We are finished here."

Travis subsided. He had seen this truth for himself. Their holdings, once rich and prosperous, were gradually falling to ruin. Slowly at first, then with increasing speed and brutality, the estate's vibrancy and air of abundance were being drained away. Slaves and freemen both were being conscripted for a few weeks' work on public projects, never to return. Tax men appeared with Roman legionnaires to reinforce their ever-greater demands for cash and produce.

"If the end is not now, then in three years," Cletus went on. "If not three, then five. The prices set by the authorities for our produce do not allow us profit. Yet the taxes continue to rise. The copper money is worthless, silver almost impossible to find, gold a legend from some earlier age. Prices for what we must buy continue to soar."

Each year they were ordered to supply the armies garrisoned in the province of Africa with certain amounts of grain and olive oil and other farm products. Even more was acquired to be sent to Rome. Prices for these goods were set and could not be negotiated. With each passing year, the amounts they were ordered to supply continued to increase. Market prices rose steeply, yet the amounts paid by official procurers remained stagnant. Taxes, which were paid according to the amount of land farmed and not income, also continued to rise. And more than half the shipments sent to Carthage did not arrive, stolen by pirates.

They were slowly being strangled.

"Our patron the consul is dead," Cletus went on. "Three years now I have written the son, begging his aid. I have received no reply. My letters to your half-brothers have also gone unanswered."

Travis was the youngest of three sons, the next in line seven years older. The other two had reached their eighteenth year during times of prosperity, and since both detested the life of a farmer, they had been sent off with full purses, assigned to go and set up stations. One was in Carthage, the other in Rome. Travis loathed them both with equal intensity.

"I am therefore sending you away." Cletus held up his hand to stop Travis' objection. "First to Carthage, where you are to ask the help of your half-brother."

"Fabian will not give it."

"He must. If nothing else, a loan of the money with which I sent him on his way. I hear he is doing well. That much he can certainly afford. From Brutus in Rome I have heard nothing at all for almost three years." Cletus slid a sealed envelope across the table. "You are to deliver this letter directly into Fabian's hands."

Travis remained reluctant to touch it. "I do not like asking him for anything."

"Nonetheless you shall do so. From Carthage, I want you to travel straight to Constantinople. Go and find out why this is happening to us, if you can. I have prepared another letter for you to deliver to the consul's son. If he will see you."

"He shall see me. He has to. You have served his family for thirty years."

"And more. But rumors tell me the son is not the father. So I assign to you a second task. If he will not see you, or will not help, then you must find for us a new home. Constantinople is a new city. A time of growth means opportunity. You shall search out such an opportunity and establish for us a foothold."

Travis stared at the letter, recalled the pride with which Fabian had loaded his two swollen sacks of silver and set off for Carthage. Since then he had not returned once, and had only written on two occasions. Both times he had asked for additional funds. The first time his father had obliged, though it had been difficult. The second time Cletus had refused point-blank. Since then there had been no word, except through passing traders. Travis asked bitterly, "With what am I supposed to seek these opportunities?"

"You will not go entirely empty-handed. Our dye process remains a secret and thus untaxed. I now have ten amphorae full of the purple, which I am sending with you."

Travis felt a flicker of hope at the news. Where their farm met the coast, the sea had carved a broad natural bay. There his father had set servants at digging a series of deep pits. Other hands freed from farming unprofitable land had gathered African sea mollusks. Travis had worked alongside them, burying layer after layer of the tiny sea animals. When the stench grew strong enough to blow his head off and ruin his sense of smell for a week, the pits were excavated, and the resulting mulch ground down to produce a treacly runoff. In all the known world, this process was the only source of purple dye. It was a color so rare it was used upon the emperor's robes and was thus always referred to as royal purple.

"I am sending Raffa and his men with you," Cletus said. "There is as little here for them as there is for us. You must try and bind them to you, find some way to show that their loyalty can still be repaid."

But Travis was not yet ready to leave behind the other news. The purified dye was worth its weight in silver. Amphorae, clay vessels used for storing wine and oil, stood as high as a man's chest. "Ten amphorae is a small fortune."

"It is all we have left. All I have to show for thirty years of tending the consul's African estates." His expression was grim, his tone bitter. "I had always expected this to be the place where I would see out the remainder of my days. Now I am not so sure." He focused once more on his youngest son. "You are not simply to sell this, mind. You are to use it as a basis to gain us a new foothold."

"An opportunity. I understand."

Cletus rose to his feet, indicating that the interview was over. But as Travis stood and turned away, his father stopped him. "You must bind Raffa's men to you," he repeated.

Travis turned back. "But how—"

"A team," Cletus repeated. "They are going far afield. The world will be new and uncertain and full of danger. They must learn to see you as a trusted leader, and themselves as a strong unit. A team able to withstand the threats of the unknown. So long," he added, "as they remain together and loyal to you."

"I think I see," Travis said slowly.

"They are to become frontline soldiers again. On the edge, far from home, and alone. They must come to see a reason to serve you as they have served me. And there is only one way to do that." Cletus stood ramrod straight, his voice a soldier's soft bark. "You must show them that you can deliver."

▲▲▲

Travis raised himself from the pallet and walked to the boat railing. He willed for his limbs to strengthen, and looked out over the sweating oarsmen. Raffa's men were interspersed among the others, serving regular shifts with the seamen. They had been called Raffa's men for as long as he could remember, though none had arrived with the warrior, and only one was actually from his regiment. Yet they shared a soldier's heritage and held to their freeman status with pride, accepting orders only from his father or Raffa. Until now.

Travis dipped a ladle into the water bucket at his feet, drank his fill, and reflected that his plan needed to bear fruit, and soon.

There had been no outright grumbling. Not yet. After all, they had themselves agreed to the journey. But the atmosphere was tense, and growing more so with each passing day. These were not young men free of ties and hungry for adventure. They were seasoned veterans, hardened by years of garrison duty and battle, embittered by a system that had repaid them with words and worthless scrip.

They had agreed to this voyage because of his father's request and Travis' pledge of shares in any booty. They were wise enough in the ways of this world to see that there was no future for them upon the estate.

Yet already they missed their families, their comforts, their routine. And they made their anger known as only old soldiers could. Orders were carried out in sullen slowness, and only after moments of tense deliberation. Duties were shirked. Time at the oars was now openly despised. Time at leisure was spent in quiet discussion, the glances cast his way ranging from resentment to burning contempt.

Travis turned, so that his back was to the ship, and stared out over the open waters. He could watch the sea for hours. Clouds became his friends, easing the sun's weight and dressing the waters in gentle shadow-colors. Each hour brought a different creation, all of infinite horizons. Sunsets were worlds of rich copper and diamond-bladed water-mirrors, with crests of foaming gold. Evening was a universe of stars, when sleep came and went in waves as gentle as the boat's motions. At night Travis floated upon a bed of liquid black, the wind echoing the half-formed mysteries within his mind.

The shoreline varied from day to day. Green farmlands alternated with tongues of desert that reached out from the south, laying a dun-colored swath as broad as a day's sail was long. On such days the heat rose to consume them, an invisible adversary who lived in the endless empty silence. Then the gentle green returned, and with it reassuring signs of life. Then hills, then more farmland, then another great stretch of golden emptiness. Until the past few days, when the shoreline had been transformed by tall and menacing cliffs.

When Travis had first arrived at the ship, the ship's captain, a seafaring gnome called Arubal, had watched the men lower his litter to the deck. He had accepted the letter from Travis' father, read it, and tossed it to his mate. Arubal had turned and contemptuously spit over the side before demanding, "So you're the cur of Cletus?"

"I am."

"Pity you didn't inherit your father's strength. How much do you know of the sea?"

Travis struggled up on one elbow, cursing the weakness that imprisoned him. "Almost nothing."

"Never take your eye off her. That's your first lesson."

Arubal was a small man, compact and square and solid. He had the blackened skin and steady eye of one wed to the sea. "She's a jealous goddess, and if she catches your attention wandering she'll do you in right quick."

"I want to go—"

"I know all about that," Arubal snapped back. "Your father himself was down here not five days ago. You'll be wanting to stop first in Carthage. I told him the same thing I tell you. The waters between here and Carthage are cursed. We should make way straight for Sicily, and from there to Constantinople."

"We can't," Travis replied quietly. "I have to stop in Carthage."

"Then we're all dead men," the captain declared flatly. "The sea god has pirate minions scattered all along this coast, and they'll be sending my ship to a watery grave, and us to the doom of a slavemaster's whip." Another spit to leeward. "I told your father the same thing, and he called in a lifetime of favors and promised me a bag of silver. You have it?"

Travis nodded at Raffa, who hefted the sack tied to his waistbelt.

The captain snorted glumly. "So it's adventure at sea you're after, is it?"

"I have a plan," Travis said quietly. "The pirates have been a thorn in our side as well."

But Arubal was not ready to hear him. "Well, you had best pray to all your puny landlocked gods that you don't pay for your thrills with your blood."

Travis signaled to Raffa, who offered one rock-hard arm and helped him rise to a seated position. Travis waited until the captain reluctantly met his eye, then quietly told him what he wanted.

Arubal responded with a more careful inspection. "Substitute half my men for yours? They'll be bitter about it, make no mistake. Wouldn't put it past the first of them to sell the information of where we're headed."

Travis nodded. "Exactly."

The assent caught him off guard. "So what kind of men are these?"

"Men you will like," Travis replied. "Men you can trust."

The eyes narrowed. "Not an hour's worth of experience on the oar among the lot, I'll wager."

"Nor sail," Travis agreed. "And their first time under way should be when we leave harbor."

"I'd be the laughingstock of the whole coast," Arubal protested.

"That," Travis replied, "is exactly what I have in mind."

Travis sighed his way from his reverie, eased muscles which tended to knot whenever he remained in one position for too long. He glanced landward, saw only sheer rock ridges crashing down to half-submerged stone teeth. Where they might find a place to moor for the night was anyone's guess. Since the port of Kalidia, three days back, the coastline had resembled a storm-tossed sea. Beaches had disappeared. Tall cliffs now fell sharp and jagged to the water's edge.

Their last easy night had been spent beneath the Kalidia fortress. The harbor had been full of grain barges, readying the spring harvest for export to Rome. Three full legions crammed the surrounding beaches and filled the town to overflowing. They had anchored well away from the activity, watching as one grain caravan after another arrived and began off-loading, all under heavy guard.

The arrival of the African grain shipment was a major event in Rome's calendar. It was the lifeline for much of the common populace. A safe shipment meant both food and stable prices for another season. Travis had stood his first watch that night, or part of it, and had observed the countless watch fires being lit. In the last light of a dying day, it had appeared that the entire coastline was ringed by flames and glinting armor. Such shipments remained safe only because of the soldiers' constant vigilance. Yet that massing of Rome's might left the rest of the coastlands unprotected, a vacuum within which the pirates could move at will.

Leaning against the rail, his face turned seawards, Travis sensed Raffa's approach. The old soldier eased himself down beside Travis on the seaward railing, and murmured, "Watchers."

Travis felt struck by a lightning bolt of alarm. Before he could rise and turn, however, Raffa stilled him with one hand and the word, "Wait."

After an endless time, Raffa finally said, "All right, easy now. Roll about and stretch. Fine. Look to your left. A tree grows in a rough cleft, the roots clinging to the rock."

"I see it."

"Walk your eyes ten paces to the right. A knoll with a topknot of shrub."

"One of the bushes wears a blue turban." Travis found his breath suddenly hard to come by. "And a broad-beaked fellow perches by the nearest tree."

"They have found us," Raffa said, his back still to the coast-line. "Or we them."

Travis stretched again, this time fighting against tired muscles turned overtense, and said quietly, "Prepare the men."

They finally anchored in the day's gloaming. The entire boat sighed with relief when yet another point revealed not more cliffs falling remorselessly into unprotected waters, but rather a natural harbor. The point threw a muscled arm sea-wards, offering a windbreak twice the height of their mast. A thousand paces farther north, a row of rocky teeth stopped the currents from pushing them onto shore. In between these two barriers the waters were relatively placid, the wind gentled.

As the anchor sank home, Raffa said, "I'd wager we're far from the first victims to choose this as their final haven."

Raffa was soft-spoken and excruciatingly polite. His de-meanor was pleasant, his smile ready. But his hands bore the coarse imprint of sword and spear, from years of war and hundreds of battles. His features were rough and strong and brutally handsome. He was not big. He did not need to be. His compact frame held a concentration of force so potent that even the grandest of centu-rions addressed him with caution. His hair had grayed to match his watchful eyes. The same eyes that gave nothing at all away, save a constant watchful courtesy.

Travis motioned for the captain to join them and said, "Raffa thinks this is a trap."

"Aye, this seabed is littered with the bones of the unwary," Arubal agreed. "And the air heavy with the stench of their unavenged deaths."

"If they come after us," Raffa went on, "it will be tonight."

"We're anchored far enough out that no arrows launched from shore can reach us," the captain offered. "And the men are taut as bows at full reach." He looked about, muttered, "This is what they've been waiting for, a perfect haven for surprise and death. I wager there are spies on permanent guard back at Kalidia, just waiting for the likes of us."

"Have the men take great care," Travis warned, trying to keep his voice as steady as the others. "Pass the word. No searching the banks, no weapons, no warning that we are ready."

"I'll be having your own men stow the oars and sail. That should lower the pirates' guard a notch, seeing as how these soldiers of yours still move like novices on first watch. For all our sakes, I hope they fight better than they sail." Arubal started to turn away, then stopped to looked hard at Travis. "You've grown up on this voyage. I wager by the time we arrive in Carthage, I'll call you lad no longer." His customary pessimism resurfaced with a scowl. "That is, if we arrive at all."

In principle, the Roman Empire encircled the entire Mediterranean Sea, from the Gates of Hercules to the wastelands of the destroyed city called Jerusalem. In reality, there were gaps, especially along the southern coasts, and these gaps grew broader with each time of upheaval. And just such a time was upon them now.

For over two centuries, a change of emperor had meant bloodshed and strife and rivals vying for ultimate power. In their struggle to ascend the throne, pretenders drew legions away from their customary watchdog duties and flung them headlong into bloody struggle, pitting Roman against Roman.

In such times, breaches in the empire's armor became gaping holes. Pirates and bandits and raiding parties spawned and spread with raging abandon.

Eleven months before, Constantine the Great had died. His passage had sent shock waves throughout the empire. Since then, generals and relatives had vied for power, moving legions about like game pieces, leaving the entire empire trembling with fear of what might yet come.

Chaos already snared the empire's outer reaches in a festering grip. In the provinces of Africa and Numidia, travelers upon inland roads were threatened by raiding desert tribes called Berbers. Only caravans traveling under the consul's orders, and thus shielded by a detachment of Roman soldiers, moved in relative safety. Towns and villages scattered about the vast fertile regions of the interior were all but cut off, save for the twice-yearly grain shipments.

This should have meant that produce from Cletus' own estate, situated as it was closer to the sea, would rise in price. But the warring legates demanded ever more grain to feed the legions, grain taken at swordpoint and at prices kept artificially low. So as prices rose for all the estate was forced to buy, the value of their produce did not. And what they did manage to produce and keep from the tax men, more often than not was lost to the pirates. The result was a slow death of the richest farmland in the Roman world.

Pirates had infiltrated the lost reaches between Alexandria and Carthage since the empire's early days. With the imperium fraying about the edges, they now stalked ever closer to the city-state's borders. Spies roamed the streets and hovered about the ports and reported all back to their masters. Here as elsewhere, honest men paid the price for the empire's gradual collapse.

●●●

With the coming of night, the wind died. The sea became so calm as to appear oiled into a mirror for the stars. A single cloud rested overhead, a silver shadow-island floating in a heavenly sea. The loudest sound was the gentle creak of timbers. The air was close and filled with the overpowering odors of fifty men living in cramped quarters. They lay sprawled in the haphazard carelessness of the undisciplined. The sentry leaned against the bowsprit, his slouched and snoring form clearly silhouetted against the night. He had not moved since hissing his quiet warning.

The pirates attacked in the last hour of night watch, when the world was at its darkest. They came in three longboats, the oars greased and moving in timed cadence, barely seeming to disturb the water. From a slit in the stern-tent's side panel, Travis watched and cursed the fates who had destined him to face his first time in combat lying down.

Their boat tilted slightly as the first pirate nimbly hoisted himself over the side, a hawser gripped firmly between his teeth. As his head appeared over the transom he froze and searched the shadows. There was no movement, no sound save for a single groan, a snore, a creak as the boat shifted over a solitary wave. The pirate turned, motioned once, then climbed over and made his line fast. Other shadows rose and slipped onto the ship, silent and dark save for the occasional glint of starlight on blade.

The shadows became so crowded along the side that newcomers had to shoulder their way in, and the first covey began drifting out among the sprawled forms. Travis looked toward where Raffa crouched behind the brazier, and received the single nod. He raised himself up on one elbow and shouted with all the pent-up tension that the waiting had caused, *"Now!"*

18

His word was caught up by fifty voices roaring in reply. Short-swords flashed and bit. Screams of surprise and panic and pain rose from the invaders.

"The boats!" Travis struggled to rise. "Don't let them escape!"

Archers untangled themselves from the fray and raced for the bow. Travis and Raffa joined them and rained feathered lances upon those struggling to cast off and flee. One of the boats had already chopped through its hawser and started to float away, its oars tangled and useless. A trio of Raffa's men leapt overboard and swam for the free-floating boat. Five more pounced upon the next group trying to flee and clubbed them to the deck. Torches were lit, and the melee quieted to moans of the wounded. Travis watched the trio scale the drifting boat's side, accept the wounded oarsmen's surrender, then to the cheers of their shipmates aim the vessel back toward their own ship.

Yet when the vessel drew within the torchlight's reach, the cheers faded to silence. The vessel's bowsprit was carved into the most hideous mask Travis had ever seen. The face was half man, half beast, with bulging eyes and horns painted blood red. Great teeth shone on either side of the lolling tongue. The face was painted mottled green and black and orange, a ghastly mélange. In the flickering light, the face seemed to leer in deadly rage, ready to strike and devour.

Travis turned to the other two pirate vessels, now lashed alongside, and saw the same mask carved there as well. He pointed and called, his voice carrying clear over the suddenly breathless night, "Cut down the heads!"

With alacrity men sprang to action. They straddled the bowsprits and shinnied to the end, where they bared their blades and hacked at the wood. A great cry of anguish rose from the pirates. "Bind the prisoners," Travis ordered, and continued to watch the men's progress.

Only when the first head splashed into the sea did he turn away.

CHAPTER II

I have no interest in being a spy," Hannibal Mago declared. "Neither yours nor anyone else's."

"I have nowhere else to turn," replied Magirus.

"Then it is simply not intended to be. To assign me such a task would be to invite disaster." Hannibal Mago was named after the two most famous of Carthage's ancient *sufets* or warrior kings, and had the build of a battle-hardened soldier. Tall and lean, his only beacons of advancing years were traces of gray in his hair and lines like knife slashes down both cheeks. He had never served in the army, naturally, since the only army operating in this or any other province was Rome's. And nothing could ever have induced Hannibal Mago to respond to Rome's call to arms.

"It is precisely because you are blunt and direct that I am positive we shall succeed." Magirus was the recently elected leader of Carthage's larger Christian community, and with the pastorate came the title of bishop. It was a title Magirus used only reluctantly, as he held those who had come before in awe. Tertullian and Cyprian were two such bishops who had set examples and established teachings for the entire Christian world. A brilliant man himself, with the ability to knit together a diverse and argumentative community, Magirus was slender and frail in body only. His mind and spirit were robust and powerful. "Do not go to act. Go to listen. Remain in the background, take note of all you see and hear, then return."

This natural humility of Magirus had attracted Hannibal to the new church leader, and was the reason he had allowed himself to be assigned the position of church elder. Perhaps if he spent enough time around the man, the qualities might rub off on him. "And if I am unable to learn anything?"

"From what I hear," Magirus replied grimly, "you will have no trouble whatsoever learning what is going on. Church activity has become the business of every gossip and street-corner wag."

Hannibal found his defenses crumbling. "Constantinople is so far removed from my normal trade," he protested, "I shall have no contacts of any use."

"So much the better." Clearly Magirus had prepared himself for Hannibal's objections. "That will grant you the perfect excuse for asking advice and information from all and sundry."

"But Constantinople," he complained. "It is the other end of the empire. I could be gone for years."

"Weeks," Magirus corrected. "Leave now, with the spring winds behind you. Return before the autumn storms. You will either have what we need to learn or it will not be accessible."

"And who will look after my affairs while I am away?"

"Your wife," Magirus replied promptly. "She was the one who suggested I ask you to go."

Hannibal's wide shoulders slumped in defeat. "I am trapped."

"See it as an opportunity," Magirus responded. "Both to serve our community of the faithful and to learn what will happen now that the emperor is dead."

Hannibal eyed the bishop. "You have heard something?"

"Rumors. None of them good. Have you met the emperor's sons?"

"Never."

"A pity. It would be good to know their mettle. Never mind." Absently he drummed his fingers on the vestry table, a gift from a local churchgoer. The wall behind him still bore the jagged edges of fresh-cut stone. The entire church and basilica, in fact, looked only half finished. Neither man minded in the least. It remained a delight to have such a public center of worship, no matter what its minor flaws.

Following his own conversion, one of the Emperor Constantine's earliest acts was to declare Christianity no longer an outlaw sect. The result was an explosion of church building throughout the empire, as communities of faithful emerged from cellars and catacombs to celebrate in public.

Magirus demanded, "How much do you know of the latest crisis?"

For a moment Hannibal thought the pastor spoke of the empire, and the weather-beaten merchant knew an instant of keening fear. Civil war remained a living memory for men of his age, a horror without equal. Already nervous flutters were creating havoc within the markets, leaving the poorer freemen wondering if they would be able to afford their next meal. Then Hannibal realized his friend spoke of the church. "Almost nothing."

"Again, this is not a bad thing," Magirus said, his gaze inward, his words a spoken thought. He focused on the man across from him. "The name they have given this threat is Arianism, after a priest of Alexandria called Arius."

"I think I have heard something."

"Of course you have. And here is another word. Gnostics. Remember that, old friend. Not one sect. Many. More than all the tribes of Africa province. All believing one thing or another. Most in opposition to one another, with a fury as fierce as that they show toward the true church."

"They are tied together, the Gnostics and the Arians?"

"Some, and only somewhat. That is my guess. The lines blur, and my news is dated. I must rely on what allies in Alexandria pass on to me, and too often they send word only of what they wish me to know." He stood and began pacing the length and breadth of the narrow vestry. "But here is what I think. These Arians remain our opponents, first and last. I speak with some evidence on my side, but not enough. What I can tell you for sure is that the eastern cities are centers for both dissent and for orthodoxy and threaten to explode at any moment. Whatever is transpiring will be ringing loud and long in the courts of Constantinople."

Hannibal Mago felt as he always did when faced with matters of the burgeoning church—out of his depth and helpless. "I understand almost nothing of what you have just said."

"Just so," Magirus said, immensely satisfied. "No subterfuge could offer us a better cover than your ignorance in these matters."

"Us? You will come with me?"

"I am too publicly joined with Athanasius, the bishop of Alexandria. He appears to offer the staunchest barrier to this tide of heresy. If I were seen in your company, many doors would immediately be shut in your face."

Athanasius. Another name that meant little besides a niggling impression that he should know more. "Then I shall be alone. My wife remains too frail to travel."

"Not alone." Magirus resumed his seat and leaned across the table. "I suggest you take Lydia."

Hannibal retreated behind a merchant's mask, his features abruptly stonelike and unreadable. Lydia was his eldest daughter, and an active member of the local church. Far more active than himself. "This is an order?"

"Of course not," Magirus said impatiently. "When have I ever been so bold with you? It is an entreaty. And advice."

Hannibal rose to his feet. "Then I shall take it as counsel, and give you my answer soon enough."

"Lydia is keen of eye and sensitive to the winds of change," Magirus continued, rising with him.

"She is also headstrong and opinionated and more trouble than her mother."

"She will prove to be your strongest ally."

"Or my downfall. I am unsure I could survive such a voyage."

Magirus covered his smile with a discreet cough. "Think on it, brother. That is all I could ask. And discuss it with your blessed wife."

Hannibal left the church compound, turned his back to the glittering waters of the Carthage harbor, and entered the winding maze of lanes. His church was the largest in Carthage and was built upon the foundations of Juno's temple—Juno being a minor goddess who had lost almost all followers in the previous generation. Still, the cramped neighborhood of hovels and twisting streets bore the old goddess' name. Each sector of the overcrowded city was named after the god whose temple dominated its center position. Except this one. Although Constantine had authorized both religion and church, still the provincial leaders were reluctant to do anything as permanent as rename a portion of their ancient city the Jesus Quarter.

Even the assignment of this particular derelict temple as site for their new Christian basilica was an intended slur, since the Juno Quarter was one of the city's poorest. In point of fact, the church felt most comfortable where it was, as one of its most central works was serving the poor, and many of its believers were drawn from their ranks.

Of the poor there were many, both here and elsewhere. Roman society cared little for the beggared, offering neither food to the starving nor medicine to the ailing. The empire's harshest side was often not shown to slaves, whose masters were bound by law to feed and clothe them, but to the landless freemen, who hung ever suspended from the slender thread of chance, their greatest worry in such uncertain times their next meal. No, the church was well placed.

The rubble-strewn way suddenly opened and emptied into the Meleareth sector, noisy and active. Hannibal walked by shed after shed, each fronted by a partially finished boat. He skirted a group of blue-robed Meleareth priests who splashed blood and chanted incantations over a vessel. Once the blessing was completed, the ship would be made watertight with hot pitch, then rolled over great logs down to the waterside. Hannibal paid the priests no mind. The city of Carthage, like all communities throughout the empire save Constantinople, was home to priests of every imaginable ilk. There was neither profit nor sense in wasting anger on this fact. No, the dangers rocking the swift-growing Christian communities lay elsewhere. Especially now.

Even the Emperor Constantine had recognized this. Before his own conversion twenty-five years earlier, any citizen convicted of Christianity suffered one of a hundred lingering deaths; the crime was atheism, a title given to any worshipper of a criminal sect. Constantine knew it would be impossible to transform the empire from its pagan state to one where only Christianity was permitted. For much of his life, he continued to allow sacrifices to be offered in his name to the Unconquered Sun and had this god's symbol stamped upon some of his coinage. Until his final years, he even did not object to pagan temples being dedicated to his own divinity, so long as there were no human sacrifices. Beyond outlawing this one ancient habit of appeasing gods with human blood, Constantine did not seek to convert the Roman people with laws. Instead, he granted Christianity equal status with all other sects, offered money and land for the building of churches, then tried to convert by example.

And his example had done much. Cities such as Carthage were now estimated to be as much as one-fifth Christian, a staggering amount for a sect just twenty-five years out of the catacombs. The smaller towns and outlying estates were still largely pagan, however, with many Christians living in both loneliness and fear. Converts among provincial slave populations often still suffered the lash for their faith.

● ● ●

Hannibal skirted the central Roman garrison with his eyes downcast. His grandfather, both the first of his family to become Christian and the founder of their trading business, had purchased Roman citizenship in order to further his business. But nothing could have induced the old man, Carthaginian to the bone, to show the empire a shred of allegiance. Hannibal shared that contempt and loathing. No matter what the Christian creed might call for, he would never forgive the Romans for having publicly tortured and killed his own father during the Emperor Diocletian's period of religious persecution.

He crossed before the city's forum, passing the governor's palace and the temple of Esculapius, and entered the sprawling area known as Megara. This district contained many of the city's larger temples, and more than its share of wealth. The people of Carthage were shipwrights and merchants and traders and makers of profit. They invented the world's first scrip, or money—made of thin strips of leather, stamped with the seal of the merchant whose name and reputation granted such worthless items actual value. The scrip was easily transportable and well-suited to their adventurous spirit, for the Carthaginians were also known as the greatest explorers who had ever lived.

Beyond Megara, Hannibal arrived at the Esculapius Quarter, which stretched inland from the forum. This district contained the central market and most of the great warehouses, where the trade and wonder of all Africa province was displayed.

Hannibal stopped before his own entrance portal. Before he could raise his staff, his servant Demetrius swung open the great door. Demetrius responded to Hannibal's grave thanks with a grunt, showing his resentment over having been left behind. He hated the idea of his master walking unattended through the maze of danger and deceit that surrounded the church compound. What was more, he prided himself on knowing all his master's business, and having church affairs discussed in secret was almost more than he could bear. The two guards he had sent to follow Hannibal could assure his safety but not fill the gap in his knowledge. Demetrius shut the door behind his master, still bearing a grudge.

Hannibal noted his servant's displeasure and started to speak, then spotted his daughter. She walked across the central courtyard with arms full of writing skins; they flopped about her in long ink-stained streamers. Hannibal found his ire returning. "Lydia!"

The sharpness of his tone was enough to back Demetrius up a step. Good. Let the old man think it was because of his dispatching guards against his master's express orders. Hannibal watched his daughter approach. "What is all this?"

"The Nubian traders have arrived," she said, her voice calmer than normal. And quieter. Incoming caravans were normally cause enough, in Lydia's mind, for frantic shouts and orders and feverish activity that upset everyone within reach, servants and animals included. "I have seen to their needs, and I was going to begin checking their wares."

Pleasure at the news could not staunch his smoldering frustration. Berber bandits had all but closed the roads leading south, and this was the first caravan that had arrived from Nubia in months. Still, the matter raised by Magirus could not wait. He waved Demetrius away. The old servant took a reluctant half-step back, fairly certain that he would not be refused confidential information twice in one morning. Hannibal lowered his voice and demanded, "Has your mother spoken to you about this voyage?"

To his utter surprise, there was none of Lydia's usual evasiveness, nor any wheedling or insistent pushing. Instead he faced a clear-eyed young woman who met his stare and calmly replied, "Last night."

A woman. With a stab of sadness, his heart's wisdom told him he was facing not just his daughter but a grown woman. He was not ready to lose her, his favorite child. "Magirus thinks I should take you to Constantinople."

"I would like to go," she replied. "Very, very much."

"That is it?" He could not help himself. "No tirades? No shrieked threats of calamity if I do not do as you wish?"

Even her smile was womanly. "Would they do any good?"

"Perhaps. I am not sure." The wound of his heart's warning unsettled him as much as her own mysterious calm. "Are you all right?"

"Fine."

He tried for anger, could manage only a hollow protest. "I object to you women scheming behind my back."

"No one has schemed, Father. Magirus came to us for advice. Mother said he had to speak with you, but she thought you should go."

"And take you with me."

"She is too weak to travel herself. But she wants you to have the family's help."

Hannibal stared at this stranger who was his eldest daughter. His prize. That was what he often thought of her, when her bossy nature did not infuriate him beyond measure. His prize. Lydia had taken the place of the sons he did not have and given him a trusted right hand. She was bright, friendly, a fierce negotiator, and forgot nothing. Not for the first time, Hannibal gave thanks for the freedom Christianity had given women. And woman she truly was.

It was not for nothing that Rome had declared Christianity an outlaw sect. Within the Roman Empire and the Christian church stood two moral structures in direct and total opposition to one another. That one would eventually destroy the other was doubted by none.

Roman moral values were based upon the family. Within the family, the *paterfamilias* ruled supreme. The father held almost unlimited power. He could try his wife and children in his own domestic court, and inflict upon them any punishment up to and including death. His unwanted babies could legally be exposed in the arena or on the mountainside, to either die or be picked up by landless freemen and bathhouse masters too poor to afford the purchase of child slaves. The father was the *only* legally recognized person, the only voice, in the family. It was the father who held all authority. It was his business to give orders, and the family's only duty to obey.

The apostle Paul had not been persecuted for saying that children should obey their parents. This was so self-evident to the Roman world that it need not even be mentioned. What was bizarre was how this Christian teacher had coupled the order with another, stating that parents must not provoke their children. Paul's crime was worsened by his ordering men to love their wives. Giving balance to time-honored laws, and the implied freedom that it offered to women, was something never before heard of within the empire. No other god, no other sect, no other provincial law, had ever granted women such powers. To Roman eyes, the Christians' attitude toward women was as scandalous as their demand that worship of other gods must cease.

Hannibal focused once more upon Lydia, and suddenly found himself furious at being trapped into taking a journey he knew was useless before it began. "I have now decided. You are not going."

She raised one lofty eyebrow, and in that movement became her mother. "No?"

"It is my decision. You are not to go."

"So." Still there was no anger, no tantrum, nothing he could point to and use as a reason for making his statement truth. "You will travel to Constantinople, a place you have never visited, utterly without contacts. You will have no allies, no one you can trust. You will do your business, and try to seek answers to questions you do not understand."

"I am the church elder, daughter. Not you."

"All the world knows that your weakness is your loathing for intrigue." She cocked her head. "So you will travel all that distance alone, and be certain you can return with the information Magirus needs?"

His own daughter, more beautiful than ever with this new poise, but a stranger. He had watched over her since birth, and yet in this moment knew her not. "I shall think on what you have said," he replied, his voice gruff with sudden sadness and the sense of his own age.

"Thank you, Father," Lydia said and turned away.

When she had crossed the courtyard, he demanded to no one in particular, "What in heaven has gotten into that girl?"

"Girl no longer," Demetrius observed.

"No," Hannibal agreed, defeated. "That much is true."

The old servant sniffed. "Of course, how could I know more, when I am kept from every important discussion?"

"Very good, Demetrius," he said, his eyes on the doorway through which his daughter had vanished. "You may go."

"How am I supposed to serve this family when all keep secrets and notions distant from me, I ask you? All my life I have asked only to serve, and here I am—"

Hannibal turned and cut off the flow with one look. He watched Demetrius make his shuffling departure, and realized the servant was too old to travel again. All his life Demetrius had stood at his side. On such a mission as this Hannibal would sorely miss the old man. He turned back to look across the courtyard, feeling the world moving faster and faster, flying off beyond his power to control or predict. No matter what the pastor might say, he was sorely troubled by the need for this journey. And even more worried by what he might discover.

Lydia settled her load of manifests on the cluttered sorting table, smiled at the matron who oversaw work in the vast hall, and marveled at both her own calm and its effect on her father. He was going to let her come. She knew it with utter certainty. He could not succeed alone. Lydia seated herself and began sorting the skins with their cuneiform script, her fingers busy with one task while her thoughts remained fastened upon something else.

Her mind was held by an instant's image. It was this memory that had granted her the first distance she had ever known from her own emotional storm when confronting her father. Hannibal was so strong, so solid, so *sure*. Lydia had often wished she could be as certain about just one thing as he was about everything. Yet now she could look at the greatest and most exciting event in her entire life, an adventure far beyond the reach of her wildest dreams, and feel nothing. Nothing save the same keening that had filled her heart since seeing the palanquin and the man it carried.

Man. He bore a boy's unlined face, but there had been nothing childlike about his bearing, or the strength and determination in his eyes.

Earlier that day, Lydia had been walking toward the city's eastern gate—racing really, having just heard that the Nubians' caravan had arrived from Libya. Three servants in full household regalia had raced to keep up, struggling to keep their ceremonial jugs from spilling. Demetrius had been given yet another reason to sulk, as she had refused his entreaties to come along, knowing the old man's shuffling gait would have slowed them down even more than the crowded lanes. She had stopped where the lane crossed the Via Saturnus, the thoroughfare running from the harbor to the city's most distant temple, when she had spotted the procession.

For a moment she feared the Nubians had tired of waiting and decided to come in unescorted, a great insult in their eyes. Then she realized that the bearers were all light-skinned, which confused her. Palanquins, the ornate carriages borne like stretchers by strong slaves, were seldom used by anyone save eastern potentates. And this palanquin was stranger still, utterly unadorned, wrapped in simple homespun cloth. Then her gaze fastened upon the young man, and her thoughts froze as solid as her step.

He was reddish-blond of hair and bronzed of skin. He rested half-sitting, half-lying, clearly injured in some way, though no wound was evident on his muscled frame.

His status was a mystery. He wore only the unadorned worker's shift of his bearers, made of the same coarse linen as that draped over his palanquin. Yet his body was oiled and his hair plaited, as though he were a noble. And he bore a sword, permitted within city walls only to warriors or Roman citizens of station.

His bearers were four armed guards who strode with alert pride, rather than the hangdog expression of common slaves. Another man walked to the front, a warrior for certain, his eyes roving, his sword unslung and grasped by its sheath, ever ready to be drawn and used. A sixth man walked two steps behind the palanquin, as watchful as the others.

All this she noticed with lightning glances that could not help but be drawn back to the young man. He looked like no one Lydia had ever seen before. Strong and fragile at the same time, his features fine-boned yet carved with bold and steady lines. Her heart fluttered like a caged bird within her ribs. She noticed the shadow-strains about his eyes and mouth, the same lines that had redrawn her mother's features, signs of a haunting pain. Yet there was also strength there, and more. The young man was alert, and *aware*.

As the pallet passed her, she searched for some sign of who he was and where his allegiance lay. There was nothing. No cross adorned either chest or dress or palanquin cloth. This meant he was probably not Christian, which would be terrible. But still there was room for hope, for neither was there a pagan sign—no bracelet with temple stamping, nor amulet, nor tattoo of dragon or god or demon. His skin was as unadorned as his dress. His only possession was a legionnaire's short-sword in a sheath as worn and weather-beaten as those carried by his guards. The sword rested across his middle, his right hand settled loosely upon the haft. An utterly strange way for a wounded man to be transported through a garrisoned city.

His eyes. Lydia desperately wanted to see his eyes. Before her mind had time to object to her heart's desire, she raised up on her toes, waved to someone unseen on the palanquin's opposite side, and called out a friend's name.

The young man's head jerked about, as did the two nearside guards. Lydia found herself trapped and inspected by three trained warriors. Then she was dismissed by all but the young man.

He held her with eyes as soft and brown as a newborn fawn's, yet filled with the same strength and determination as her father's. His focused intensity pierced her, leaving her suddenly unable to breathe. Then he turned away, and she realized she was still standing with her hand upraised. Slowly she let it sink, watching as the procession rounded the corner and disappeared.

Only then did she realize that the servants were watching her curiously. She turned to the nearest one, whose name she suddenly could not recall. "Did you not see her?"

"Who, mistress?"

"I could have sworn that was she. Never mind. Look, here is an opening." She forced her numbed limbs to carry her forward. "Hurry along, everyone."

Without stopping his continual scan of the crowd, Travis spoke to the man bearing the pole to his right. "You saw her?"

"Aye, sire," the man replied with approval. He was called Gaven and was Carthage born and raised, before hiring himself out as a mercenary and being subsequently captured and sold into slavery. He had regained his freeman status under Travis' father, and was now proud to count himself among Raffa's men. "High-born and a beauty. She walked with three servants who acted as ceremonial water-bearers. Strange to see that old custom still around. Perhaps she visited a temple to make libations."

Travis signaled for Damon, the guard stationed at their rear, to come forward. "The young lady back there."

"I saw her, sire." Clearly his servants took this renewed interest in women as a sign of his returning strength, and approved. "A rare jewel."

Travis frowned to cover his own eagerness. "Follow her and find out what you can."

"I hear and obey." The man was gone.

Travis lay back. It was as Raffa said. The successful attack on the pirates had granted him new authority. Already the men treated him as never before. And called him *sire*, the address reserved for highest officers. Indeed they were becoming his own men.

That face. She was more than beautiful. She shone with the same light that flickered deep within her dark eyes, as though the sun rose within her heart.

Raffa moved back alongside the palanquin. "Our back is now exposed." His voice carried the frown his face did not reveal.

"Five men are enough," Travis replied, shaking off the image. "They would not dare attack us here. If they are here in Carthage at all."

"A beauty," Gaven announced, bearing his share of the palanquin's load with ease. "Worth the risk."

"I do not have eyes in the back of my head," Raffa said to the others, his voice full of quiet warning. "Stay alert."

Travis nodded and focused upon the danger ahead. Now was not the time to have his head turned, no matter how great the girl's grace.

Their guide, a man they had hired to lead them through the city's winding streets, stopped at a major thoroughfare and came back to Travis. "I shall take my money now."

Travis felt the icy dagger of fear work its way into his gut. "We have arrived?"

"This is the Vicus Senis," the man replied. He was a wizened mariner, pickled a dark brown by years of sun and salt and wind. "Take this road until you reach the stretch of barren ground. The house you seek stands alone."

Travis looked doubtfully around the teeming ways. The houses were jammed as tightly together as the people and animals crowding their lane. "There is unused land here?"

"You will know it," the old man insisted, and thrust out his hand.

When the old man had hobbled off, Travis asked the guard by his shoulder, "You understand this?"

"I was a young child my last journey here," Gaven replied. "There may be something I was once told, but I am not sure." He looked to Raffa, who scouted the ways, then shrugged. "I sense no more danger here than anywhere else."

Travis signaled for them to continue, then said to Raffa, "Stay close."

They passed through yet another market, this one filled with the bleating of panicked animals and the stench of fresh blood. Immediately after, the street emptied of people. One moment they were struggling through a throng far too large for the narrow way, the next they were almost alone. A few stray people passed with lowered head and frightened step. Others clustered close to patrolling guards, none of whom walked alone. The houses remained as jammed together as ever, but disintegrated into the worst hovels

38

Travis had ever seen. He started to ask if anyone truly lived here, when a bundle of rags heaped alongside one wall stirred and groaned and extended a blackened claw. Even the hardened Raffa was touched, for he plucked a small coin from his belt-purse and dropped it into the outstretched hand. The claw retreated into the rags, and the bundle moved no more.

As abruptly as the people had vanished, the dwellings simply stopped. The palanquin passed an invisible border and crossed into a field of rubble and silence. Only the road continued as before, ancient and cobblestoned and dusty. Travis blinked in the sudden light, saw a temple up ahead. And just before it rose the walled compound of a wealthy man's home.

Raffa moved up alongside, said, "Your brother has done well."

Before Travis could reply, Gaven muttered, "The dreaded Saturn."

That drew them to a halt. Travis ordered, "Set me down. I shall walk from here." When the litter was grounded, he rose to his feet, and with the others gathered about the Carthaginian. "Go on."

"Those who worshipped at the temple knew him as Molech. Saturn was the name assigned to him by the Romans."

Travis nodded his understanding. This was common practice. Wherever the Romans conquered, they sought to bind the vanquished closer to the empire by incorporating their gods into the Roman hierarchy. The most powerful of the local gods was thus renamed Saturn, at least as far as the Romans were concerned, knowing that future generations would gradually forget the earlier names. The only time this practice was not followed was when the local god was seen to preach opposition to the new Roman masters.

In that case, as with Christianity, the sect was declared seditious, and all followers branded atheists, a crime punishable by death.

"My father spoke of this place with dread," Gaven continued. "This was a temple of many names, which was part of its powers. But the god's most common name was Baal Hammon."

"The god of time," Raffa murmured. "I knew a warrior who followed this one. A good man in his way. He said it was a religion of the stars."

"And of blood," the Carthaginian added. "That is why this temple stands alone. All others are crowded into districts that bear their names—Cronus, Ashtarte, Juno, Esculapius, and so on. The smaller the deity, the lower class the district. You have already seen this is so. The other temples stand cheek-by-jowl with shops, warehouses, baths, residences, tenements."

"Except for this one," Travis said, shifting his eyes from the temple to his brother's compound and back again.

"Baal Hammon stands alone," Gaven agreed, "isolated by fear and blood-soaked power. Not even the Romans would dare use this ground. Only those who slaughter animals live here freely, for once they were drawn from his priesthood. Those and the poorest of the poor, whose poverty robs them of choice."

"I feel eyes upon us," Raffa murmured.

Travis joined the others in searching the silent grounds. He saw no living thing. The temple stood solid and menacing in its stillness upon the hilltop. He turned back to the Carthaginian. "My tutor mentioned the Roman gods but little. Father was against our learning what he called the nonsense of parasites. If I recall, Saturn killed his father Uranus, murdered his female offspring, immolated his firstborn son, and sacrificed others as burnt offerings."

"This temple's followers adhered to such practices," Gaven concurred. Though he was a big man and strong, his voice carried a faint quaver. "In the last epidemic, a hundred children were sacrificed upon the altar as appeasement."

"Then what has brought my brother to this place, I wonder." Travis took in the massive limewashed walls surrounding the estate. "As I wonder how a man who can build such a palace for himself has nothing to spare for his own father." He started up the slope, reveling in his limbs' growing strength. "Come. I want to see this temple for myself."

"I would advise against it, sire," the guard said.

"Stay and watch the litter if you wish," Travis said, striding forward. "I for one want to see who or what my brother has chosen as a neighbor."

Within the temple enclosure, the very air seemed angry. The empty silence only magnified the sense of menace. Travis resisted the urge to turn and run, and instead started across the broad paved platform leading to the central steps. He stared up at the portico with its ornate carvings and fading colors, and asked of no one in particular, "What has happened to them all, I wonder. This place is large enough to hold a thousand worshippers. More."

"Blood sacrifices are forbidden," Raffa reminded him. "Most of the old ways are finding it hard to exist in the empire."

"My father spoke of how the Saturnians had taken over one of the outlying villages," Gaven offered, following close on Travis' heels. "There they continue with the old ways, or so it is said."

Raffa snorted. "Where would they find the victims? Even if they prey on slaves and freemen, only so many people can vanish without the soldiers being called in."

Travis entered the central hall with its lofty ceiling, his attention caught by the great stone altar. It was layered in what appeared to be blankets of thick red dust. Raffa moved up beside him, muttered, "Why are we here?"

"Better you should ask, why is Fabian?" Travis replied.

"This is not a place friendly to mortals," Raffa insisted. "Better we face enemies we can see."

"There!" Travis pointed to the distant corner.

Raffa squinted through the dusty gloom, grunted involuntarily. "Do my eyes deceive me?"

"Not yours and mine as well." Shadows did not quite conceal the faces or their fury. Each corner of the temple bore a garishly painted gargoyle, a beast with horns and snout and bulging eyes.

The guard moved forward, and gaped. "It is the same beast as adorned the pirate vessels."

Travis signaled them back outside, wondering what had brought his brother to such a forsaken place as this. Wondering also why he felt that here was something, a key, an instrument he could put to his use. "Come, let us go see how my dear brother is faring."

CHAPTER III

"W hy should I allow my life to be shaped by silliness and superstition, when here lies the only free land in all of Carthage?" Fabian said. Then he added hastily, "Of course, that does not mean that the land came cheaply. Costs in this city are simply staggering."

"You have my sympathies," Travis said dryly.

"My dear brother, you simply have no idea what it has been like, attempting to instill a bit of culture into my new dwelling. I have worked my fingers to the bone, only to have every copper I earned sucked away by these parasites called builders."

Travis hid his bitterness by keeping his gaze elsewhere. The hall in which they sat was palatial. Three walls were entirely covered in brilliant mosaics, each depicting a scene from heavenly gardens—gods gallivanting, seduction of Leda by the swan, hunters closing in on rampant stags. The fourth wall was colonnaded and opened into a vast internal courtyard. The marble frieze adorning the roof supports boasted some of the finest carving he had ever seen. "Culture," was all he said.

"Indeed, yes." Fabian lifted his beringed hand to touch his hair. His coiffure matched those Travis had observed along the streets, lacquered and curled tightly about the head. Men who wore such hairstyles also chose form-fitted robes and tunics opened about the chest and up the thigh. Many, like Fabian, completed the outfit with color applied to their faces. "I was never suited to the harsh outdoors like you." A languid gaze flickered over Travis' form. "I was always more, shall we say, delicate. On the farm I positively pined away for the cultured life."

The hall centered upon a great marble fountain. In its midst cavorted a trio of water nymphs, their naked forms intertwined about a mythical half-man, half-goat. Similar statues adorned the front foyer. Behind the fountain stood a matched pair of armed men in mock gladiatorial garb. Their muscles shone from thorough oiling.

Travis nodded slowly, as though giving Fabian's words serious thought. But in truth his mind was suddenly captivated by a rush of memory, images he had held down for many years.

He had been six years old, his mother recently taken by the wasting sickness. That morning his father had traveled with a large shipment to a port some three days' distance away. Brutus, Fabian's older brother, had been almost eighteen, and had already shown great pleasure in terrorizing the household whenever Cletus was not there to rein him in.

That day his brothers had devised a new game, cutting thin slivers of bamboo and soaking them overnight until they became supple as reeds, yet strong as leather. Brutus had herded Travis toward the goal, the pillars flanking the entrance to the main patio. Meanwhile Fabian had been charged to keep him out. Herding could be done only with the whips. Twice servants had been drawn by his screams, only to be battered senseless by Brutus. The house had then grown silent, and remained so throughout the brothers' cruel sport.

Travis struggled against his unwanted reverie and signaled Raffa forward. "I bring you a letter from our father."

Raffa's motion brought a pair of armed servants from the hall's opposite corner. When he stopped, they did as well.

"Oh, really, brother." Fabian's voice turned cold as he was forced to look upon his father's freeman client. He had never tried to mask the loathing he felt for Raffa. Brutus had also despised the warrior, which had been ample reason for the young Travis to trust the warrior fully. "Let your manservant go join the other men in the foyer. He should be so much more comfortable there among his own kind."

"Raffa comes and goes at his own choosing," Travis replied, grateful for the soldier's silent presence. Although Travis had grown to a stature and strength far beyond Fabian's, still he felt the childhood terrors too close to be comfortable facing his half-brother alone. "If he chooses to join me in such meetings, then I am honored."

"Oh, very well." Fabian accepted the letter and motioned Raffa off with a wave of irritation.

As Travis watched his brother break the seal and peruse the script, the memories rose unbidden once more. That same afternoon, his father still away, the game had started anew.

The young and terrified Travis had frantically sought a safe haven, searching as far afield as his six-year-old legs would carry him, but the brothers had found him out and punished him for hiding, then begun their game once more.

The next morning, he had found the hideaway. Like most manors of the empire's southern reaches, the house was a sweeping series of rooms built like an elongated *L* around a great central courtyard. The entrance was a tall domed portico in the third wall, bordered by two pillars of rose marble. The fourth wall was covered by a series of mosaics, which swept down and continued across much of the patio floor. The artwork was bordered by flowering vines hung from great trellises, which rose up to run along the crest of the wall. Slender pillars encircled the terrace, suggesting an oval within the square.

That morning Travis had crawled into the corner opposite the entrance, where the trellis vines and the pillars' shadows offered a crumb of refuge. When his brothers' raucous laughter sounded the alarm of another living nightmare, he slid behind the trellis itself. To his amazement, he discovered a small hole in the wall, a cave just large enough to hold him if he sat with his legs drawn up. His brothers spent the entire day searching in vain, their fury mounting to frightening levels when he was not found.

That evening, when his father returned, Cletus noted the new slash scars and demanded to know what had happened. Terrified of further ordeals, both Travis and the servants remained silent. With the passing days, the brothers turned increasingly savage whenever Travis could be found. His wounds became bloodier than mere whip scars. A simple passage down the inner hallway could become life-threatening, if he happened upon a brother when a servant was not there as witness. He began taking breakfast with his father and then, whenever Cletus was in the fields or called to the harbor, he disappeared until nightfall. The cave was tight, and Travis' back and knees hurt abominably by evening, but at least he remained alive.

Two months later, Raffa had arrived. Two months after that, Brutus had been sent to Rome. His life had been transformed. No matter how bad Fabian might be, he was nothing compared to his older brother. And Raffa had been there to see him through.

Fabian casually tossed the letter onto the low table separating them. "Dear old Father."

"He needs your help," Travis said woodenly.

"No doubt, no doubt." Fabian cast his half-brother a small cold smile. "But I absolutely insist that we observe proper decorum. There shall be no further discussion until I have been permitted to offer you refreshments."

Fabian turned to where a manservant hovered, dressed and coiffured in a fashion to mimic his master. "Hanno, go and tell Chloe to serve us wine."

A moment later the side portal opened to admit a woman-child so beautiful Travis half rose from his seat, only to subside at his brother's cold smile of satisfaction.

The young woman was scarcely removed from childhood. She was clothed in diaphanous robes that revealed more than they covered. She was indeed beautiful, her lithe young body beckoning luridly. But the perfection of her face and form was marred by the shadow of tragedy that surrounded her, and by the hopelessness that transformed her dark eyes into bottomless pits.

"Lovely, don't you think? She cost me an absolute fortune, but I believe she is a worthy addition to my household." Fabian's eyes roamed over the girl's body. She stood and endured the inspection with a face as still as death. "Serve my dear brother first, that's a darling."

Travis accepted the goblet, watched as the girl's eyes remained unfocused and distant, refusing to meet his. Her lovely young face was slack, a mask of living wax drained of all emotion, all hope. "Thank you," he said, shared pain sharpened by his own memories.

"It is an excellent vintage, I think you will find." As Chloe approached and offered him the second goblet, Fabian traced one hand up and under her robes. His look passed from the girl to Travis and back again, flaunting his new possession. His tongue emerged slightly to flicker across his lips, a human lizard tasting the air. The girl stood frozen and unbreathing, her eyes fastened on a darkness only she could see.

Abruptly he dropped his hand. "Very well, my dear. You may go." When the girl had left the hall, he raised his goblet and said, "To what shall we make a toast, dear brother?"

"To our father in his hour of need."

"Oh, yes, dear Father." Fabian drained his goblet, set it down beside his lounge. "Such a pity that his request arrived just when I was so committed to the builders and their crushing demands for money, money, and more money."

"This new request I carry is desperate."

"And I shall give it every consideration, I assure you." Fabian flicked at an imaginary crease in his robe. "Unfortunately, I remain pinned to the rack of debt. The cost of the cultured existence, dear brother. You cannot begin to imagine the burden under which I live."

Travis stared down at his untasted goblet, formed of smoked glass and spun silver. "No, probably not."

"Well, isn't this nice. My very own dear brother here in Carthage at long last. I must throw a party very soon and introduce you to all the right people."

"Thank you, but I doubt I shall be staying here long enough for a party." Suddenly Travis felt if he did not escape the stifling confines immediately he would suffocate. He rose to his feet, felt Raffa slip up beside him. "He needs your help, Fabian. Now."

"Rest assured I shall give this letter my utmost attention," he said, and gave the letter a look of amused contempt. "Must you go? What a pity. We have so much still to speak of."

"I have other business to attend to." Travis resisted the urge to turn, run, flee, rage at the heavens and at fate. "When can I expect your answer?"

"Oh, with so much else clamoring for my attention these days, it is hard to say."

"When, Fabian?" Travis said, bitter anger grating in his voice. The sound was enough to draw the two armed servants by the distant wall a step closer.

Fabian cast a glance to where they stood at the ready. Reassured, he turned back and smiled with his mouth, his eyes hard as little agate balls. "Oh, I should think four days will be enough time. Perhaps five."

"I shall return then," Travis said. He wheeled about and strode from the hall. As he passed through the ornately decorated foyer with its mildly obscene statues, his men gathered in about him. He did not stop nor slow until his long strides had carried him beyond the front gate. There he paused and took long gulping breaths of the hot dusty air. His men stood and watched in silent understanding.

When his breathing was back under control, he demanded, "Did anyone see one of the masks about that place?"

"As in the temple compound?" Raffa showed astonishment. "You think your brother is involved with the sect?"

"I don't know what to think," Travis replied, suddenly excruciatingly tired. "Except that I need a bath and a scrub. I feel as though filth has worked its way into my very bones."

Despite his fatigue and aching muscles, Travis found he could not sleep. He emerged from his tent, set in the space between the two beached pirate vessels, and wandered down to the water's edge.

One of Carthage's great advantages was its pair of natural harbors. The first held its naval fleet, now reduced to almost nothing by Rome's spring grain shipment. The second, holding the maritime vessels, was shaped like an oval with a tall island at its middle. The island held the customs house and guard contingent, as it kept all the maritime fleet under its careful eye. Travis stared out over the still waters to the island, a mere shadow in the starlight, while his mind wandered over the days leading up to his departure.

The day after Cletus had announced his intentions to send him to Constantinople, Travis had arisen as usual with the dawn. His father had been called to a distant part of the estate by another crisis, an event so regular these days that it seemed almost normal. Travis had entered the kitchen area and greeted the sleepy freeman clients awaiting the day's orders, which he and Raffa would assign in his father's absence. He had accepted the cook's tray, the one he and his father always ate from together, fed a morsel to his favorite dog, ate a second morsel himself, and walked outside alone to enjoy dawn's entry over the fields.

Suddenly Raffa had bounded out, slapped the cup from his mouth, and backhanded the tray from his other hand. And even before Travis had heard the kitchen commotion and the dog's howls of distress, even before the dreadful panic in Raffa's eyes had registered, he knew.

The poison was swift to act yet slow to show its full force, as no doubt had been planned. The numbness crept outwards from his belly, a growing chill that no fire could penetrate. Travis felt Raffa lift him and bound across the fields, bellowing for help. And he thought, this is the man who has never raised his voice, not in all the years he has been part of our family, and he truly is that, more than the brothers I know by blood, so if Raffa is to raise his voice such that it echoes up and down the land, then it must be serious. Travis' thoughts then lifted and swirled like chaff blown skyward at harvesttime, disjointed and as numb as his limbs, and as they entered the inner courtyard he managed to think how strange it was, that he could enter the morning sunlight and have the world grow so dark.

Dark it was when he awoke, the chamber lit by two braziers wafting sweet-scented smoke toward the high ceiling, and by that and the mosaics rising up the wall across from his bed, Travis knew he was laid out in his father's chamber.

"You are going to survive," his father said, after helping his son drink. His gruff tones were belied by the fatigue that scarred his face with dark wounds. "The healer has come and gone a half-dozen times, and with each visit his proclamation becomes louder. Even I am beginning to believe him."

Travis motioned toward the cup, grimaced when the slight movement drew lances of agony up his arm and shoulder and neck.

"Poison," his father said, after helping him drink again. "It seems there is no doubt."

Travis nodded his acceptance of the news, saw the answer to his unasked question there in his father's anguished gaze. He managed to croak, "How long?"

"Two full days and most of a third night." The time had aged him. He flung back the coverlet and asked, "Can you move your feet?"

Travis did as he was asked, though it cost him. "Hurts."

"The poison collects in your muscles and joints, if the healer knows as much as he pretends." His father leaned back, puffed his cheeks, clearly relieved by what he had seen. "Death comes when your lungs stop drawing breath and your heart stops beating. When that didn't happen, the healer started filling my ears with worries about paralysis."

The words crystallized his awakened state. Travis looked into his father's eyes, knew the terror of a lifetime spent trapped and unmoving within a dead-alive body.

His father recognized the tremor, said calmly, "Have I ever lied to you?"

Words from another momentous day. "No."

"Then I say to you what the healer told me, without adornment. Were you able to move even the littlest toe, there is hope. With time and effort, the poison can be worked from your system." His father drained the cup, set it down, and when the shadows masked his features added, "And pain. Movement will not come easily. The end of pain will mean that the poison has been washed away."

Travis watched as his father raised himself back up. He saw the unspoken words and understood. The pain might not fully depart, nor movement ever be fully restored.

His father turned from the second flash of naked fear, limped to the window, pulled open the sash, looked out over the fields, and said, "Have I ever told you how I came to be here?"

The sudden offer had the desired effect and startled Travis from his anguish. His father had never made more than passing reference to his own heritage. Cletus was a quiet man, secretive in the manner of old soldiers who had seen much and learned to hold their thoughts tight to their chest. "No," he whispered, "you never have."

"I have no homeland," his father said, his face turned toward where dawn's first light graced their fields. "Not as those with family or title know of such. For them, a homeland is part of their heritage, and I have none. I was born a Celt in the open lands bordering what they call Hadrian's Wall. Have you heard of it?"

Travis nodded, knowing his gesture would go unseen, not wanting to speak and break the flow. Hadrian's Wall, the grand structure erected across the entire province of Britain's northern border, was known to all who had a modicum of Roman education. The island province was home to some of the most ferocious barbarians ever to confront the Roman army. When they refused to accept either defeat or dominion, the Emperor Hadrian had his forces erect a great barrier, effectively splitting the island in two.

"The place I recall as home had no name," his father went on, "or perhaps it did, and perhaps I was told, and forgot because it mattered little. My early world was a double-dozen huts clustered about a rutted road and ringed by fields that barely fed us. Beyond the fields were the forests and the wolves and the demons who abided there, lurking among the night shadows, waiting to steal the weak and the weary away, as they did my mother on toward the end of my seventh winter. At least I think it was my seventh."

His father turned from the blind inspection of morning fields and stumped over to the nearest brazier. He stirred the coals, the light casting ruddy shadows over his haunted features. "I do not know my birthdate, which has saved me much money and distress when besieged by pestilent astrologers and priests. I remember an old woman telling me I was born in time to cry for the first snow, in the winter of the big freeze, when twenty died and only one was birthed, and even so there was scarcely enough food to feed the one who fed me.

"My mother died as women did, too weary even to complain as she departed. I scavenged for a few days after that, the youngest of six or seven, I do not recall which, the older boys fighting for a place by the cooking fire alongside my farmer father, himself too tired by day's end to concern himself over whether the youngest and weakest managed to scrape a meal from the bottom of the pot."

He limped back over to his chair, dragged it across the flagstones and closer to the bed, eased himself down with a sigh, and said, "Then my world was torn asunder, my boundaries split so hard that in one fell swoop they opened to gather in all that lay beneath heaven's reach."

Travis waited and inspected the inward-directed face, then asked quietly, "How?"

His father raised his eyes, and said, "You will have to go away. You know that."

Travis nodded. He knew.

"And soon. Soon as you begin making true progress. They will not stop with this one try. Not if they see you weak and vulnerable and still in their way."

"Who did this?"

Another puff from fatigue-slackened cheeks. "Who wishes to drive us from this land? And why? Perhaps you will find answers in Constantinople. Perhaps there are no answers to find. If not, a soldier learns that sometimes the only success is found in retreating to live and fight another day. But this much I can tell you. The tray from which you ate and drank was meant for me. Or perhaps for us both. It could just as easily have been me lying there, and without your youth battling alongside."

Travis pondered this a moment, then said weakly, "But I don't want to go."

"Aye, and that is a great boon to offer your father." They looked at one another for a long moment, father and son, before Cletus stirred himself, eased his side, and said, "You ask how my world was split apart and remade. Very well, I shall tell you. A parting gift to the only son who ever cared enough to ask. The only son . . ."

But his ears failed him then. Try as he might, Travis could not capture and hold the words he had yearned his life long to hear. Sleep reached dark hands up and about him, clogging his ears, closing his eyes, drawing him down into darkness and away.

His father was not there when he awoke. Instead, Raffa was seated beside his bed, watching him with eyes that held the same calm alertness that he had shown all the world since his arrival those fifteen years before. Without asking, he poured a cup and helped Travis raise his head. Travis forced the water through a throat so swollen and dry he choked and sprayed as much as he managed to drink. Raffa waited until he was done, settled him back, said, "You'll have to start eating sometime soon. I know it's the last thing you want, but you need your strength just the same."

Travis nodded acceptance, though just the thought of food made him gag. Raffa was up and out the door with the silent swiftness that was his stock in trade, and back before sleep could reclaim its victim. Raffa inspected the heavy-lidded face, said, "You'll need to try and fight the drug of sleep, lad. The struggle will be hard, I know. Anyone who's stood as close as I have to worldly power knows the work of the shadow hand. The road back is rough and steep, and you'll have to claw your way. But the fire of life is strong in you, just as I told your father. You should make it."

The shadow hand. A curious name for poison, Travis thought, but saved his strength to ask, "You and Father guard me?"

"Aye, you can rest easy. They won't get to you here, that's for certain. Not the ones who tainted your meal, nor the one who waits beyond the border of sleep."

Travis recalled fragments of dreams, vague shapes that had whispered nightmarish invitations to come and sup and sleep forever. He felt a chill return to his bones.

Raffa pretended not to notice the sudden sweat that brightened his face. "Your father told you of your need to leave?"

"I don't want to go."

"You're a good son, and that's the fact of the matter. But one thing is clear to the both of us. If you are to have a future at all, you'll live it elsewhere." He pulled a scroll from the belt-pouch. "Now let us see what to take with us."

Raffa's matter-of-factness helped him see it as happening, rather than something against which he could struggle. In the instant of acceptance there came a sense of turning away, of moving toward the unknown. Despite his weakened state, he felt his fear flash away like oil in an open lamp. "You will come with me?"

Again the calm, steady gaze. "If you wish."

"I could not," he replied truthfully, "do this without you."

Travis ate, or allowed himself to be fed, then found the effort of holding back his fatigue to be too much bother. He pulled sleep back up and around him like a blanket.

The day passed like a door opening only for swift bright glimpses. When he again fully awoke, it was to the thrill of a double blessing. The pain had eased, and he knew for certain that he would live. How he knew did not matter. That he knew was enough.

"Just like your first birth," his father said, helping him drink. "You return to this world in the safety of night."

Travis lay back, feeling strength course with the cool broth outwards from his belly. "You were telling me of your childhood."

His father laughed, a rare sound. "You pass so close to death's door that even I can hear your name being called. And you return wanting to hear the old tales."

"You had trouble surviving that first winter," Travis pressed.

"Aye, I did that," Cletus agreed, his face hardening with the onset of memories. "But I did not die as the villagers expected. The old women kept me alive, though how exactly I do not recall, since they scarcely had enough for themselves. Then that spring a wondrous thing happened. I was gathering wood out beyond the village perimeter, as close to the forest as I dared go, when suddenly there was a great crashing, rending noise. I was certain it was a bear or a dragon or something large and ferocious enough to make a meal of a small, scared boy. Then what appeared but a pair of men on steeds.

"It was the most magnificent sight I had ever seen," he said, his eyes shining. "The pair wore uniforms of burnished leather with swords and shields and helmets and breastplates of gleaming metal. Their steeds snorted and pranced, as proud and strong as the men. They were from another world, so far above anything I had ever imagined that I knew I looked upon the gods themselves.

"I did not think, I did not look back. I raised my hands above my head and ran toward them, shouting words I do not recall. One of the men laughed, a great booming sound, then reached down and grabbed my outstretched hand and swung me onto his horse. I wrapped my arms tight around him, certain that I was about to be borne off to heaven." He chuckled at his own young folly. "Instead, I rode back to the Roman army camp, where I soon learned how to polish leather and make metal gleam and fight for scraps around the camp followers' fire.

"I grew into a likely enough lad. Shaggy, if I recall correctly. I joined up when I was sixteen or thereabouts, a mere formality since by then I'd been training with swords and shield and lance for nigh on five years. Between my labors, that is, taking up the wooden training tools and having at it with the other lads. Not that injuries couldn't happen with wooden staves for swords. They could and they did. Only with wooden blades they were seldom fatal.

"I survived the rough-and-tumble of being a camp follower, and I joined the ranks as one who neither knew nor cared for another life. It was all I expected, a decade or so in the legions, then whatever came after, a soldier's grave most likely. It was enough. That single day was as far as I ever cared to look. Then fate reached down once again and plucked me from the ranks."

He rose and stumped to the window. "We were on patrol with a visiting consul to please, when the Celts fell upon us, all hair and screams and battle-axes and stink. Their first assault ran through us like a hot knife through butter. I saw the consul fall, and I moved without thinking. I say this for certain, though it all took place more than thirty years ago. The consul fell, slipped in the blood of a fallen comrade most likely. I saw him go down, and saw too the stave lifted and centered for his heart. And I leapt and bore the wound myself."

Cletus turned back from the window, lifted his tunic, pointed to the great circular wound now healed into a darkened leathery depression. "Here it went, under my ribs, just as my sword took off the barbarian's head, long swinging red hair and all. I thought I was dead, but fate was not done with me yet. Then and there on the battlefield, surrounded by the cries of wounded and the stench of battle, the consul knelt beside me as they drew the spear from my side, and called me a brave man. His man, if I survived. Which I did. Lying there while the consul's own healer cauterized my wound with steaming pitch."

Cletus walked back over and sat down. "I passed blood for a while and tasted bile for well over a year. But I survived, and the consul honored his pledge. In time he gave me this land of his to manage, and the right to call the position mine for all my life and that of the generation to follow. And then he gave me his favorite concubine's daughter for a wife."

Travis struggled to sit up, was stilled by his father's restraining hand. "Your first wife? The mother to my half-brothers?"

"The consul was a shrewd man," Cletus replied quietly. "Very shrewd. He moved men and armies like others use stones on a gaming board. His Africa estate was too far away to visit often, and his favorite concubine was fearful of her daughter being sold as a rich man's plaything. So he wed us, both to honor me and keep me honest. It was not a choice I would have made myself, but choices seldom are. I agreed because I had to, as did she. But she hated it here, far from the delights of the city and the intrigues of court. In truth she would have been far better off belonging to another man than to me."

"And you could not divorce her," Travis said. "You could not escape. Not and still honor your pledge."

"She fed her sons on her own bitterness." Cletus rose to his feet, started for the door. "There was little I could do except be who I was, and hope at least one would not turn against me."

Travis forced himself up on one elbow. "And my mother? What of her?"

His father stopped, turned back. "Your mother was a gift, she was. Daughter of a neighbor now long gone. He was a northerner like me, from Gaul. She had your light hair and a spirit like a brilliant flame. Over her I have no regrets, save that she passed on before me."

"You loved her," Travis said quietly.

"Love? Where in this hard land is there room for love?" His face set in the resigned lines of an old soldier. "You have much of her in you. Which is why I have kept you here almost too long. Now rest. The new day soon comes."

Raffa entered the tent when the Carthaginian sun was so high it shone bright and hot on the roof. "Our watchmen saw you battle your night ghosts down by the waterside, so I've let you sleep. But it's almost noon, and this tent of yours is an oven. If you want to sleep more, do it outside where there's a breeze."

Travis struggled to focus, found himself drenched in sweat. Then he recalled the plan that had come to him just before sleep arrived, and rose to his feet. "How many pirates do we hold as prisoners?"

"Seventeen unharmed, two more badly wounded. Another did not survive the night." Raffa poured him a goblet of water, watched him drink, reported, "Just done the rounds. All appears well, but Septimus has gone missing. Probably reveling with one of the bath mistresses. Saw a pair of them sniffing about last night."

Travis stripped off his sweat-stained garment, accepted the bucket from Raffa, and poured the water over his head. "Bring the pirates to me one at a time. When they leave me, they cannot be seen by the others again."

Raffa's expression grew watchful. "Why?"

"Something came to me in the night." He wiped himself down, the rough linen cloth scratching yet pleasant. "Bring them in shackled, ready for the slave market. Let them all know that's where they're headed."

Raffa watched him, a glimmer of something new in his eyes. The objection Travis half-expected never came. Instead he observed, "We'll have to post extra guards if we tell them that outright."

"Fine." He slipped another fresh tunic over his head. "But keep yourself free. I want you in here with me. And two others. Choose those who truly can be trusted with our lives, for by being here they will hold our fate in their hands."

Raffa did not move. "You have a plan?"

"Perhaps." Travis eased himself down onto the leather camp-seat, reached for the bowl of fruit, and felt his strength begin to drain away. "When will this cursed weakness leave me?"

The glimmer was still there as Raffa turned toward the tent's entrance. "It is doing so," he replied, ducking his head, "even as we speak."

CHAPTER IV

I should be getting back," Septimus said, sweating badly now.

"Grant me the pleasure of your company just a moment longer," Fabian replied, his voice an even drawl. "Tell me now, why was it not possible to warn us of their plans to ensnare the pirates on the way here?"

"Master, I have already explained that." He glanced outside the window. "The longer I am here, the harder it will be to account for my absence."

"Indulge me," Fabian insisted, sprawled easily upon his silk-draped lounge. He kept Septimus standing before him, ignoring the man's growing nervousness, his orders backed up by the pair of muscle-bound guards stationed to either side. "My memory, you know. It is these pressures I am forced to bear."

"We were only told of the plan ourselves once we were under way," Septimus repeated, flickering a glance at the guards, armed and tensed and at the ready. Beyond them lolled the servant known as Hanno, dressed and coiffured as always in imitation of his master. "You must believe me."

"Of course I believe you," Fabian said, his voice soothing, his eyes hard as stone. "Why should I not, a servant as loyal as you? It is only, well, you must understand, this lapse of yours has placed me in a most uncomfortable position. My allies are extremely displeased. Angry, really. They blame me for this little lapse, since it was I who urged them to await Travis' vessel, and I who requested its capture."

"Master, I speak the truth. There was no way to escape; we were all watched and ordered to watch each other." Septimus was a small, wiry man whose life had aged him far beyond his years. He stood straight and unbending with a soldier's discipline, but his eyes were held captive by the same fear that showed in his face. "In every port, we anchored well apart from all other vessels. The plan was to let all see how poorly we handled the oars, yet keep word from escaping that it was because legionnaires were working the vessel."

"Yes, well, I must say my dear brother's subterfuge worked all too well. My allies planned to attack a relatively poor, unarmed vessel. And they paid heavily for the error."

"Please, master." Septimus swiped at his face. "I do not care to know more than I must. You ask for information, I deliver. That is enough."

"Ah, but no longer, I am afraid." Fabian inspected grapes nestled in a bowl embossed with gold leaf, chose one, slipped it into his mouth. "You see, Septimus, the pirates insist upon retribution. Yes. I am afraid it is not enough to send your apologies." Another of the glass-eyed smiles. "You will have to go and explain your actions in person. For your sake, I do hope they choose to believe you."

The first pirate brought before Travis was a wiry, one-eyed weasel. His fetters granted him just enough play to take shuffling half-steps. His arms were roped to his sides, the knots so taut his hands were already puffed and swollen. His rapidly shifting glance showed a man who knew where he was headed, and frantically sought escape.

Travis sat on his elevated pallet, propped up with two cushions so he was just below eye level. He waited as long as his own nerves would allow, then stated flatly, "You follow the old and forbidden ways, you and your kind."

At the words, the pirate's head jerked upright and his body stilled. He watched his questioner, his attention focused on this unexpected development.

"I have visited the old temple. The symbol was there on the bow of your boat. Baal Hammon demands what is no longer permitted, is that not so?" Travis saw Raffa's eyes widen slightly. Good. It pleased him enormously to know he could surprise the old warrior. "I want to enter your village."

"Impossible," the man sneered. "You would be the next sacrifice to Molech."

"Then you shall be taken from here and sold this very hour in the city's main slave market," Travis replied calmly.

The pirate studied him. "And if I were to do the impossible?"

"You shall be freed, with five silver sesterce pressed into your hand." Travis nodded toward the open flap. "But be forewarned. I shall ask the same of all your mates. If your stories do not match, you will not only be sold but branded beforehand."

The threat had no effect except to narrow his one good eye even farther. "How do I know I can trust you?"

"Ask anyone here. They will tell you I stand by my word."

Nervously the pirate shifted his eyes toward Raffa.

"Travis son of Cletus is a man of his word," Raffa said, his voice soft with promised death. "For myself, I would reward you with my knife across your throat."

Travis made as to relax himself farther into the cushions. "Now then. I want to know when and how such a thing would be possible."

Travis stepped up beside the guide. "Here? You are sure?"

"There is only one trader Hannibal Mago," the man replied, extending his hand.

Travis inspected the door with mounting dismay. The main portals were high enough to permit a man to ride his horse through with spear upraised, or for a camel to pass through fully laden. That was not what disturbed him. The door was marred by great ax strokes, the wood splintered and then carefully repaired, as though the owner wished to show all the world what had been done. At head height a fiery torch had been used to brand a great cross deep into the wood.

A Christian, and a fanatical one at that. Travis had never met one, but from all he had heard, he would find no help here.

"Sire." Gaven approached. "The young maiden yesterday."

66

"What about her?"

"If I understood him correctly, Damon followed her here."

"Worse and worse," Travis muttered. Then there was no hope of having her either. Christian women were notorious for looking at none outside their sect. Angrily Travis raised his sword, and pounded the heavy timber with its pommel.

The face cage, a small barred aperture set in the middle of the door, opened to reveal a bearded old man. He squinted at Travis, gave the stranger's simple dress and worn sword a cursory inspection, and snorted his disgust at being disturbed. Without deigning to speak, he started to close the portal.

Travis was in no mood to take any such nonsense. Before the old man could slam the door shut, Travis unsheathed his sword and slid it between the iron bars. The old man squeaked in alarm and jerked away from the blade.

"Travis son of Cletus to see your master."

"Eh?" The old man was not without dignity. He drew himself erect, remaining at a safe distance from the gleaming blade, and said in lofty Greek, "What manner of screechings are these?"

It was common for educated Greeks, even those raised as slaves, to consider both the Latin language and all who used it barbaric. But this was slowly changing, since the Emperor Constantine had spoken no Greek whatsoever, yet had been known throughout the empire as an educated man. A soldier, but an educated one. For a servant to speak thus was intended as a slap in the face.

Travis smiled mirthlessly. The expression coming from behind an unsheathed blade must have carried a warning, for the old man took another half-step back. "Travis son of Cletus to see your master, the merchant Hannibal Mago," he repeated in excellent

Greek. He then switched to neo-Punic, the local language, restricted to Berbers and outlying villages and the poorest of marketplaces. "And you understood me the first time, you senile old fool."

"Fool, is it?" The face clamped down into well-used furrows. The old man wheeled about, snapped, "Then you can just stand there and eat dust until the guards are summoned, young pup."

"Call your guards, and there shall be more than the blood of sacrifice scattered across your portal," Travis shouted, his rage pushing the old man back yet farther. "I have not traveled across desert and sea to be treated thus."

"What is this?" A woman's voice carried across the courtyard.

Travis withdrew his blade at the sight of the young maiden from the market street. She in turn stopped cold when his face came into view. They stood and stared at one another for a long moment before she turned back to the slave and said, her voice trembling slightly, "I asked you a question, Demetrius."

"The stranger drew a weapon," the old man muttered.

"Only after being treated in a loutish manner." Travis made no attempt to hide his bitterness. She was as beautiful as he first had thought. And, as a Christian, utterly unattainable to the likes of him. He offered a curse for all temple sects and the way they drew in the women.

"Open the door," she ordered, her voice growing stronger.

"But, mistress—"

"Must I shame our house by doing so myself?"

Resigned, the old man walked forward, slammed back the bolts, then turned away, leaving Travis to push open the door himself. "I shall summon the master," he said, shuffling off. "And the guards."

She paid him no mind, but rather stood regal in her bearing and looked at Travis with the greatest, darkest eyes he had ever seen. "Greetings to you, stranger."

Travis sheathed his sword and bowed deeply. Continuing in Greek, he said, "Travis son of Cletus at your service. I beg forgiveness for bringing disharmony to your home, mistress."

"There is nothing to forgive." She nodded to the men, taking no visible note of their arms and guarded stance about him. "Will you and your men take refreshment?"

"Water, if it is not too much trouble."

"We can do better than that." She turned, and at some silent signal a handmaiden appeared from the colonnaded shadows. "Bring sherbet and fresh fruit for our guests."

"There is no need for you to go to trouble on our account," Travis protested, continuing the formalities. His heart filled his throat, making each breath an effort.

"It is no trouble." A braid intertwined with silver threads started at each temple and connected at the back, holding her long black hair in place. Her shift was simple, yet as elegant as her poise. Her neck was long and graceful, her chin delicate, her lips full and pale and untainted by coloring. "I am Lydia, daughter of Hannibal Mago."

"An honor, mistress." Travis bowed a second time, then rose to see an older man as seamed and steady as old oak come stomping into the courtyard. He wore a short tunic, unadorned save for a single silver shoulder-clasp in the form of the Christian cross. The old servant shuffled two steps behind, a fresh gleam in his eye. Travis drew himself erect and waited for the storm.

"What's this I hear of a sword being thrust upon an honored servant of this household?" The man planted himself before Travis, corded arms on hips.

"Demetrius no doubt deserved whatever this gentleman gave him," Lydia offered.

The patron raised one stiff hand, clearly intended to silence his daughter, but mistaken for a signal by others, for instantly guards separated themselves from the sharply drawn shadows.

"Blades!" Raffa's voice snapped out the one word, then shoved the startled patron back as he and the others drew their swords and formed a barrier about Travis.

"Hold!" Travis stepped out and in front of Raffa. "Sheath your swords."

"Sire—"

"Do so," he ordered. "Either these are allies or we are departing. Either way, there is no danger here."

Raffa nodded and straightened and slipped his sword home. Reluctantly the others obeyed his hand signal. Travis turned back and met the patron's gaze, ignoring the stance of his guards. The air surrounding him was taut with explosive tension. "I apologize for the actions of my men."

"It is not your men's actions that concerned me." His eyes remained steady on Travis, as though nothing untoward had happened. "I asked you a question."

"We have traveled long and hard," Travis said, feeling the girl's eyes on him, resisting the urge to look her way. "We have met much resistance, and fought pirates only six nights back."

"Pirates!" Lydia's voice rose a full octave at the news.

But Travis was not finished. "It is only through the alertness of my men that I stand before you today. As for myself, I too have suffered attacks, from within and without. I share the strain of my men." He looked directly at the old servant, who stiffened but did not move. "For any slight given members of your household, I offer my humble apologies."

"Accepted," the patron said, his words clipped by the same tension that still gripped the courtyard. "Do you hold evidence of the pirates?"

"Father," Lydia protested.

"Three of their ships," Travis replied, a touch of pride ringing through.

One eyebrow lifted a fraction. "You captured three pirate vessels?"

"And nineteen of their men," Travis added. "Fifteen of whom are headed for the slave market this very afternoon."

"The palanquin," Lydia said. "I saw you being carried by your men. You were injured?"

Travis shook his head, allowing himself to look in her direction, reveling in what he found there. He replied simply, "Poison."

"Why do you come to me?" the patron demanded.

Reluctantly Travis turned back to the stalwart old man. "I and my men have asked around. All with whom we spoke said Hannibal Mago was both a man of power within Carthage and a man to be trusted. We are in need of an honest man."

Still he showed no willingness to disengage and welcome the strangers. "You are stopping here long?"

"A few days only," Travis replied. "We are on our way to Constantinople."

Lydia's gasp was matched by her father's involuntary start. The patron swiftly recovered, drew one hand to his shoulder, and bowed. "Hannibal Mago, trader of Carthage."

"Travis son of Cletus, at your service."

Hannibal motioned once, and the guards relaxed and drew back. The courtyard's tension instantly eased. "This sun is burdensome. Perhaps your men would take their refreshment in the hall. Demetrius, see to these men's comfort."

"As you say, lord." A world of doubt was contained in the old servant's voice.

Hannibal Mago's grace and formality were matched by a solid power as he waved Travis forward. "Welcome to my humble home."

"There is a celebration of the full moon," Travis told him. "The entire village takes part. This information was confirmed by three other men."

"Three other pirates," Hannibal corrected. "What makes you think they can be trusted?"

The chamber in which they sat, as the rest of the compound, spoke realms about the people who dwelled here. Their house was clearly ancient, filled with property collected over many generations and handled with easy familiarity. The high stone walls were bare save for a wooden crucifix, a symbol of the Christian sect. The long table flanking their trio of chairs was covered in scrolls and manifests. Beneath the flooring came occasional sounds of goods being moved about the great warehouse. To Roman eyes, the fact that the business was part of his home estate would suggest that the patron had once been a slave. But Travis thought otherwise. He recognized in the man's casual strength the same disdain for Rome's pompous customs that his father held.

"Their freedom does not come unless our raid is successful." Travis sipped his goblet of sherbet, fruit dried and ground and stirred into water. It was cool, refreshing, and far less satisfying to his mind than wine. But it was all that had been offered. "All the village gathers at midnight. According to the captives, we should enter safely." He hesitated, then repeated the words spoken by all four, "Unless the god sees us."

A servant came in, bowed, searched among the papers on the desk. Travis watched him from the corner of his eye. There was none of the fearful servitude he had found at his brother's estate, nor the secretive darting about and spying and subterfuge that indicated a divided household. Instead there was the humming bustle of a busy, successful, solid enterprise. To his surprise the servant then approached and bowed again, but instead of bending next to his patron, he approached the *daughter*. Impatiently Lydia whispered a few words, watched as the servant went back and picked up a half-opened scroll. She nodded once, then turned back without acknowledging the servant's final bow.

Hannibal inquired, "The god?"

"According to some legend, this Baal Hammon or Molech arrives at the festival, and takes on human form." Travis struggled to ignore Lydia's presence. It was not only her beauty and her watchful silence that unsettled him. He had never known a woman to be present in such discussions, clearly privy to all her father's affairs. "No doubt just another ancient superstition."

"Yes." Hannibal Mago was a most imposing figure, his strength undiminished by the years that had grayed his close-cropped hair. He was not tall, but bore himself with a general's casual authority, adding greatly to his stature. "You are not troubled by such supernatural threats?"

"Temples and sects draw upon the weakness of man and his fears of the unknown," Travis said, using his father's words. Only afterward did he recall the cross burned into the door and added hastily, "Although I have heard the Christian god is different."

"Indeed," Hannibal said, glancing his daughter's way.

Travis understood both the glance and the girl's lowered gaze in response. Futile desire grated in his voice as he demanded, "Can I count on your help?"

Hannibal turned back, inspected him, offered, "I could bring this up with the council."

"Do," Travis replied, "and you shall perhaps destroy our plans, and possibly us as well."

"I see," he said slowly. Then, "There is a man who aspires to the council. A certain Fabian. His father is also said to be named Cletus."

"My half-brother," Travis said grimly.

"Ah." The gaze became keener. "You have no doubt paid your respects."

"Yesterday."

"And you discussed this with him?"

"The matter," Travis replied, his words bitten short, "did not arise."

"Your brother has bought his way into the proconsul's own tax syndicate. Did you know that?"

"No, I did not." Tax syndicates were a delight of the rich and the stuff of nightmares to the local citizenry. Proconsuls, the title given to provincial governors, were responsible for providing the emperor with a certain amount of tax each year. They auctioned off the right to collect these taxes. A few syndicates operated honestly, most did not, especially in such unstable times. The winning syndicate was ordered not to overburden the population, but little attention was paid to such orders. Visiting legates sent to oversee taxation were bribed, their reports falsified. The syndicates then taxed the local peasants and shopkeepers and landowners and free craftsmen all they could bear and more, with the local garrison ordered to back them up.

"Well, no matter." Hannibal inspected the depths of his goblet. "Some feel that Fabian bids to join the aristocracy. I for one think his action holds a baser aim."

"Profit," Travis said, knowing he was being tested.

A single nod, more of the cautious inspection. "You are residing with your brother?"

"Alas," Travis grated, "my business holds me to the port with my men."

"Your men, yes. A most interesting collection. They call you sire, I note." A glance at Travis' simple garment. "You are of royal blood?"

"Hardly." Travis stole a look toward Lydia. She remained still and watchful, her eyes raised up to him, a look so deep he longed to turn away from this talk and watch her in return. "My father was a simple soldier. He now manages a consul's estate. Most of his and my own men come from an army that has forgotten how to care for its survivors."

"And the title they bestow upon you?"

"A gift."

"Interesting." Another warning glance in Lydia's direction, this one not returned. "Your brother says little about his background, but fosters rumors that his family holds to noble ties."

"I am not surprised."

75

"Did you also not know that your brother now finances wine and spice shipments?"

Travis blinked. Wine and spice, along with gold and certain perfumes, were the most precious of goods coming from the Africa provinces. "Paid for through his tax profits?"

"Impossible, as his entry into the syndicate was only months ago. Strange, is it not, that the son of an estate manager might begin financing such cargoes and purchase a share of the city's richest tax syndicate, all in one season?"

But Travis was not yet prepared to let the other news go. "Do you know if any of his shipments have been attacked by pirates?"

For the first time, there was an easing of the cautious inspection. Hannibal Mago leaned back, sipped from his goblet, and replied, "During this season and the two before, there have been more attacks than all the past three decades combined. None upon grain shipments bound for Rome, mind you, and not so often that the empire would be forced to marshal its forces here. For the moment, we remain one of many brushfires throughout the provinces. The pirates are called a minor irritation because the attacks seem uncoordinated and do not affect the government's own ships. But some of us who have suffered at the pirates' hands think otherwise."

"You have not," Travis said, "answered my question."

"To my knowledge, your brother has had a remarkable run of good fortune." Another sip, then the decision. "What is it exactly that you require to put your plan into action?"

"Not soldiers," Travis replied. "If what I have been told is true, we shall do best by acting with measured force. I seek allies who can be held to only what force is necessary, and not an ounce more."

Hannibal nodded slowly, then said, "I have certain acquaintances who are no strangers to force. They are also as tight with their words as you."

"A knowledge of the terrain and how to move quietly would help us greatly," Travis went on. "When we succeed, a quarter-share of any bounty for me, a quarter for you, and the remaining half to be shared equally between all who take part, plus those of my men who stay behind on guard duty."

"*When* we succeed," Hannibal echoed.

"There shall be no need for any of us to consider the alternative," Travis replied somberly.

"Very well. I think this can be arranged." Hannibal rose and drew Travis with him, then motioned for Lydia to remain where she was. Travis had no choice but to bow and follow, risking a final glance as he swept from the room.

When they were out in the connecting hallway, Hannibal continued, "I must ask because they will want to know. Why do you do this?"

"My family and I have suffered at the hands of these pirates." Travis hesitated, then finished, "And I could use the money."

"As with all else you have said, it rings with a steady honesty. I like that." Hannibal led him back outside, but before they passed the columns and reentered the blazing sun, he stopped and said more quietly, "Your brother is profiting from the move against the pagan temples as well. He is buying up those women who before would have been hired as temple prostitutes." His dark eyes glittered from the shadows that cast dagger-lines over his sharp features. "He supplies many of the taverns near the port."

"My men shall be warned as soon as I return," Travis said, understanding him perfectly. "I am in your debt."

● ● ●

Lydia entered the half-light of her mother's room. She resisted the urge to march about, fling open the shutters, do what she could with tension and energy to banish the smell and the closeness and the vague sense of approaching death. She had never known anything as hard as this, standing and watching as her mother wasted away. "Mother?"

"Come over here, daughter." The voice was quiet yet alert.

"I don't want to disturb you."

"Come."

She shut the door, and with it felt her accustomed energy and drive slip away. It was not just illness that she met in these shadows. Here was a different form of truth. Her mother's illness and Lydia's own helplessness forced Lydia to see her constant activity for what it was, a mask. She used it to cloak her own insecurities and fears and lack of answers. The confidence dropped away, revealing a young woman who felt her entire being filled with the tumult of unanswered doubt. "How are you?"

Her mother waved the question away, reached over as Lydia seated herself on the side of her daybed, and grasped her hand with surprising strength. "What is this I hear of battles in the courtyard?"

"There was no battle. Who told you such nonsense? Demetrius? He should be whipped."

That brought a smile. "Ah, so the other bit of nonsense is true, then."

Lydia looked down at the frail hand in hers, the skin translucent in the half-light, the bones delicate as a small bird's. "His name is Travis. Such a strange name. Such a strange man. He is the same one as the man on the pallet."

"The one who drew your attention in the market the other day?"

Lydia nodded, unable now to raise her eyes, fearful of finding the same warning she had seen coming from her father. "His men call him sire, and not because they must. There was a moment when Father's guards made a threatening move, it was all a mistake, but you should have seen them react."

"These men of Travis?"

"Yes. They surrounded him in an instant, so fast I felt my heart stop. I watched their faces. They would have willingly died to defend him. He stopped them with one word." She took a breath made shaky by the memory. "He was poisoned. He did not say, but I think by his own brother, the man called Fabian, the one Father detests who wants to weasel himself onto the council. And Travis was attacked by pirates, but he captured three of the boats and some of the men."

When there was no reply, Lydia forced herself to raise her head. To her surprise, she found her mother smiling. "This reminds me of when you were a little girl. You loved to tell stories you had heard. But if you were excited, the story became muddled, with the beginning at the end and the end in the middle and the middle left out entirely. Your father used to laugh until he cried."

Lydia did not smile in reply. "He is sailing for Constantinople."

"Ah. Then here is indeed something to think about." Her mother looked worried for the first time. "He is not one of us, I take it. Otherwise someone would have said this by now."

"No." The word was little more than a sigh.

"And yet you meet him by chance in the market, then he arrives here. Were you followed?"

"I don't know. Perhaps. He says he heard Father was an honest man. His purpose seems genuine."

"Indeed, it is hardly logical for a man courting my daughter to bare blades upon entering the front gates." Her mother turned a gaunt face toward the shuttered window and said quietly, "Perhaps there is something intended here."

The tiny flicker of hope burst into a flame so passionate that it brought a burning to Lydia's eyes. "You truly think so?"

"Perhaps, I said." Her mother turned back, inspected her daughter, and sighed. "My beautiful, willful young lady. Of all the men in our community of faithful, all those seeking your hand, all the families who would beg to join with ours." Another moment, then, "Tell me of him."

"His hair is the color of a sunset," Lydia said, her chest so tight the words caught and emerged as little musical breaths. "Red and gold at the same time, a color I have never seen before."

"A Gaul, perhaps," her mother murmured. "I have heard of such."

"His eyes are the color of a forest glade, yet clear as crystal. He is tall and slender, yet strong. He carries himself as Father does, full of power."

"Yet he is young."

Lydia nodded. "My age, perhaps a few years more. But he holds himself as one much older and speaks with Father as with an equal. His voice is quiet. He does not treat his men as the Romans do their slaves; you can see they are his friends. Even when they bore his palanquin they spoke with him and guarded him because they wished it so."

"If what you say is so, then he is of singular quality." Her mother seemed reluctant to say the words. "Very well. Tell me all that has happened this day, all that you saw, all that you heard."

Lydia looked at her mother, so frail and yet so strong, and whispered, "Then what?"

"Then we will pray together, you and I," she replied, "and ask the One for answers to what appear to our earthly eyes as impossible mysteries."

Carthage was a city wed to the sea. It ran lengthwise along the coast, the inland borders marked by hills, academy, theater, and temples along a great lake.

Carthage was a city of people. Well over half a million humans made up the noisy, surging mass who cloaked themselves in smoke and dust and noise and heat and stone.

Carthage was a city of temples. Gods of every description, from the bloodthirsty Punic beasts to the secretive Greek mystery sects, all had their dwellings. Those who had found favor with the Roman masters were housed in prominent places, their old Carthaginian and Berber names translated into the Roman hierarchy. The others, the ones whose past legacy dripped with the blood of human sacrifice and unspeakable acts, were relegated to the hills and plains that ringed the inner city.

Carthage was a city of grandeur. The governor's palace fronted the forum, or central square. Across from it rose the capitol, or primary temple. The plaza was rimmed by statues of former emperors and African proconsuls. That of Constantine still held pride of place in the center, though the emperor was now dead. When it was deemed safe, the head would be struck from the central statue and a new one set in its place. Twice already the festival had been postponed, as rumors of wrangling and plots and counterplots continued to sweep through the empire. Each arriving ship brought more news, all of it sending tremors through the community.

Carthage was also a city of layers. Above rose the newer Roman structures, proud and prosperous and domineering as their builders. Below, especially in the city's poorer quarters, lay the remains of ancient Carthage. Much had been destroyed, but not all.

Carthage was built upon ranks of rocky hillsides. During its first two thousand years, the rocky cliffs had been penetrated by a maze of man-made caverns. Some formed stalls and storage rooms. Others housed beggars and thieves and the poorest of freemen. Berber hillsmen seeking work had claimed many and guarded them zealously. Not even the Roman census takers penetrated far into those gloomy depths. It was a dark world, possessor of many secrets.

Hannibal continued the argument with himself as he scrambled hastily down winding ways. It was the perfect solution to both problems, yet he was reluctant to believe he was actually attempting this contact, and doing so alone. Hard as it was to admit even to himself, he was afraid.

"Why should we trust this man?"

"I can give you no answer," Hannibal replied, seated in the smoky cavern, the air fetid with the closed-in force of so many tightly packed bodies. "Other than the fact that I do myself."

The cowled and bearded figure inspected him across the fire. "You will be going with us?"

"I will," he answered, not having decided until that moment.

"This is not your type of battle," the bearded man sneered. "If what the man says is true, you will find yourself leagues away from your markets and counting houses."

Hannibal ignored the slur, as he had so many others from this man and his minions. "I must see if what he says is true. Magirus has asked me to go to Constantinople. This man's ship travels there."

"So. You take your orders from the bishop now, do you?"

"I accept *requests* from all my Christian brothers," Hannibal replied, the effort of clamping down on anger costing him dearly. "Including you, Ettaba. You and your desire to own lands of your own. A village where you and your people can live as you choose, worship as you please, and be free from what you find so disagreeable in our Carthage church life."

The berobed figure pondered deeply. He was cut from peasant Berber stock, short and sparse of frame, his skin dark and hardened as old leather. "There is a rumor that Donatus is returning to Carthage."

"There are rumors everywhere, most especially now." Hannibal strived to conceal how the news rocked him. The return of Donatus would be nothing short of disastrous.

Donatus was the second bishop of Carthage and leader of the larger community, at least in numbers on high feast days. For the remainder of the year many of his members traveled, as he did himself. Most of the Donatists were drawn from the discontented freemen, landless Berbers, and the angry and rebellious village dwellers whose hatred for the Romans was not diminished by having a Christian upon the throne.

Dwellers of inland villages were known as Berbers, and their dress declared both tribe and region. Theirs was a heritage even more ancient than that of Carthage, and they remained a sullen and surly lot. The Romans spent fortunes annually on endless skirmishes with these sword-wielding warriors dressed in long flowing robes. Desert bandits emerged without warning and disappeared just as swiftly, leaving only the fallen in their wake. They were known as the desert scourge and were as roundly cursed as the pirates. Their skin was dark, their women beautiful, and their enemies held close for generations. Becoming Christian had not made them any easier to deal with, even for those who shared their beliefs.

Donatus himself had been away from Carthage for almost two years, traveling from one small community to another, using his great personal appeal to hold the fractious Donatist movement together. In his absence, a semblance of calm had fallen over the Carthage Christian community, as many on both sides wished for peace, especially when the empire was threatened with cataclysmic upheaval. Many, but not all.

Hannibal sat erect and stone-faced, watching the Berber across from him. Ettaba was leader of a group known to some as the *circumcillian*, roving bands of landless freemen who pressed their angry cause with fists and stones and clubs. Hannibal's entry was possible only because of his father's legacy. Because his father had been martyred, Hannibal remained a mainstay of the fragile peace between the two Christian communities. Yet entering the Carthage caves was a risky move, taken only because of what Travis and his plan had to offer.

"Land," Hannibal repeated, offering the greatest lure he could to such as these. He kept his eyes on the leader, but cast his voice out to all those half-hidden listeners. "Land of your own. An empty village, protected and isolated from the hand of Rome. I would myself see to the proper registration of ownership."

Dark eyes glittered gold and hard in the firelight. "You would do this for us?"

"You have my word."

"Then you shall have my answer with the dawn." Ettaba rose to his feet. "We salute all who have remained loyal to the Christian ideals, Hannibal. We accept as one all who hold fast to the truth, even until death."

"That," Hannibal replied dryly, rising with him, "neither of us has been called to confront."

"Your blessed father was a saint, a martyr whose place has been assured for all time in heaven. You should give thanks for his sacrifice."

"I would rather give thanks for our own deliverance," Hannibal replied, "and welcome into our fold all who now might seek the truth."

"This attitude of yours threatens yourself and your family's good name," Ettaba snapped.

"If so," Hannibal replied, striving for calm, seeking no quarrel when he was so close, "that shall be a judgment for God and God alone to make." He bowed to the stern-faced Berber and departed. Only when he was well clear of the fire's light and the cave and the silent, watchful circle of men, did he draw his first full breath in what felt like years.

CHAPTER V

The day was spent in frantic preparation. Hannibal came and went like the wind, collecting material to be transported back to the harbor, outlining his plans in greater detail, watching as Travis gained Ettaba's grudging approval. It was not until after the noonday meal that he found a moment of quiet and privacy to confront his daughter.

She was binding together another group of masks, purchased by discreet servants from a number of different market stalls. Masks remained a part of Carthage's tradition and were used at numerous festivals. Their darker history was conveniently forgotten. Thus buying a dozen or so from each of several stalls did not draw undue attention their way.

"He is a man wise beyond his years," Hannibal said.

"Yes." There was no need to ask of whom her father spoke. Lydia continued with her tasks, sensed his questing gaze, knew she was unable to hide what she felt. Not from her father. "He is."

He smiled briefly, understanding his daughter very well. "You will take advice?"

Lydia stiffened against the coming attack. Suddenly the arguments she had carefully marshaled began melting away, leaving her heart exposed and trembling. A pagan. She was falling in love with a pagan.

Hannibal took his daughter's silence as agreement. "Teach him only what he wants to learn."

The words were so unexpected she jerked as though slapped awake. "What?"

"He is not only wise," Hannibal told her. "He is aware. He will see the flaws in our religion, as this is the way he has been trained to see all the world. He will seek the weaknesses, and unless we refuse the convenient cloak and instead meet him with open honesty, he will use what he learns to condemn and criticize. I know such men as these. The world has taught him only to be strong, to defend, to struggle. We must seek not to shield ourselves, but rather to disarm him with truth."

Her defenses opened before his genuine concern. All the fear, all the worry, all could be exposed before the strength of her father. She whispered, "I'm so afraid."

"And I am afraid for you," he said somberly.

Lydia felt a single tear escape from her burning eyes and trace its way down her cheek. "What am I to do?"

"Hide nothing from him. It is the only way." He waited to be sure she understood what he was saying. "Let him also hear the bad from you. Let him see that you are aware of the flaws within what is supposed to be kept holy."

The burning crept down from her eyes to her heart. He was not speaking to her just as his daughter. For the first time, he spoke to her as an adult. As an equal. She took a deep breath, but it was not enough to erase the trembling from her voice. "And if, despite this honesty, he uses it against me?"

"Then we lose," he said simply, glossing over nothing. "But if we seek to show him only what is good, only what we know is the truth, without acknowledging all that he finds about him, we have lost him for sure. At least this way we have a chance."

"A chance," she whispered. *We*, he had said. We win, or we lose. She was not alone. Another tear escaped and trickled down unnoticed.

"I like this man," Hannibal admitted. "He is of singular quality, and may someday make a true leader of merit."

Despite the pain and the fear, she had to smile. Singular quality was his way of classing the finest trade goods.

His face gentled. "You have not lost your humor. Good. Do you love him?"

Again the words failed. She made do with a single nod.

"Well," Hannibal sighed. "Know that whatever happens, I am here with you."

By mid-afternoon the constant activity had left Travis so exhausted he stumbled over both his feet and his words. Ettaba watched the transition with narrowed eyes, until Hannibal finally explained he was fighting off the effects of a poisoning. Immediately the Berber's tone changed, and he joined his voice to the others in insisting that Travis go and rest.

His sleep was so deep that when he awoke to daylight he thought for a moment that he had only slept an instant, and delighted in returning to strength so swiftly. Then he noticed the sun's angle upon his tent roof, and realized he had slept an afternoon and a night and most of the next morning.

He stormed from the tent, found Raffa walking toward him, demanded, "Why have you let me sleep?"

"The supplies are loaded," Raffa reported, ignoring his ire. "Our men have cast lots and assigned duties. It was good to see such grumbling from those left behind on guard duty, even when they are to receive an equal share."

"I have lost almost an entire day," Travis groused. "With departure this very afternoon, and a thousand tasks left to do."

"The thousand tasks are done. Those Christians are good workers, I'll give you that. As for letting you sleep, we are going into battle. I would rather have you rested and alert, and leave the preparations to other hands." Raffa glanced behind Travis, said, "Another has been waiting for you to awaken."

Travis turned to find Lydia approaching. She smiled a greeting, asked, "How are you feeling?"

"Better," he admitted. "I am sorry to be such a weakling."

"Raffa has told us how lucky we are to have you here at all," she replied. "Are you hungry?"

"Very."

"A good sign." She glanced down at the wooden bowl in her hands. "I have been preparing a meal for you over by the port garden."

"That is indeed kind." Travis started to move away, noticed that Raffa waited to speak. "One moment."

"Septimus has still not returned," Raffa said quietly.

"You have searched the area?"

"Men have scoured the city and found nothing." The crusty warrior looked worried. "Two days and counting. It is too long."

Septimus was a relative newcomer, with them less than a year, and one who maintained a distance to all, even to Cletus. Travis thought of Hannibal's warning about the port's tavern girls, and said, "My half-brother Fabian has much to answer for."

"You think he is behind this as well?"

"Again, I do not know what to think." Travis pondered the choices before him. "If we wait and miss the tide, our next chance will not come for another month."

"Preparations have moved too far," Raffa agreed. "And Septimus has been gone since before the plans were laid."

"Then we continue," Travis said, committing himself. He knew the thrilling rush of adventure on the wind. "Have those who stay behind keep on sharp lookout."

"And take another turn about the district when not on watch," Raffa agreed and moved away.

Travis followed Lydia by the trio of captured longboats. The Christian hillsmen gathered silently about their own fire, well removed from Travis' men. Eyes followed their movements in heavy watchful silence until one tribesman called out, "Ettaba says you speak the hill tongue."

Grateful for the chance to speak to them, Travis replied in neo-Punic, "That is true."

"Word has it you were struck by the shadow hand."

"Do not worry," Travis answered. "I will be ready when we attack."

His response was met by grins of approval. "Is it true what we hear," another demanded, "of land for us to choose from?"

"That is what was told to me." The law was clear. All property belonging to sects resorting to human sacrifice was forfeit. "But we will not know for certain until we arrive." He looked around the gathering, saw the turbans and rough-weave robes and hungry expressions of landless Berber tribesmen. He knew the watchful caution, understood their inbred reserve.

Travis gave the short bow of equals, and said formally, "It is good to know my men and I will travel with ones such as you." He was pleased to watch the men stand and respond with the hillsman salutation, hand to heart and lips and forehead. He turned away, found Lydia watching him solemnly. As she led him to a small garden bordering the entry to the port, she asked, "How did you come to speak the Berber tongue?"

"My father uses many of them in the times of planting and harvesting. I also had a nurse from the hills when—" he hesitated, surprised at himself. He had been about to say, when his mother had been taken ill. That was a time he seldom thought of, much less shared with another. Instead he finished, "When I was young."

If she noticed the lapse, Lydia had the wisdom not to say anything. "They are a closed and difficult people. It is remarkable to see them begin to accept you." She looked up at him. "My father was right. You have the makings of a good leader."

They passed beyond the border of date palms and entered a narrow green point lying between harbor and sea. The mountains south of Carthage rose strong and mighty from the water, a great ocher barrier separating the blue below from the blue above. At her direction, he settled on a multicolored carpet near the stone seawall. "Yesterday Hannibal used a word to describe the tribesmen."

"Donatists." She nodded her thanks to the servant watching over the food, the gesture a clear dismissal.

"The Donatists are a tribe?"

"No." She swept off the covering. "I hope you enjoy it."

He looked over the various bowls, knew instinctively she had prepared it all with her own hands. "This is a feast."

She smiled, offered him a plate of unleavened bread, then sat back and watched him eat. The food was excellent, their silence easy. Lydia ate little, content to sit and watch and share the day.

Only when he began to slow did she ask, "Do you truly wish to know more of the Donatists?"

He shifted his weight back against the wall, inspected her openly. Her face was too full of planes and angles to be beautiful in the classic sense. Her nose jutted, her chin was chiseled and direct, her cheekbones taut and slanted, her lips too full. But there was such life, such energy in her that a sleeker shape would not have suited. "It would be good to know more of my fellow travelers."

"The Donatists are a group within the Christian church. They are constantly causing trouble for my father and the other elders."

He saw the shyness masked behind this brisk talk of things more distant and marveled at his ability to understand. "And yet your father went to them for help?"

"They are fighters. That we know for certain." She hesitated for a moment, then asked "Have you heard the story of Jesus of Nazareth?"

"There were a few Christians among my men," he replied. "This is the god who was born of man, yes? Like the Greeks say of their old gods."

"No, not like that. This is no legend. Nor was it simply *a* god. This was *the* God, incarnated as man. He was born so as to die for our sins."

Travis watched the play of emotions across her face, wondered at this willingness of his to listen to such talk. "I see that you believe it was so."

"That surprises you?"

"Everything about you," he replied quietly, "baffles me utterly."

She masked the sudden flush by brushing back her hair and saying briskly, "Some eighty years ago, the Emperor Decius started a great persecution throughout the Roman world. There was a famous bishop of Carthage, Cyprian, who was one of the emperor's strongest opponents. Under the Emperor Valerian the persecutions became even worse, and Cyprian was publicly tortured and killed. We call such believers who die for their faith martyrs."

"I have heard the word."

"Valerian's persecutions lasted nine years. Afterwards there was a time of relative peace, with sporadic persecution but nothing ordered by the emperors themselves. Then came Diocletian, the emperor but one before Constantine, and with him empire-wide persecutions started all over again."

Lydia stopped to sip from her goblet, then continued, "Each time, Christians were ordered to publicly offer sacrifices to the divine emperor, to worship him as a god. If they agreed, they were released. If not, they were tortured and then killed. Their homes were looted, their land and possessions confiscated, their churches burned. Entire Christian communities were destroyed."

"Of this I have heard as well," Travis said quietly. "It has puzzled me why they did not simply agree and get on with life."

"Some did," she confirmed. "Some made the public sacrifices, then later claimed that they continually prayed to the one true God. Some purchased false certificates of sacrifice from temple priests. Others refused, living in terror or fleeing the cities, leaving all behind."

"Your door," Travis said. "I remember now. Your door was axed open."

"My grandfather." Lydia lifted her chin to steady her face. "My father's father refused to accept the orders and chose martyrdom. He was burned at the stake in the opening ceremonies of gladiatorial games, as a sacrifice to the emperor and the Roman gods."

"I am sorry," he mumbled, not knowing what else to say.

"My grandmother fled to the mountains, along with many of the others who refused to bow to the emperor's dictates. It was a hard time. Very hard. My father will not speak of it. He was a young man when they returned, protected by Constantine's new edicts. The local governor was forced to offer restitution, and my father used this money to rebuild the family trading business."

"But nothing could bring back the old man."

"No." She turned her face to the sea, sat there for a long moment. Then she straightened her shoulders, patted her knees with both hands, and continued in the familiar brisk voice. "The Donatists believe that any who bowed to the emperor's edicts and made the sacrifices are apostates. The word signifies someone who has turned against God. The Donatists say this is a crime that can never be forgiven, and that such people and their offspring are to be banned from the church forever."

Travis narrowed his eyes in concentration. All this was new to him. Not the story. Such battles and intrigues were a part of the empire's history. But this was a battle within a religion, and not one played out by bickering priests.

"Others, known nowadays as moderates, say that all who are willing to publicly confess their sins and do penance should be invited back. The Donatists call this offer an apostasy as well. In some cities they condemn any bishop or pastor who agrees to this. These extremists refuse to take communion with any who do not adhere to the Donatist belief, and have accused the moderates of not being Christian at all."

Travis listened with the sense of hearing two tales at once and understanding neither. Arguments between priests and wizards and acolytes were constant, as were poisonings and intrigues and public denunciations and bloody battles. But these were not priests; these were traders. Yet they spoke of this conflict as though it affected them all, and affected them deeply. "And in Carthage?"

"My father and a few of our friends have stopped them from going so far. He as much as anyone has the right to condemn and yet refuses to do so. He says that the danger does not lie just with those who left the church and return, but for those who are coming to the church now. How will these newcomers be tested? Are all who did not know persecution to have their faith questioned?"

"Your father," Travis said, "is a wise man."

"Yes, he is. But the Donatists are constantly complaining about him and his position. They want him to join their camp. And he refuses. He supports the other bishop, a man elected by our church, and has become a church elder. We offer welcome to all new believers. This is another source of friction, because our church is growing very rapidly, while the Donatist community does not."

"I don't understand," Travis said. "Your father is a priest?"

"An elder," she corrected. "He helps the pastorate. It is a wearying task, and thankless. He is attacked on all sides." She looked worriedly at him. "Am I doing the right thing, telling you this?"

"Yes, of course," he replied, not understanding. "What could be wrong in wanting to learn?"

Something in his reply seemed to comfort her. "Many believers are drawn from the lowest classes," Lydia went on. "This is true of both the Donatists and us. Poor freemen, clients, slaves. Most cannot read. The Donatists feed upon this and search out the angry and embittered. They say that a rich Roman cannot be both emperor and a true Christian. They deny everything done by Constantine to help the church. We disagree. We feel that having the legal freedom to open our doors to all people everywhere can only be a good thing."

Slowly Lydia shook her head. "But they use this argument as a focal point for gathering together both people and power. The *circumcillian*, those men gathered back there, are becoming very difficult. Twice they have started running street battles in Carthage. My father is hoping that by finding them land of their own, they will become less troublesome."

"Is all this why your father travels to Constantinople?"

That startled her into reserve. "What makes you think we wish to travel?"

"The way you both reacted when I said that was where I was headed." She had said *we* want to travel. He tried to keep the eagerness from his voice. "I ask only because if it is so, I would be honored to offer you both place upon my ship."

"That is for my father to decide," she replied vaguely. "And if he does travel, wherever he goes, he goes as a merchant."

"Of course," Travis agreed, knowing there was more, knowing now was not the time to search it out. He turned and looked out over the waters.

"What are you thinking?"

He focused upon her, said gravely, "That I am glad your father will be sailing with us tonight."

A hand touched his shoulder, and Travis was instantly awake. "Time," Raffa whispered.

Travis raised himself up, stifled a groan. His body was stiff and bruised from sleeping on ground that had rapidly lost its warmth with the sun's passage. He looked around. His men were struggling to their feet, stretching clenched muscles, moving with the practiced silence of trained warriors.

They had sailed through the night and the day and another night, mooring toward noon on the likeliest stretch of beach the rocky coastline had to offer. The weather had stayed with them, clearing and granting a steady wind. Still, the Berber were no seamen, and the trip had weighed heavily on them. After a cold meal, the men had thrown themselves down on whatever level spot of rocky ground could be found. They had slept as the dead, for most the first real sleep they had known since leaving Carthage.

Another cold meal without benefit of firelight or hot drink, then the boats were pushed off and the sails unfurled. They traveled in the three former pirate vessels, boats designed along ancient Punic tradition. There was no keel. Instead, a single great plank ran down the boat's center, jutting farther and farther into the water the closer it drew to the stern. This served two purposes, both stabilizing the boat and permitting it to be beached, as a Roman ship could not be. The boats were twenty-five paces long and twice as wide as a man was tall, their sleeker lines granting both speed and flexibility. As long as there was neither strong wind nor heavy seas, the vessels were ideal for swift and silent passage.

They missed the opening entirely on the first run. When they arrived at the mountainous isle that, according to the pirate's warning, meant they had gone too far, some of the men passed half-heard forebodings among themselves. But the captain took note of Travis and Hannibal's shared determination and ordered them back, piloting the lead craft in so close that the rocks appeared to graze the end of the leeward oars.

Travis pointed through the gloom and hissed, "There."

The captain cast him an approving look and piloted them in. The way was marked by a Punic mausoleum, just as the pirates had said, but almost invisible now in the darkness; it was a three-story tower with a lion's head carved at each corner and a crown denoting its royal occupant. The sails were furled, and three sets of paddles extended from each side.

The cleft through which they paddled was hewn from a sandstone cliff by eons of harsh winter storms. The rock was veined and brittle and colored like stone-bound fury. They moved at a snail's pace, poling themselves forward, the oars scrabbling for hold on opposing walls. A hundred paces farther on, the way suddenly opened into a shallow pool. A half-moon beach of fine pink sand reflected the day's dimming light. Another boat was beached. But there were no guards.

As quietly as possible, they disembarked and pulled their boats up and out of the water. They climbed the steep hillside along a track hollowed into shallow steps. Each clink of metal or stumble brought quiet hisses. But the only sounds they detected, the only movements they saw, were their own.

At the clifftop, they came not upon another rise as Travis had expected, but rather a broad cultivated plain. The mountains, which from below had seemed to shoulder up directly to the cliffside, were in fact a league or more distant. The plain dipped like a bowl, the natural slope perfect for irrigating crops. It was an ideal location for a secret and self-sufficient village. Travis glanced at the faces around him, saw that others were thinking the same.

Nestled up next to the mountain's base was the town. Silently Raffa sent two of his men out as point guards, then nodded to Travis. He checked the group. All were tense, set, watching him. He met Hannibal's eye, received a nod in reply. Travis hefted his club and pointed them down toward where the village nestled in growing shadows.

Each man carried a stave that could be used as a club, but that might be taken for a walking stick if challenged. Each also had a mask slung by leather thongs about his neck and a metal amulet bound to his forearm. Raffa's men, experienced warriors who could be trusted not to use more force than necessary, also carried swords and bows and arrows wrapped in burlap.

Carry with you the sign of Tanit, the pirate had said. She is the sister-goddess of Baal, and shares his thirst for blood. Wear it upon your arm or around your neck. And bear a painted mask. Thus will you be known as acolytes and be granted entry.

When the pirates had been taken back, Travis had asked of Gaven, the Carthage-born guard, "What are these masks for?"

"Rumors," the man had replied uncomfortably.

"Tell me."

"They say the god's demon servants enter through the masks, and take possession of their bodies."

Travis fought down the clench of fear. "We will face a field of demons?"

"We will face men," Raffa said. "Every barbarian tribe I have ever fought carries such demons into battle with them. They still bleed as mortals."

SIGN OF TANIT

By the time they arrived at the village perimeter, the stars were a silver wash across the dark sky. The moon was still hidden behind distant hills, with only a ghostly glow indicating where it would soon rise.

They stopped and gathered beyond what once had been the city wall. Now the stone was crumbling and used as a lean-to for animal stalls and sheds. They crouched near crumbling structures of mud and straw, and studied the swarm of revelers streaming from a single great watch fire toward the city's main portals. Their dancing had a drunken, lunatic quality.

A sudden gust sent smoke spilling over them. Travis' chest felt stabbed by fire. "The air stinks," he whispered, struggling not to cough. "My nostrils burn, and it hurts to breathe."

"Kif," Raffa said quietly.

"What?"

"I know of this," Hannibal said from his other side. "It is a weed akin to hemp, grown up in the hills. Some of the pagan ceremonies call for bales to be thrown upon the fire. The smoke is said to invite dreams."

"The smoke is deadly to a warrior," Raffa hissed. "Tell the men to stay upwind if they can."

Orders were passed, masks fitted into place, and the band started forward. They joined the last of the stragglers, their presence unchallenged. Travis tried to match the weaving loose-limbed walk, pretending to lean heavily upon his stave as he passed under the gateway. His mask cut off almost all peripheral vision, but by swinging his head from side to side he managed to keep careful watch. Beyond the first line of houses, he peeled off to one side, waiting behind the shadow of a dwelling's stone wall for the others to join him. He glanced about and saw an utterly unroman town. Two of the empire's most common structures—columns and marble statues—were absent. No building stood higher than two stories, and all were built of small stone.

"Ready," Raffa whispered.

"Stay to side streets," Travis said, motioning to the others.

What statues he saw were of wood or clay, and none depicted humans. All were of great mystical beasts, fanged gargoyles with horns and leathery wings. All were painted the most garish of shades, red and orange and ocher. All were loathsome in their frozen fury.

Bas-reliefs set into walls and street corners and temple buildings were the same or worse. Winged creatures hunted men and animals, crushing them with demonic weight or carrying them off alive and screaming. They depicted a world beyond human power to control, predict, or conquer.

The sign of Tanit was everywhere, in house foundations, over doorways, in stubby street markers. Stone coffins too small for anyone but infants were set along the city's ceremonial ways. Tiny lives given in sacrificial payment for the town's survival in this hostile realm.

There was no mistaking the center of activity. The temple compound was set upon the town's main square, which was all ablaze with torches and bonfires. Travis followed Raffa's stealthy scramble around the light's perimeter, stopping at regular intervals to leave behind cohorts of men.

Behind the temple was a central warehouse, a common enough place for holding public stores. Raffa checked carefully, then quietly forced the door. Travis scouted the street, his chest heaving like overworked bellows. The mask was more than hot. It clung to his face like a branding iron. He glanced at the men gathered about him. Though painted differently, each of the masks was essentially the same. They held lurid gawping expressions, eyes out of kilter and mouth opened lewdly. The colors were hellish, red and brown and orange and black and angry.

Raffa hissed them inside. Travis checked the interior, saw no movement, spotted the stairs notched into the side wall. Together they climbed, then moved toward a window overlooking the plaza.

They looked out upon bedlam.

Men and women gyrated in and about the bonfires. Great billowing plumes of smoke rose when bales of greenish-brown weed were tossed upon the flames. Primitive instruments of hollowed reeds were played by dancers and by robed individuals standing around the central altar. The sound was harsh and angry, like swarms of bees whose attack was timed to the rhythm of a dozen drums.

Arms and legs jerked spasmodically as the music's pace increased. Faster and faster trilled the flutes and drums, harder beat the bare feet on the dusty stone.

Suddenly a trio of tambourines rose and shivered in the firelight. The flutes trilled in reply like dying birds. Then nothing. The music stopped as abruptly as if cut off with a blade. But the dance continued, the only sounds now those of stamping feet and huffing breaths.

Then a cry escaped from a strangled throat. Travis had never heard an eerier sound. A full-throated scream followed. Then another. With each a body jerked somewhere in the procession, all limbs extended and akimbo, as though struck from behind with a spear. Yet none fell.

"I don't like this," Travis whispered.

"Nor I," Raffa murmured. "The very air is angry."

Travis shivered in reply. His own breath sounded alien to his ears, a softly hissed warning that they did not belong.

The people remained erect and taut as puppets pulled by more than one set of hands. Further bloodcurdling shrieks sounded, more bodies became suspended in tension, until the entire square was filled with statues of flesh and bone.

In the deadly silence, the crudely shaped door behind the central altar creaked open, and out stalked what could only be the head priest. It was instantly clear why the overly high door had been carved as it had. The priest wore an ornate headdress, taller than he was and broader than his extended arms. The carved headdress-crown was overlaid with silver and fringed with great feathers. Even if hollow, which it did not appear to be, it had to weigh more than the priest himself. Yet in spite of his advanced years and emaciated form, the priest did not stagger. He *stalked*.

He crouched and swung and hunted, feral like a human cat, swinging back and forth, his face covered by a mask descending from the headdress and carved into a dragon's snarl. His arms were extended into talons as he spun and weaved his way through the frozen throng.

Then the music began again. Strident and wild. The crowd leapt as one and howled with maniacal glee. Their clothing was unwrapped and flung skyward like giant ribbons. The masks were tossed aside, needed no longer. No mask could compare to the tortured frenzy locked into their faces.

Gradually the writhing half-naked bodies formed two long lines, leading down and out from the central altar. There the head priest danced, supporting the headdress' deadweight on one leg, his other leg extended at an impossible angle, and gyrated in a tight circle. As he moved, he spun a pair of gleaming swords.

Doors slammed back at the square's other side. The undulating mob's howls reached a fever pitch as seven bound forms were dragged, screaming in sheer terror, toward the altar and the priest and the waiting blades.

Travis stiffened, heard Raffa's indrawn hiss of surprise as he too recognized the first bound and shrieking form as Septimus, their man who had gone missing.

Travis craned through the window, checked the periphery a final time. Just as the pirate had said, there were no guards. He ducked back, noticed that Hannibal had slipped away from his station beside Raffa. Travis turned back to the scene below them. The lines of writhing figures slowed the sacrificial prisoners' progress by clawing at them with talons and teeth. None of the half-naked forms were armed, save the high priest, who stood with blades poised high.

Yet Travis could not move.

He looked at Raffa, willing him to give the signal that he himself could not. The warrior did not move from his bent-over sweating posture as he watched the screaming procession below. Travis leaned farther over the window. Yet still he hesitated, held back by the implacable force of rage that bound itself tightly around the arena. A force so potent and deadly it seemed more real than the prisoners' shrieking as they were lashed to the bloodstained altar.

"In the name of Jesus Christ, the Lord of All," boomed a great voice from below, and suddenly the plaza froze a second time. Hannibal stepped into the ring of firelight, his stave raised high. "In the name of the Messiah, I banish all evil, all demons of air and fire and spirit from this place!"

A great sigh rippled through the plaza. Bodies seemed to gradually grow slack, only to be stiffened by a great cry from the priest, who hurtled himself at Hannibal, blades raised and aimed for his heart. Hannibal stood straight and stern and waited until the man was within reach, then rapped the blades away with one swing, and cross-swung with all his might. The blow knocked off the headdress and felled the priest, who suddenly was nothing more than a little old man.

Travis bounded down the stairs, Raffa and the other men on his heels. By the time they arrived at the plaza, it was over. The stone courtyard was surrounded, the few revelers who had even tried to escape clubbed senseless.

Hannibal nodded at Travis' approach, said quietly, "Perhaps you should send men to look for rope. We will need to bind many to ensure that they do not escape."

"I . . . yes." Travis directed his men, then turned back and said quietly, "How did you do it?"

"I? Do?" Hannibal's look was keen as a blade of light. "I myself did nothing."

Travis looked out over the throng, now groaning and weeping and helpless in their unarmed, unclothed state. The sense of rage and danger had vanished. "I could not move," he confessed.

Hannibal's gaze did not waver. "Perhaps it is not enough to stand alone, not even for one as young and strong as you."

"I don't understand," Travis stammered.

"No," Hannibal agreed solemnly. "I see that you do not. But seek the truth with an open heart, and perhaps in time you shall."

CHAPTER VI

I t was long past midnight when they arrived back in Carthage. The night was chilled by a rising wind off the sea. They answered the guard's halloo with the call of recognition, entered the merchants' harbor, and rowed quietly to quayside. Travis stood in the bow of his own boat, surpervising the transfer of men. The Donatists who had helped man the extra vessel clambered ashore; most had elected to remain in the village and lay claim to their new holdings. Which was a good thing, as the boats were so packed with booty and captives that every large wave sent water splashing over the gunnels. Travis watched Hannibal dispatch Ettaba's men, returning their farewells with a general's grace.

Ettaba and two of his lieutenants stepped forward into the flickering torchlight. "You will stand by your word?"

"Tomorrow at first light," Hannibal replied. "We shall meet at the governor's palace and make your claims public."

"I am learning to expect nothing but the truth from you, Hannibal Mago. You are indeed a worthy son of your father."

The Berber leader inspected him with a keen eye. "I confess that this and your acts at the square leave me questioning much that I have said and done."

Hannibal was the same height as the others, and yet to Travis' gaze, his aura of calm strength granted him a far greater stature. "Christians are commanded to be brethren and live in harmony, are we not?"

"Aye, it is true," Ettaba murmured, ignoring the startled glances cast by his two lieutenants.

"And so the Donatists excuse their actions by accusing those who disagree with them of not being Christian at all." No anger was there in Hannibal's voice, no condemnation. Nor was any needed. "You judge us, you condemn us, you usurp God's authority and call us apostates. But are you perfect in your own worship? Do you lead lives filled with the Master's command to love?"

The Berber's grimace showed how much the act of listening cost him. "I must think upon what you say."

"We are all human," Hannibal said, his voice calm and quiet as the night. "We must, all of us, accept that the answers we find most comforting are only *part* of the truth, and that the *whole* truth is God's and God's alone. Learning this lesson is the first step toward living in peace with all our Christian family."

There was a long silence, broken only by the soft lapping of waves upon the hulls, and the sigh of a rising wind. Finally Ettaba drew himself erect. "I would argue with you, Hannibal Mago. But I have spent the return voyage thinking of what I witnessed. With my own eyes I saw the Spirit's power move within you. This I cannot deny." The Berber's gaze remained direct and steady upon

Hannibal. "So I bid you good night, Hannibal Mago. Know I shall carry your words with me, and ponder them long and hard."

Travis watched the exchange of bows, waited until the Donatists had melted into the night, then said, "Even after they have helped you, you do not find ease among these of your own sect."

Hannibal turned to him. "I do not care for those who attempt to make Christianity exclusive, no matter what their reason." He walked over to Travis' boat and leaned on the gunnel. His back to the boat and the weary men, he continued quietly, "When my father's father first came to Christ, there was another group going about their excluding business. They were called Montanists, and they claimed that unless a person experienced the Holy Spirit in a way which could be seen and identified, they could not call themselves believers. Others, my grandfather among them, said that how the Holy Spirit chose to reveal Himself, in silent mystery or in powerful signs and wonders, was the Lord's choice and not man's."

Hannibal rubbed a weary hand across his neck. "Mind you, this came about while the church was beset by an empire that detested it and wished it gone. My grandfather failed to understand how we could reach out to the world when we were so divided among ourselves. I share this opinion. I do not think simply because Christianity has been declared legal that our woes are finished. The world still remains unsaved."

"I hear your words," Travis replied quietly, "and yet you may as well be speaking in some utterly foreign tongue."

"I am not good at such explanations," Hannibal agreed. "I believe in the Lord of All, and I believe that He sent His blessed Son to save man from his sins. For me, that is enough. For more, perhaps you should ask my daughter, whose mind is far sharper than my own."

Travis nodded his agreement to the night, and said what had been on his mind for the entire return journey. "When you entered the plaza and spoke the magical words, I could not move." He had to stop and swallow. "I was afraid."

"I too felt the urge to give in to fear," Hannibal confessed, "but the Lord has told us to seek His strength at times of weakness. As to my words, there was no magic. It is a gift to all believers, the right to call on His name."

Before Travis could respond, Hannibal turned to the boats pulled up alongside the dock and raised his voice. "To all who have followed false paths, the Lord reaches His hand out to you in invitation. The Lord offers no condemnation to those who acknowledge that their ways have been wrong. Only forgiveness, and entry into eternal life."

Travis was glad the darkness covered his alarm. Several times during their return journey, Hannibal had spoken thus, an entreaty to captives and conquerors alike. Many raised their heads and listened, as did some among Travis' men. But none chose to respond.

Hannibal waited a moment in silence, the wind rising about them and drumming a steady beat with the halyard and the furled sail. Then he turned back to Travis and said more quietly, "A request. I am more in need of silver than of further trade goods. Would you permit me to take the chest as my share? I will value all the goods tomorrow and apportion them fairly."

"Of that I have no doubt," Travis said, and meant it. Among the plunder had been found a small chest of the silver coins called *sesterce*. Travis glanced back to where Septimus sat, surrounded by booty and the other captives. His mind flitted nervously over what the next day would bring. "A part of it, certainly. And perhaps all. I care little whether I travel with silver or goods. But my father is in need of coin. Tomorrow I will see what help my brother offers. Then I will answer your request."

"I could not ask for more," Hannibal said, and remained where he was. "A final request, if you will permit. We Christians prefer not to be called a sect. The word signifies one of many, and we consider our faith to be that granted the truth of eternal salvation. *The* truth."

"I will remember," Travis said. He stood and watched in silence as the older man turned and was enfolded by the night. There was so much there that he did not fathom.

They rowed quietly back to the center of the harbor and moored well apart from all other boats. Soon enough the passengers settled down to wait for sunrise. The loudest sounds were the creak of hawsers, the slap of water, an occasional groan from their prisoners, and the wind.

A free space had been formed in the stern of Travis' vessel by the bales of goods returned with them. It was a pirate's hoard of every imaginable item, carpets and swords and bottles of perfume essences, goblets and spice boxes and ingots of iron. But no food or wine or even water. No discussion had been necessary for all to agree that nothing edible within the village would be touched.

The return voyage had been strangely subdued, given the richness of their haul. Even after a half-share to the local government, their allotment would be considerable. Yet all had remained touched by the eerie quality of the night's events. All but Hannibal.

Travis sat on the stern railing, separated from the other men by the pile of booty, and watched Raffa drag Septimus back toward him. The man remained bound and bowed. He had scarcely raised his head the entire return journey, sitting amidships with the other bound prisoners, saying nothing. Now he accepted Raffa's prodding without protest, stumbling over the plunder as he sought to keep his balance with fettered hands.

Travis waited until Septimus was seated on a bale directly before him, with Raffa standing alert and watchful alongside. "You have betrayed us. Your life hangs in the very balance," he said quietly. His words were plucked by the rising wind, and carried no farther than the soldier seated before him. "The truth, and swiftly."

"My wife," Septimus murmured. With his head bowed, a small bare spot shone at the crown. He was a slender man in his early thirties, wiry and silent. "My child."

"What of them?"

"They are slaves in Fabian's household."

"You never told me you were married," Raffa growled, and could hold his anger back no longer. He cuffed Septimus and snarled, "You fool. Did you not even consider that we could save them?"

Septimus did not try to defend himself. "You could also have killed them."

Raffa raised his fist again. Travis snapped quietly, "Hold."

The warrior lowered his arm, growled, "Did loyalty count for nothing?"

"Not when the lives of my wife and son were in jeopardy."

Travis waited until Raffa had subsided, then turned his full attention upon Septimus. "Tell me."

"I and my family were sold into slavery," he said, his head bowed so low the words were spoken to the gunnel.

"You told me you were a soldier," Raffa spat.

"That I was," Septimus replied. "But I was also a gambler. A bad one."

"You could not meet your debts," Travis supplied.

"And two years after I left the emperor's service I was sold," Septimus agreed morosely. "I and my family. Fabian acquired us. He is an evil one, your brother. I know. I have lived in his household. He cares for nothing save his pleasures and his money."

"Did he arrange to have me poisoned?"

"That I cannot say. I beg you to believe me. When it happened, it was my first thought, but if so it was done by another's hand." Septimus raised his head far enough to dart a glance at Travis. "All I can say for certain is that Fabian loathes you. And Cletus. The mention of either name is enough to fill his face with bile."

"But until this journey I had not seen him in nine years. Longer. Neither has my father."

"It does not matter. He bought me because I was a soldier, and he knew of Raffa's men. I was sent down to spy upon you both. Word was sent back and forth by a certain grain merchant."

"Spy upon us?" Travis shot a glimpse at Raffa. "But why?"

"That I do not know. He told me nothing save that I was to spy upon you, to report everything, especially when either of you would be traveling by land or sea in the direction of Carthage." The head raised once more, for a fleeting look of naked appeal. "That was all he said to me, beyond the fact that if I failed to do his bidding, my wife and child would suffer long and lingering deaths."

"He set us up," Raffa said, his voice a threatening rumble. "He informed the pirates of our passage."

Travis ground down with his gaze. "Is this true?"

A reluctant nod. "I did not know it at the time, I swear this on the head of my child. If I had, would I have agreed to travel with you?"

Travis turned about, stared at the gradually lightening sky so long that Raffa finally asked, "What should I do with this one?"

"Mercy, please, masters," Septimus begged. "What I did, I did for my wife and son."

Travis turned back with a long sigh. "My head is aching with too many thoughts."

"It has been a long voyage," Raffa agreed. "We can let this wait until after a time of rest."

"No, we cannot," Travis decided, shaking off his fatigue. "Rouse the men. This sunrise shall be shared with my dear half-brother."

"It should wait until we are fresh."

"Again, no." Travis rose to his feet. "Such news will spread like wildfire. And I wish for Fabian to hear this first from me."

Travis found the foyer crowded with more than his own men. He refused the sleepy servant's curt invitation to enter and be seated, choosing to stay within the safety of the others. But even here, memories attacked him. He leaned against one of the obscene statues painted in lurid flesh tones, and glanced across at Raffa, who stood guard beside a slender figure cloaked in a cowled dark robe.

Travis suddenly recalled the day of Raffa's arrival at his father's estate, and remembered anew the bellow with which his father had greeted the scarred warrior. Cletus' cry had been so loud it had caused havoc among the maids. Travis had remained hidden behind the trellis, watching with the caution taught through avoiding his brothers' wrath.

His father shed real tears that day, the only time Travis had seen that happen in all his young years. He embraced the stranger, calling his name over and over while the stranger just stood there, smiling his amiable smile. It had been very strange, that smile, far too gentle for a man of such strength and danger.

But that was not why Travis recalled the day so vividly. No, what had shocked him most was that his father had then turned directly toward him, looked through the trellis as though it were not even there, motioned once, and said, "Come here, son."

Travis had been so shocked and frightened that he could not move.

"It's all right, lad," his father said, his tone gentler than Travis could ever recall hearing. "The boys are away. Come out."

As Travis forced his legs to unfold and carry him out, he heard his father say to the stranger, "He is the youngest."

The stranger spoke for the first time, his voice as amiable as his smile. "And your favorite."

Travis felt his numb legs falter once more when his father did not deny it. "His mother died last year. I have tried to show no preference. I know the other two. They are savage, and have terrorized the servants. Given half a reason, they would do away with him."

Raffa inspected the scar on Travis' shoulder, the result of a blow meant for his head that he had only partially avoided. "They are hard on him."

"I suppose my feelings must show," his father agreed. He turned to Travis and inspected him gravely. "Have I ever given you less than the truth?"

"No, Papa."

"Then listen carefully. This is Raffa. He is my friend. I want you to make him your friend as well."

Travis looked up at the stranger. His travel robe was clasped with the same legionnaire's badge that his father kept on the table in his private chamber. His legs were caked with dust from the road, his wrist-guards almost black with ancient sweat, his hair disheveled and his beard carelessly cropped. Deep lines of strain and fatigue furrowed out from his eyes and mouth, and laced their way across his forehead. One hand was draped across the hilt of his broadsword as though it had rested there forever. He was no taller than Travis' father, yet his wiry frame appeared immensely strong. Strong enough even to protect him from both brothers.

"He is a man you can trust," his father went on. "He has saved my life more than once. He will save yours. Do you understand what I am saying?"

For some reason Travis felt the tears come unbidden. He shamefacedly wiped them away. "Yes, Papa."

His father nodded once, then turned to Raffa and said, "Welcome home, old friend."

The next morning Travis had risen at his accustomed hour, when the sky's few clouds were transformed into golden heralds of the coming sun. Their estate was a fragile strip of green that bordered the endless desert. Dawn came to their home in gentle stages. Mist rose like night's whispered farewell from the irrigation canals, veiling the sleepy world in layers of shy splendor. Fruit and olive trees stood at silent attention in long rows along the canals, guarding the flocks of wheat and cotton and corn and grapes. The house was silent, the world safe. Travis ate a breakfast of cold dates and curds and well water, standing at the small window of his loft, surveying the fields and hearing the birds and the animals sing their raucous greeting to the day.

Below him, the door leading to the house's main chamber clattered back, and his father came into view. Cletus whistled up the pair of hounds who were his constant companions, bent to fasten his sandals, hefted the spear he used as his walking stick, and limped toward the outer portal. Travis turned from his window, plucked up his sandals, and started down the winding stairs.

But just before the outer door, he froze to a halt.

Arrayed on the floor were four knives, from a slender dagger no longer than his hand to a true warrior's blade, long as his forearm and serrated with vicious diagonal crossings.

But that was not what held him fast.

Leaning against the stone door frame was a legionnaire's short-sword. No dress weapon, this. The hilt was molded to the warrior who had long gripped it. The blade's razor edge bore metallic rainbow-arcs caused by years of whetting. The scabbard and soldier's belt lay coiled at the floor before it, scarred and darkened with sweat and dust and old battles.

Travis reached for it, was surprised to find how heavy it felt. He needed both hands to hold it out in front of him.

"Gaul," rumbled a voice from the shadow-well behind the stairs. "Two years fighting the Huns. Before that, guarding

Hadrian's Wall and battling the barbarians who poured over from time to time. That was where I met your father. After that, a year in the frozen north, worse than crossing the Styx, that was."

Travis lowered the blade, turned to find Raffa watching him with glittering dark eyes. "Is this yours?"

"Aye, that it is."

Travis had spent the previous afternoon and evening shadowing the man, watching him with the wary caution of one who has known little affection from adults. Toward evening his curiosity had drawn him too far from his lair, and his brothers had caught him out in the open. But before they could land the first blow, Raffa had been there, a wiry beast of a man, catching them up in arms strong as iron and tossing them into the canal. Saying nothing, answering their curses with silence, just standing there alongside Travis, as solid and protective as a rock wall.

Travis' eyes tracked back to the sword. "Teach me," he said softly.

"A warrior's blade requires a man to use it. A boy, now," Raffa took in the array of knives with a casual wave, "he can protect himself with any of these. But the bearer of a warrior's arms has to know how to take care of himself."

Travis lifted his eyes to meet Raffa's for the very first time. "I want that," he said.

"If you want it, then say it," Raffa replied.

Travis kept his look steady, though it was hard. "I want to be a man."

"What in the name of all the gods has possessed you to arrive at such an hour?" No amount of primping or makeup could mask

Fabian's flaccid features and sunken eyes. His voice strove for anger, but could only deliver a whiny petulance. "Not to mention barraging my door with hammer-blows and threatening my servants with a forced invasion."

"I merely wished to share the dawn with you, brother," Travis said quietly.

"How kind. Some other time, perhaps." Fabian squinted at the dark, cowled figure but could not make out the face. He backed a step away from the guards' looming mass. "Last night I dined with friends and did not retire until quite late. So if you don't mind "

"Ah, but I do, dear brother," Travis said, stepping closer. "As a matter of fact, I positively insist. You see, it is the day when you promised to have a reply to our father's request for aid."

Fabian's laugh had a forced quality. "If you expect to barge in here and threaten me into rash acts, you are sadly mistaken." With a sweeping motion to his robes, he drew himself up to full height. "I am connected to the highest strata of society. Any threats will be dealt with most harshly, of that you may rest assured."

"Threats? Who spoke of issuing threats?" Travis motioned to Raffa. He stepped forward, one hand binding the cowled figure to his side. Travis kept his eyes fastened upon his brother's face as he reached over and flung back Septimus' hood.

His brother screamed and would have fallen, had his back not struck the doorpost. "You!"

"Two of my vessels are piled so high with pirate booty that the gunnels are almost under water," Travis said, his voice lashed with quiet fury. "We brought almost sixty prisoners as well, who will be presented to the proconsul himself before being offered up for sale. I am positive he will be most interested in listening to *anything* I have to say."

Fabian clutched at his throat, took a trembling step away from the doorjamb and into the main hall. Travis followed, his men close on his heels. "Invite us in, dear brother. I am sure a sunrise will do you a world of good."

Travis watched as Raffa stationed guards at regular points through the hall, by the fountain, and out onto the patio. Four more men were stationed outside the main gates. His brother was cornered, and utmost caution was required.

Even before Fabian collapsed on the bench, Travis pressed the attack. "I am certain Father would be extremely grateful to hear that you had found it possible to help him."

"Yes, most certainly." Fabian swallowed nervously. "I am gratified to report that I have managed to gather, ah, two hundred silver sesterce—"

"A thousand," Travis said, easing himself down, adjusting the sword to nestle alongside.

"But that's . . ." Fabian's voice trailed to nothing as Raffa sidled around so that Septimus faced them both. The captive's expression was venomous as he stared down at his former master. "Ah, yes, that will take some time."

"Now," Travis said.

"I, ah—"

"Perhaps some of my men could help you look through your belongings and see if there might be some articles of wealth you have overlooked."

Fabian's eyes flitted about like that of a trapped animal, hunting for a way from the snare. Up to Septimus, over to Travis, then to the men standing poised and ready around his veranda. His shoulders sagged as he called, "Hanno."

The coiffured and perfumed servant arrived with the alacrity of one well trained at listening in doorways. "Master?"

"The three bags in the wall cupboard beside my bed," Fabian said, his shoulders drooping farther. "Bring them."

"But—"

"You heard your master," Travis snapped, then motioned to Gaven. "Go and ensure that he does not lose his way."

When the servant had departed, Travis turned back to his brother and said, "I am also in need of a good house-servant. Perhaps you, a man of culture, can help me."

"Indeed, brother." The eyes roved with panic-stricken speed. "Yes, anything. You need but ask."

"Septimus has family here. I understand his wife is a good cook."

"Certainly."

"Naturally, she would wish to travel with her son."

Fabian rose to his feet. "I will go and see to it myself."

A single glance, and three of Raffa's men crowded in. "Attend me, brother. I am sure one of my guards can find the servant."

Reluctantly Fabian returned to his seat, waiting in ever-increasing agitation as a man left and returned with a servant. In mumbling tones Fabian passed on orders to find the serving woman.

"Thank you," Travis said mildly, feeling his hand aching for the hilt of his sword. "Just one more small matter."

"Anything." Weaker now.

"That lovely young serving girl."

Fabian stiffened as though pricked with a knife. "What?"

"Of course, of course, you have so many." His eyes drilled into his brother with the force of a branding iron. "The young one who served us during my last visit. What was her name? Oh, yes, I remember now. Chloe."

Fabian's features took on a waxy sheen. "You, ah, but—"

Travis leaned forward until his face was a mere hand's breadth from his brother's, and hissed, "I want her. Now."

By the time they returned to the city's center, the lanes were clogged with early morning crowds. People walked with the sleepy quietness of those who wished for another hour of rest. Occasionally the flow slowed and crammed and complained softly, the way blocked by an overloaded cart, its horse plodding slowly, the iron wheels scraping and creaking over the uneven stones.

Travis was gritty with anger and fatigue. His ire felt ancient, a burden he had carried all his life. All he saw seemed tainted with his bitterness. The city looked tawdry and garish, its painted beauty only a mask for that which lurked in every shadow.

The young girl, Chloe, appeared a perfect victim of the city, he thought. She stumbled along in wide-eyed fear, the cowled robe now flung about her almost naked form. She glanced his way, terror-filled eyes asking questions she dared not even speak. Travis sought to rise above his inner turmoil, and smiled in her direction. "Peace," he said quietly. "You will not be harmed."

But her fears and the uncertain future did not allow her to truly hear what he said. She turned away, her slender finger clutching the robe to her throat, her eyes flitting like two captive birds.

Travis felt himself suddenly sickened by it all. By the city and its veneer of lurid charm, masking a cesspool of evil and pain and wrongful desires. By the lustful glances that his men cast over Chloe's frightened form.

By the spell he could feel being cast over himself as well.

Travis found himself struggling not to be swallowed up by the city's power, to hold himself apart, to remain an individual even here. But in truth he felt the city weaving its way into his being, and knew if he stayed, he too would be snared by its endless siren song. It was as the Romans said: Cities were indeed gods.

He stopped abruptly. Two of the men whose eyes were more on Chloe than the road collided with him. "I must see to another task before returning."

"You are tired," Raffa counseled. "We all are."

"None need come with me." His voice grated harshly in his own ears. "I go to see the trader Hannibal. The girl comes with me."

A fleeting look of dismay over several of the guards' faces strengthened his determination. Raffa rewarded him with a single nod, the most approval he ever showed, and the words, "I will come."

"No. Return to the ship with the silver. Guard it well. It means life or death to my father. The rest of you return with Raffa." Travis turned his attention to where he had avoided looking, and felt his anger burn more brightly. "Septimus."

The slender man stepped forward, his wife refusing to release his arm even then. She and the young boy clutching to her skirt looked haggard with exhaustion and fear. Septimus himself still bore the mark of his night of terror. He stood with shoulders bowed, his eyes not rising from their inspection of the road at his feet.

"You lived with us," Travis said harshly. "You saw who we were and by what traditions we shaped our lives."

"We accepted you as one of us," Raffa added, anger burnishing his tone to sharpened steel. "We treated you as an equal."

Septimus neither replied nor raised his head. "You ate my father's bread," Travis rasped. "You accepted his coin. You called yourself his client. He rewarded you with all that he had, treating you as he did his own."

His wife's hollow eyes roamed from one hard face to another. Her mute appeal choked the words in Travis' throat, halting him before he could speak and banish them. He stood and looked at her and the child and the man with his bowed head, and felt torn in two. His anger surged and pushed him to order the man away, penniless and broken. Her silent entreaty kept him still. He looked away, unable to face her raking gaze any longer, scanning the crowds surging around them, looking on the stalls being set up along either side of the road. Then it hit him.

He motioned Raffa forward, unleashed the neck of one sack, drew out twenty sesterce. Even in his confused and angry state he noticed how cool the coins were, how heavy.

He reached over, lifted Septimus' limp arm, let the coins fall into his palm. "You have shown yourself to be an accomplished spy. Earn my father's forgiveness by spying for us."

The look that rose in the woman's eye somehow left him feeling utterly exposed, and irritated by his own actions. His voice grated in his own ears as he said, "Set up a stall here. I will send word to my father that you will handle all his goods, both those he needs to buy and those he has to sell. Send all information you can gather back with each shipment."

For the first time since leaving Fabian's house, Septimus dared raise his eyes. The fearful hope was so great that Travis was forced to turn away. "I go," he said abruptly, grasping for Chloe's arm, and walked off.

"Sire," called Gaven, rushing after him. "I would walk with you."

"Walk, then," he said gruffly, turning a corner, and another, running away from he knew not what. Stopping then, he realized he was utterly lost. "Guide me."

"A right at the next thoroughfare, sire," Gaven replied, then ventured, "Raffa has said that you hold the seeds of a great leader. I did not believe it myself, until now."

"I was a fool," Travis said bitterly.

"All the men will speak of this deed," Gaven replied quietly. "And none will call you foolish for acting as you did."

His confusion and fatigue and rancor did not allow him room for a reply. Travis walked as fast as the growing throngs permitted, pushing away both weariness and thought, striving futilely to ignore the girl's faint whimpers and wisps of perfume, wanting nothing more than to be away. Out on the open sea again, where the world was pure, and life simple, and his mind not bursting from an invisible storm.

He knocked loudly on the burned and scarred portal, then stepped back. He passed Chloe's arm over to Gaven, and waited. When Demetrius opened the face-plate, he gave a short bow and said in formal Greek, "A good morning's greetings to you, Demetrius. I would have words with your master."

Silently the old man opened the door and stepped back. "I will see if he is available," he replied, his tone as formal as Travis'. "You will take refreshment?"

"Thank you, no, I—" Travis stopped as Hannibal stepped from the shadows and walked across the courtyard. Another bow, then, "Excuse the intrusion, but I and my men must begin preparations for tonight's departure."

A quiet gasp turned him to his right, where Lydia stepped from the storehouse's main doors. Again there was the sense of being torn in two, knowing what was right and yet feeling utter confusion at the same time. There was no chance for him, not here, not with her. All the empire knew of the Christians' demand for union only between members of their sect. Travis felt bitterness flood him as he bowed in her direction, before continuing to Hannibal, "My father's instructions were to make all haste for Constantinople. I dare not tarry longer."

"Of course," Hannibal said mildly.

His words seemed to push his daughter forward. She took three steps toward them, one hand rising as though to clutch at the air between them. Hannibal reached over and gently grasped the hand, drawing her close to him, stopping her forward progress. He adopted Travis' formal tone as he replied, "It would be unwise to stand between a son and his father's orders."

"I ask that you come to the boat and value the goods."

"I will do so."

"There is something else," Travis went on. "I ask to leave all the prisoners in your care. If the proconsul declares them chattel, I also ask that you sell them for us."

"Thank you," Hannibal replied, "but I do not deal in slaves."

Travis did not attempt to mask his surprise. A merchant who refused to deal in something that guaranteed a profit was beyond his ken. "This is something to do with your Christian god?"

"Some of us think so. Others disagree."

Again that disconcerting frankness. "Do you hold no slaves of your own?"

"All within this household are freemen."

Travis covered his astonishment by turning and motioning for Chloe to step forward. The young girl had the wide-eyed trembling stare of a frightened fawn. "I would ask that you take this girl as a servant."

It was Hannibal's turn to show genuine surprise. "You are giving her to me? Why?"

"A gift," he said, and realized that the words were not enough. He reluctantly explained, "My brother has," he glanced at the terrified young girl, then went on, "used her badly."

"Your brother," Hannibal said slowly. He looked at the girl, went on, "I believe I have heard talk of this one." His voice gentled as he asked, "What is your name, child?"

"Chloe," Travis replied, when it was clear the girl would not. "You are an honest man. I ask that you treat her well."

"She will be safe here," Hannibal said, keeping his voice gentle and his gaze upon the girl, the assurance meant for her. He motioned to the hovering Demetrius and instructed, "See she is bathed and fed and sent to bed."

The servant stepped forward and said, "Come along, child."

It was only when the old servant began to lead her away that the girl seemed to grasp what was happening. Her fearful eyes turned toward Travis. He tried to hold down his angry fatigue as he said, "These are good people. They will treat you well."

"This is a Christian home," Demetrius agreed, tugging on the girl's arm. "You can rest easy now."

The girl broke away with a sobbing cry. She fell to her knees beside Travis, and rained kisses on his hand. The action only increased his sense of surging confusion. He lifted the weeping girl as gently as he could, felt his own desire surge at her helpless submission. He pushed her into the servant's arms. Indeed the city's lure was great.

Travis looked up to find Hannibal watching him strangely. "Fabian is said to have spent a fortune on her. He simply gave her to you?"

"I took her. As punishment. He . . ." Travis hesitated, then finished, "My brother offended me. And angered me by the way he treated her."

Hannibal glanced at his daughter. When he turned back, there was a new depth to his dark eyes. "I would ask that you join me for refreshment, Travis son of Cletus. I will not hold you over-long."

Travis hesitated a moment, then surrendered. "Very well."

When Travis was seated in the cluttered office-room, Hannibal served the younger man a goblet with his own hand. "I am a simple man, given to simple speech," Hannibal said, then stopped. He glanced at his daughter, who sat erect and silent with the inner will of one long bereaved. He sighed his way over to his own leather-bound chair, seated himself, and went on, "Listen, you. I am thinking that in the fullness of time we could become friends."

Travis noticed Lydia's slow awakening, though he kept his eyes on the father. For some reason the words helped ease his own burden of fatigue. "I am thinking the same."

"Alas, time is not a friend of ours just now. Nor is tradition. Most of my fellow Christians would not consider friendship with a nonbeliever to be a rightful act. But I disagree. We have all fallen short of God's call to holiness. Who am I to say where I would be, were life to have presented me with your past and view of the world?"

"You are many things," Travis replied. "But simple is not one of them."

"Time is not an ally," Hannibal repeated. "The world moves, and we with it. Whether there awaits the abyss of civil war, or a new day of hope beyond the horizon, only God knows." He fastened Travis with a steady look. "I would thus say that we should cast aside the chains of time, you and I. And call one another friend, here and now."

"I agree," Travis said. "More than that. I am honored."

Hannibal stood and extended his hand. "Then may the Lord God bless this moment, and may the fullness of time show us that we have been right to go forward calling one another friend."

"Amen," Lydia said, rising as well.

Travis stood with them, felt his hand taken within an iron grip. Such reassurance was there. Such a sense of steady force. His mind went back to the night and the plaza and the dance of masks, memories that were never far from him. "I feel that there is much you could teach me."

The sense of rightness strengthened with his words. Travis felt his fatigue retreat, a shadow left in the sunlight beyond the chamber's portal. His hand gripped by a man whose ways were an utter mystery, watched by a woman whose appeal was matched only by her barriers, he felt at peace. A new friend.

"I would ask that you delay your departure," Hannibal said, releasing Travis' hand.

"Why?"

"Tell me." Hannibal strode to his cluttered table. "What do you intend to do with these pirate vessels?"

"One will be dispatched to my father's home with a letter and assistance. Some of my men must accompany it."

"I hand over to you my share in the newly captured vessel. Send that one, leaving us three here." Hannibal looked up from his sorting. "If trusted sailors could be arranged for your shipment, would you reconsider and hold all your men here?"

Travis watched the older man. *Us?* "If the sailors truly are trustworthy, all but a few. Perhaps."

"I know a good captain, one who lost his ship to the pirates. An honest man, a Christian, one I have known all my life. But he is also too limited in his travels for what I have in mind, having never traveled farther than the coastline of our region." Hannibal bent back over his skins and scrolls. "I have also just received my largest shipment ever from Nubia. A caravan arrived the same day as you. They joined four consignments together. Four. And traveled with a small army of guards."

"The bandits have been horrible," Lydia offered, her voice small.

Travis risked a glance her way, saw an appeal spoken directly from her heart to his. "I am well aware," Travis replied, "of this problem."

"Lydia, what have you—" Hannibal's voice trailed off as she walked over, reached down, and immediately plucked out a single scroll. "Ah, of course. Here it is." He unrolled the document and began droning, "Amphorae of myrrh, honey, frankincense, dyes, copper, pepper, spices, bales of woven goods, opals, onyx, sapphires, scented woods, even a few unshaped nuggets of red gold. The list is staggering. Not to mention those of the pirates' goods which are worthy of transport to more distant markets." He dropped the scroll to his side, the long end trailing to the stone floor. "I would hire your vessels."

Travis' eyes widened. "All of them?"

"Whatever space is remaining in your holds. I am choosing to take this caravan's arrival and your own as a sign," he replied. "The first shipment to make it through in almost a half-year. Coming on the day that a young man pounds on my door and offers me the solution to a problem that has plagued me for years."

Hannibal glanced at his daughter, and this time he smiled. He turned back and said, "I would travel with you, Travis son of Cletus. I and my daughter. We seek passage with you to Constantinople."

CHAPTER VII

Hannibal sat at his wife's bedside, his hands clasping and unclasping in his lap. This was proving to be the hardest moment of his entire life. Far worse even than the fears he had known as a child, fleeing into the catacombs.

He would never forget that time, his mother's calm and love totally lost behind a mask of terror and tension and fatigue. She had dragged him on long after his little legs had wanted to give up and let him collapse to the rocky soil. Half-walking, half-running, a great crowd of them stumbling over poorly marked tracks, racing out of the city southward to the cliffs and the caves and safety. Hearing the screams and smelling the smoke wafting on the wind, urging the exhausted people on to ever greater speed. No, it had been bad then, but not so bad as now. At least then the terror had been shared.

His wife sensed his mood. That was one of her many gifts, this ability to see him as others did not. "I will be here when you return." Her voice offered quiet promise. "Who knows, the time alone may even help me grow stronger."

He looked down at her. This was not a fear over the journey that would begin on the morrow. This was a fear of loss. "But what if—"

Maria stopped him with a single shake of her head. "I am not dying, husband. Ill, yes, but that is a state we have both learned to live with."

"You are my strength," he murmured.

"There are things I have learned while lying here," she said, only half speaking to him. "Times have come and gone when God has so filled this space that there was scarcely room here for me. I saw then how this suffering of mine is something I shall take to Him as a gift. My lessons He will treasure. My life He will give meaning."

She looked at her husband and smiled. "Then the feeling vanishes, and I am left wondering at all the mysteries I thought I had come to understand. Trapped once more inside this frail and puny form."

Hannibal stared at her, beyond words. She had never spoken to him like this. Yet it came as no surprise. He felt he had always known this of her, somewhere deep beyond the level of thought. She had spent days beyond count imprisoned within these four walls, and yet in her immobility had moved farther along unseen paths than he could even imagine. "I shall miss you with all my heart."

"What distance can there be between those who love God?" She laced both her hands about one of his. "May our gracious Lord fill you with strength and wisdom, my husband. Know I shall be ever with you in prayer and in love."

Fabian looked up from his writing desk. "You are ready?"

"I have been ready," Hanno replied dryly, "since you ordered me to prepare in haste yesterday."

"It proved more difficult than I had thought to arrange a vessel in secret." Fabian folded the skin with expert motions, turning the four corners inward and pressing down hard. "Not to mention arranging a cargo suitable for such a voyage. One that would not raise suspicion over chartering a vessel for a straight run to Constantinople. And the cost, by all the gods, the cost."

"All the city is speaking of Hannibal and your brother's exploits against the pirates," Hanno said coyly.

"I know very well what the city is saying," Fabian said grimly. He dripped wax on the letter's edges, then stamped and sealed them into place.

"There is talk in the marketplace of the proconsul writing an official introduction to the emperor himself."

Fabian shot him a venomous look. "There are times, my dear servant, when I wonder why it is that I put up with you."

"Because you can trust me." Hanno smoothed the robe across his breast. "You have neglected to mention how the not inconsiderable expenses of your trusted servant will be met."

"I have neglected nothing." Fabian hefted a leather bag, the coins clinking gently. "There shall be the same again upon your return."

"I am yours to command," Hanno said, taking the sack, his fingers busy counting through the soft skin.

"Indeed." Fabian handed over the letter. "Directly into my brother's hands. No one else."

"I have acted as your messenger before." Hanno made the letter disappear. "Does Travis think that Brutus is still in Rome?"

"He did not say, but I would assume so." Fabian pointed at the sack Hanno continued to finger. "A third such sum if you reach Constantinople before Travis. I have told my brother to confirm this in his reply."

"I shall pray that the gods grant my vessel wings." Greed drew his delicate features into taut lines. "Anything else?"

"Yes." Fabian rose and drew close. The look in his eyes caused Hanno to draw back an involuntary half-step. "Whatever welcome Brutus prepares for my dear brother, I want you to watch it all carefully. Then I want you to return and report it to me. In precise detail."

To Lydia's surprise, her mother was smiling as she entered the room. The expression was so unexpected that it pulled her from her own distress. "What is it?"

"You and your father," her mother replied. "You make such a pair. So strong and sure to the outside world. Then you come in here, and what do I see? Sorrowful faces and heartsore voices and weaknesses brought out only for me."

"You are stronger than both of us," Lydia replied, crossing over to the bed, seeing the truth of her words more clearly than ever before. "And wiser."

Her mother was a long time in answering. "This is not my first illness. I was laid up soon after your birth, and once after that, and three times before. I warned your father before we were wed that my health was not good. He insisted on marrying me anyway. My parents were relieved, but thought him foolish."

Lydia settled her mother's hand into her lap. As she looked at the wan and frail face, she had a sudden insight—not of something new, but of something seen yet never before truly realized. She did not look *down* upon her mother. No matter that the woman was lying and unable to rise unaided, no matter what the posture. Lydia looked up to her mother, and always had.

"This room is not a prison," her mother was saying. "My body is. I have often lain here and wished for freedom. Sometimes it has even come, little hints of a future unchained from fever and pain. And with each such time of grace comes a lesson. Like steps of a ladder, leading me higher and higher, ever closer to Him."

"Don't leave us," Lydia said, her voice near breaking. Giving no heed to her own departure. Knowing there was nothing to compare the two. "Please."

The grip on her hand tightened reassuringly. "I have promised your father that I will be here for his return. You shall take care of him for me?"

"Yes."

"He is a wise man, and good. But sometimes he forgets to see beyond whatever his concern of the day might be. As do all men." She inspected her daughter's face. "You shall take an old woman's advice?"

Lydia started to protest that her mother was not old. But she was met with a look of such timeless wisdom, such unconditional love, that she could only nod.

"My beloved and headstrong daughter, there is only one way to know a true bonding with another. I do not speak of the bonding of passion, nor the bonding of happiness, nor even the bonding held together by the strength of your human will. You are young, and think the moment is all, and your strength is enough to see all things through to their rightful end."

"Mother—"

"No, don't interrupt, I beg you. Hard as it may be for you to hear these words, I beg you to listen. As a parting gift to your ailing mother." She waited until Lydia had settled, not only in body but in mind as well. In a quieter tone she went on, "The only bonding that is truly *beyond* time is when both you and your beloved have come to see the freedom of faith. Then there is the ability to leave self behind. And only then is there the possibility for a *true* joining. Love without this awareness is always in danger of being torn apart, isolated, suffocated by the burdens of life's turmoil and concern for self."

They departed with the midday tide, and by dusk were far beyond sight of land. Windswept blue stretched out in every direction, each rolling wave a billion burnished mirrors. The sunset was grand as only a sunset at sea could be, a great sweep of colors bursting with such silent power that not even the horizons seemed broad enough to contain it all.

Night fell with gentle abandon, the wind lessening with the light until even the captain was heard to sing an ancient chantey as the torches were lit. Across the gathering dusk, answering lights appeared on the three other boats, flickering assurances that all was indeed well.

They would not take the most direct route to Constantinople. They could not risk taking the captured vessels upon rough and open seas. Instead, they would travel first to Sicily, then hug the coast eastwards.

The voyage from Carthage to the southwestern tip of Sicily was the second shortest passage across the Mediterranean; only the Gates of Hercules at the sea's entrance was more constricted. Even with the boats heavily laden, and with the rowers spread out thinly, the journey would take just over two days if the wind held, three if not. From there the island's southern coast would be hugged all the way around to Syracuse, where in seven days' time they hoped to put in for fresh water and provisions.

Travis and Captain Arubal spent the journey's first hours studying their course on Arubal's salt-encrusted skins. The maps showed nothing but the Mediterranean's coastline, but there they were precise. The captain's stunted fingers traced their way with cautious optimism, pleased with the way the sea was treating their departure, offering them both untroubled sky and a fair wind.

From Syracuse they would make the brief passage to the tip of Italy's boot, then follow the southern shoreline around to the Straits of Otranto, which connected Italy to the Greek coast. This last passage on open seas was even shorter than that from Carthage to Sicily. Yet this did not mean they could lower their guard, not for an instant. The fingerlets that formed the southern Greek coastline were riddled with rocky passages and treacherous currents, even in the relatively storm-free season of early summer. And there was always the threat of pirates.

Here Arubal had squinted into the sun, as though seeking answers far beyond the horizon, and offered a cautious note of optimism. With four ships and constant alertness, there was less chance of water-borne bandits taking them for easy prey. And once across the Otranto Straits, they would never be more than a half-day's voyage from a safe port.

Travis had nodded at the news, hearing only the adventure's call of strange names and unknown lands, and had pointed to the map's great blank space stretching outwards from the Straits of Hercules. "What is here?" he had asked.

"Dragons and great winds and seven-headed beasts," Arubal had replied, rolling back his skins. "Best you keep your mind occupied with the dangers that lie ahead, not those beyond the ken of man."

Travis stood at the stern railing, looking back over the three boats that remained in close and steady contact. Lydia stood by his side, while Raffa and Hannibal engaged the captain at the far railing. It was as close to privacy as they could have on such a cramped vessel, and somehow the others' studied gift of isolation made her closeness even more intimate. Travis took a deep breath of crisp sea air and allowed himself the momentary gift of hope. It was indeed the finest night of his life.

Lydia's hair was caught by a sudden gust and wafted into his face, an exciting silken lash. Shyly she tucked it back behind her ear and raised her face to the night. Travis followed her motion, the breeze a heady wine in his nostrils. The indigo blanket draped across the sky was pierced by a million tiny silver-white lights, all shining from the mysterious world beyond.

"I feel such a novice next to you," she confessed quietly. "I have seen so little of the world."

He had to laugh. "Before this journey I had never been beyond the borders of our neighboring market village, and that only twice a year."

"And yet you seem so," she searched for a word, settled on, "worldly."

Travis was glad for the night to hide his flush of pleasure. "Old soldiers, friends of my father and friends of friends, they stopped in from time to time. I learned to creep in as close as the shadows permitted and listen to stories of how the empire was crumbling. It was an exciting way to learn of the outside world. I heard tales of bandits and marauding Berber tribes slowly choking off the roads."

"This I know," she murmured, "all too well."

"The soldiers told how their garrisons were often battling one another, caught in the struggles of leaders who hoped to become emperor. That was why many of them left Rome's service before reaching seniority. They grew disgusted with the corrupt politics, and the vacuum this created."

"This is where your men were garnered?"

"They are called Raffa's men. It was my father's idea, putting a soldier in charge of soldiers."

"And yet they call you sire."

"Only since this trip." He hesitated, then confessed, "Sometimes I can scarcely believe they are speaking to me when I hear the word."

"It suits you," she said quietly. Then, "Tell me of your home."

"It is a consul's estate and was once a grand place. It lies a half-day's journey south of Lepcis, a fifteen-day reach from Carthage."

"Was?"

"Times have been hard." Briefly he described their troubles, his words chilling the night breeze. "I carry a letter from my father to the consul's eldest son, begging for his help."

"You do not sound hopeful."

"It is not the first letter. My father has never even received a reply."

"What is his name?"

"The son?" Travis had to search his memory. "Titus Octavian."

"I shall ask my father," she offered. "Perhaps he will have connections who can help."

"That would be wonderful."

"Do not raise your hopes. Father has never been to Constantinople, and has had little contact directly with the new regime. But still there may be allies."

"That is more than I have."

"You have much, Travis son of Cletus," she said softly and returned her face to the heavens. "You have much."

"I have the night," he agreed, "and you to share it with."

Instead of turning back his way as he had hoped, she kept her face upturned, and said to the night, "'Lift your eyes on high, and see who created these, the One who brings out their host by number. He calls them all by name.'"

He recognized the sound of a memorized chant, and asked, "This is from your temple scrolls?"

"It is called our Bible," she said. "The prophet Isaiah wrote those words. He was one who predicted the Messiah's coming birth."

For reasons he could not fathom, he did not mind the fact that this night's discussion was not headed as he planned, nor directed by his hand. He said quietly, "Tell me."

●●●

Dawn was the proper time to arrive in Syracuse.

They slipped into a silent harbor shrouded in a morning mist, which lied in its promise of coolness. The damp clung to everything, creating colorless jewels which beaded and dripped. The city was half-formed shadows hanging above an invisible sea. All of its poverty, all of its scars and intrigue, everything lay hidden beneath the gentle morning veil. It was a silent world, one where dreams and wishes seemed as real as the port they entered.

They were only seven days into their voyage, but already the ships' routine had become a balance requiring few words and fewer orders. Their haste to complete the morning's tasks and visit the city added speed to their movements. Anchors were set so that the boats rested within hailing distance, yet were set far enough apart that a change in wind would not swing them into contact. By the time the four boats had heaved to and moored, the mist was beginning to burn away. Yet neither official craft nor water-borne merchant had appeared as expected.

Travis joined Raffa and the captain by the bow, squinted as a brilliant shaft of morning light pierced the remaining mist, and asked, "What is it?"

"Too quiet," Arubal declared gloomily. "There's danger ashore."

"We need fresh supplies," Hannibal said, joining them. "Water especially."

"I'll row in with two men," Raffa offered. "Take the lay of the land and report back."

A piercing shriek wafted across the water, followed by other voices raised in panic-stricken alarm. Travis gripped the railing and leaned forward. "What was that?"

"There!" Raffa pointed to where a flat-bottomed fishing skiff was being poled toward shore. He hallooed loudly, then demanded, "What is amiss?"

"Ruin," the lean poler called back, not missing a beat. "Doom for all."

"This won't do." Hannibal fingered open his belt-pouch, pulled out a pair of silver pieces and raised them over his head. "Two sesterces if you will do us a kindness and approach!"

"There is no kindness to be found here," the leathery man replied, but reluctantly guided his skiff about and poled alongside their bow.

Hannibal tossed the first coin, and when it was caught asked, "Do you know the merchant Silas Galerius?"

The man inspected the coin in his hand, then allowed, "I know him."

Hannibal tossed the second coin. "Find him, tell him that Hannibal Mago of Carthage has arrived and awaits him at the main dock. Show him the pieces, and say I promised you another from his own purse."

"I will do this," the fisherman replied, and poled for shore.

"Hannibal and I will go ashore with four guards," Travis declared. "All others are to stay here and hold off any who try to board until we learn what it is we face."

Hannibal stood in the bow of their skiff, his eyes scanning the shoreline. Syracuse was his main entry port for goods not intended for Rome. His merchant partner Silas had been his father's partner before him, and a good man, though getting on in years. The long central dock drew within hailing distance, yet still he could not see the merchant's bent figure. Only chaos was there to greet them.

The closer they came, the louder grew the clamor. Figures appeared here and there, racing helter-skelter, but in no pattern that he could discern. They did not seem to be fleeing from something, nor all moving in a single direction. There was a jerky aimlessness to their movements, as though—

"Looks like a city awaiting invasion," muttered one of Raffa's men, busy on the oars yet with eyes and ears trained on the shore. At Hannibal's request the main vessel had taken on a small rowboat; it was this they now used. The guard scanned the dockside, said, "Isn't this a garrison town?"

"A full legion," Hannibal affirmed. "I contracted to supply them, not five years ago."

"Well, there's no sign of them now."

Hannibal recalled the rumors of civil war, felt a chill grip his gut. "I hear no battle."

"No, nor I." Travis stood alongside him, his voice taut as the hand that gripped his sword's pommel. "But something is very wrong."

A lean man in rich robes as gray as his beard limped down the quayside and waved his silver-topped staff at the approaching boat. Hannibal pointed and said, "Can you put us there?"

Before the boat was docked and tied, the merchant was already waving them up. "Come, come, there is no time to lose, no time."

Hannibal pulled himself upright. "Greetings, Silas."

"Ah, ah, of all the times for you to arrive." The merchant was fairly dancing in place. "Had I but known, I would have told you to wait, but no, how could I, I did not know myself."

Travis directed two men to come with them and the others to guard the boat, then joined Hannibal on the quayside. Hannibal gestured ceremoniously and said, "Travis son of Cletus, may I present my partner, Silas Galerius."

But the merchant had no time for politeness. "Come, come, there is panic on the streets. Not even the garrison can promise us safety. Or you. Which is your ship?"

"Those four," Travis said, a trace of pride to his voice. "Two cables off, moored in deep water."

The merchant granted them scarcely a glance before starting back down the quay. "That should do, I suppose."

Hannibal stared as six armed guards fell in about them, giving Travis' men a single hostile look before turning their attention outwards. He questioned Silas, "Six men for a journey of half a league?"

"Had I but more. Wait! Quickly, in here." He drew them into a hooded doorway as a trio of women raced by, shrieking with dismay, blood streaming from furrows they had apparently dug in their own foreheads. The screeches remained a long time after they had disappeared, then nothing. Silas Galerius poked his bearded face out into the empty street, scouted in both directions, then motioned them forward. "Careful now."

Hannibal found his legs as unsteady as his voice. "I have seen nothing like this since the last plague."

"Were it only that," Silas said, scurrying down the cobblestone lane. "Here, here, this way is better." They turned into a way so close that three of them could not walk abreast. "There were riots last night, two of the main thoroughfares turned into battlegrounds. Fires everywhere."

Hannibal followed the old merchant through another turning, his breath coming in gasps from more than just the haste they made.

"But what is it?"

"Chrysargyron. For all Italy." Silas fled up a steep rock-lined slope, then realized that Hannibal had frozen to a stop at the turning. He wheeled about, motioned frantically, and hissed, "There is no time to lose."

"That is impossible," Hannibal said dully, not moving.

"If you value your life, you shall not stop to discuss this now," Silas pleaded. "For all our sakes, hurry!"

Travis gripped his arm, helped his legs restart, demanded, "What is a chrysargyron?"

"Who is this young traveler that he does not know of the empire's greatest curse?"

"Travis is a landsman. His father runs a consular estate," Hannibal replied impatiently. "What you are telling me is impossible."

"And yet I tell you the truth," Silas shot back, scurrying on, his guards hard pressed to keep track with his winding course. "The legates arrived yesterday, the rumors three days earlier. The garrison has been split in two, half preparing the instruments of torture even as we speak, the other half quelling the riots with bloody dispatch."

"But there was a chrysargyron only three years ago!"

"A new ruler, a new tax," Silas said, stopping at a corner as the lane crested the steep ridge. He leaned against the building, clutching his chest with one hand, his eyes scanning every direction. "There is also word of a new punishment. Anyone caught lying about their holdings will have their mouths pried open, then filled with molten lead."

"But I had heard of treaties," Hannibal protested, not wanting to believe the news.

A guard urged, "We should move from here."

"A moment's rest. I am too old for such panics." The merchant pushed himself erect and tottered forward on tired legs. "Constantine's three sons are supposed to share the emperor's throne. This you have no doubt heard. The third, Constans, has been given power over Italy. It is he who has ordered this new scourge."

"Tell me the money is not being raised for war," Hannibal pleaded.

"That I cannot do." The merchant straightened and hustled on. A hundred paces farther, he stopped before a pair of great doors and rapped once with his staff. Instantly the doors swept back, and the group hastened within.

Hannibal scouted the courtyard, saw every sign of calamity and affliction. "This can not be so."

"Go to the central forum and see for yourself, if you dare," Silas puffed, easing himself down on a chair supplied by a servant who bowed and ran off, eyes streaming panic. "Already the first victims are being stretched upon the rack. Clearly the officials have come with stern orders from their new ruler."

Hannibal found he could no longer ignore Travis' questioning gaze. "The chrysargyron is a tax imposed only upon city dwellers. It is also called the silver tax, for only in gold or silver coin may one pay. And gold coin is almost impossible to find."

"Silver as well," moaned the old merchant. "I have traveled the length and breadth of this city, and there is none to find. None. And my own coffers are empty."

Hannibal gave the merchant a probing glance, saw only genuine distress. He turned back to Travis and continued, "For centuries it was the land that was taxed, and since only the wealthy could afford much land, they carried the most burden. And this could be paid in kind."

"But the land has been taxed until the trees themselves groan," Travis said bitterly. "The *ingum* and the *caput* are the scourges with which my father's life work has been brought to nothing."

"A few years ago, a new tax was announced," Hannibal went on, "one paid every fifth year by those who lived and worked in cities and towns, and all who dealt in commerce. The chrysargyron it was called."

"The curse of Constantine," Silas groaned.

"Sadly, it is so," Hannibal reluctantly agreed. "It was intended to act as a balance, spreading out the burden of taxation. Even Italy lost its exemption, only the second time in history the home provinces were ever taxed." He sighed. "But it has not worked. Not from the outset. This tax is paid in coin, and coin is much easier to manipulate by corrupt tax officials than grain or oil or wine. Governors suddenly found people willing to spend fortunes to gain places upon the tax syndicates, and for one purpose only."

"Profit," Travis said. "Like Fabian."

Hannibal studied the young man. "Is it possible that he may have heard of this new chrysargyron, and thought it might eventually reach to Carthage?"

"I have no idea," Travis replied, meeting his gaze.

"It would mean access to the highest corridors of power," Hannibal mused. "Could he have contacts in Constantinople, ones which—"

A throat-wrenching scream lofted over the courtyard wall, a shriek that went on and on and on. It was answered by moans and cries from all about them, inside the compound and from dwellings on every side.

"I know nothing of my brother's activities," Travis said, once his power of speech returned.

Hannibal nodded acceptance, and returned to his explanation. "This corruption has had terrifying results. Children have been tortured before their parents in order to exact information on possessions and secret hoards. Servants are bribed or tormented until they inform on their masters. Those with grudges speak lies, then stand and watch as their enemies are executed, all the family's holdings taken by the state, all the family sold into slavery."

"Doom, doom," moaned Silas, dropping his head into his hands. "All my wealth is in goods, and now there are no buyers. None."

"In Carthage, our only hope has lain in careful preparation," Hannibal continued to Travis. "Precise records, copies lodged with officials, allies at every level of local government."

"And a hoarding of coin," Travis said.

"Your share of the pirate goods was a fair exchange for the chest," Hannibal replied.

"I believe you," the young man said calmly.

In those words came the first sense of rightness to the terrible day. Hannibal turned to where the old merchant sat. "Rest easy, Silas. I will take your goods for coin."

●●●

Following their speedy departure from Syracuse, Hannibal remained morose and isolated for a day and a night and yet another day.

Silas the merchant had lost no time stampeding his household into action. Hannibal had been careful but firm. He repeatedly insisted upon an honest measure for honest coin. One team had been sent out for provisions and water, another to hire another ship and man it. Seamen had fair leapt at the chance to escape the horror, most not even asking the destination. Merchants had been dumbfounded by travelers willing to pay not only in coin, but at a fair price.

A contingent from their vessels had rowed over to help cart the goods back to the ship. No urging to make haste had been required. The screams and wails had continued unabated. By nightfall all had been made ready, the newly acquired goods stowed in what was now their fifth ship. When Hannibal had stood at quayside and counted the heavy silver coins into Silas' hand, the old merchant had broken down and wept. They had sailed from the port immediately, the night sky ruddy from fires burning uncontrolled in two segments of the city, screams lofting high and long on the chill wind.

Travis was forced to wait until the second day to approach Lydia and ask what was troubling her father. In preparing their departure from Syracuse, it was decided to split the new seamen among all five vessels, doing the same with Raffa's men. Travis, Raffa, and Arubal were to spend each day traveling upon a different vessel, holding careful watch, keeping the new seamen honest and gauging their mettle. Hannibal was to remain with his daughter upon the central and largest vessel, the only boat outfitted for the transporting of women.

On the second day Travis claimed duty on the main vessel, primarily because he wanted to be near Lydia. None objected. Their growing affection was evident to all. Yet Travis could not mistake the cloud of gloom surrounding Hannibal, and asked her about it.

Lydia was long before replying, "He wishes for all the world to be Christian."

"I don't understand."

"No," she sighed. "Neither do I. He is a man of great strength, and one of his strongest points is his simplicity of faith. He feels that since the emperor declared himself Christian, all the old problems should have been erased. Centuries of corruption and evil practices, all wiped out overnight."

"Your words make no sense," Travis said. "I feel as though I am being told a riddle without answer."

"Then go to my father," she said, facing him full on. "Pull him from his gloom with questions."

Hannibal stood by the aft railing, staring out over Italy's southern coast. Rocky shoreline gave way at regular intervals to pebble-strewn beaches, where fishing craft lay upturned alongside drying nets. Fields of dusty green stretched out into the distance, olive trees and fruit orchards and vineyards ranked in orderly rows. The vista was lit by brilliant sunshine, the sea a blue as deep as the sky. The five boats of their little fleet were lined up fore and aft like a string of wooden pearls.

Hannibal neither turned nor spoke as Travis approached. His shoulders remained bowed with the same weariness that stamped itself upon his features. Travis stood and tasted the wind for a time before venturing, "Your daughter is worried to see you so troubled. I as well."

"The empire is an island surrounded by a sea of chaos," Hannibal said to the distant shoreline. "The waves of rage and envy and war nibble away at the edges. Either you fight continually, building back what is being eaten away and remaining strong from the struggle, or you are doomed to watch the island be washed away. It is the same for the church. How can either remain strong if corruption is allowed to devour from within?"

Travis thought back to Hannibal's stubborn insistence that Silas place a fair price on all his wares, then did the same with both the ship owner and the seamen. Treating strangers as he did his partner. Taking advantage of none, though desperation would have made doing so proper in the eyes of many. Travis wished for some way to describe how this had touched him, but could only say, "Your daughter has been trying to explain certain things to me. But I find myself more confused than before she spoke."

"Yes? Something troubles you?" Hannibal's tone was more bitter than Travis had ever heard. "Good. I am glad. It is good to know that I am not alone, that there are others troubled by matters within the empire and the church."

"She has told me some of this God-made-man. I am reminded of the martyrs. It seems that your religion is based on courting death."

Hannibal wheeled about. Fatigue smudged dark lines under his eyes. "This is a surprise? You find life such a blessing, such a gift, that you would prolong it when you know that paradise waits upon the other side of death?"

"I know nothing of the sort."

"Then you lack vision," Hannibal snapped, and turned back to the railing.

Travis refused to let the tone push him away. "I ask these things of you because I seek to understand."

"Such things you would be better off asking my daughter."

"I am asking you."

Hannibal sighed. "I am a simple man. I believe what I believe. I do not bother my head with answers to questions I can scarcely form."

"Perhaps," Travis ventured, "that is why I would like to sample your words."

Reluctantly Hannibal turned away from the gently rolling sea. "Lydia has spoken to you of the Savior?"

"She tried. I confess to having understood almost nothing at all."

"It is not a thing for understanding with the mind alone. Either you accept and seek to learn through the experience of knowing God within your own life, or understanding will ever be denied to you."

"And yet there must be some understanding before such a step can be taken," Travis countered.

Hannibal nodded slowly, for the first time appearing to be pulled from his self-defeating reverie. "There was a famous teacher of Alexandria by the name of Clement. The Bible, our holy book, tells us that all men were made in God's image. Sadly, man fell from grace. But this does not change the fact that man, even fallen man, contains shattered fragments of this perfect image. These shards are present in each of us, to a greater or lesser extent. Some people have goodness, others bravery and courage, others aware-ness and wisdom. But the shards remain incomplete and unfinished, unless the individual makes the decision to let the One repair the damage."

A glimmer of light returned to Hannibal's dark eyes, a rekindling of the familiar spirit. "By the gift of His Son, God in His infinite wisdom and eternal love has granted us, the unworthy, a gift of salvation. This is what Christ offered the world, and the central law by which we Christians stand and claim the gift of ultimate truth. Not a deed done by us. Not a return to infinite wisdom from our own imperfect knowledge. Not a forming of perfection from our own fallen state. No. A gift. Granted to us because the Lord has chosen to bring man back into grace, not by what we do, but by what has been done for us. And it is only through the gift of Christ's sacrifice joined to each heart through genuine faith that we are restored to our rightful place."

Hannibal turned back to the railing, and as he did the shadows returned to cloak his features and draw the morose brooding tone back to his voice. "Yet where is the healing for this scarred and battered empire?"

CHAPTER VIII

Five days beyond Syracuse was the second Sabbath of their journey. At Hannibal's request, the boats moored at dawn in a tiny rock-hewn cove. Travis watched as Christians from each of the boats gathered in the main vessel's stern, saw the smiles and the clasped hands and the welcoming bows. The gathered knelt together in a tight cluster. An ethereal light, soft as mist, seemed to emanate from the little group. Travis tried to think of it as nothing more than the growing dawn, yet felt the light in his heart far more than saw it with his eyes. It spread until the entire aft section was bathed in soft luminosity. Clearly others felt this change, for the ships' normal chatter gradually died to a respectful hush. In the resulting silence Travis tried to listen to what was being said, but the voices were too quiet for him to catch the words. Yet the light remained and beckoned, the words they shared a lingering mystery.

It was his day to travel upon the largest vessel. Once they were again under way, Travis approached Lydia and was greeted with a smile so open and sweet it twisted his heart. She said, "I was thinking of my mother. The Sabbath does not seem the same without her."

"Hannibal told me she is not well."

"Her health has never been good." Lydia turned her gaze back seawards. "Once when I was little I asked my mother how she could bear being ill so much. She had been in bed then for a very long time. I was too young to know the measure of days, I only knew it was too long. Weeks certainly. Possibly months. I would come to her every day, and she would ask me questions and then tell me a story, if she had the strength. Sometimes she could not speak without difficulty, and then I would pretend she had asked me the questions anyway. I remember it was such a day. I talked as long as I could, but I was young and I grew impatient. I asked her how she could stand being sick so long. Did she not grow angry with God?"

Travis waited for a time, then when she did not go on, he pressed, "What did she say?"

Lydia had difficulty answering. "All she said—" Lydia was forced to stop and take a shaky breath, then she went on. "All she said was, 'Though He slay me, yet will I have faith in Him.' I waited and waited, but she said nothing else. She did not want other words to come in the way, I know that now." She shook her head. "Even if I live to be a thousand years old, I will never be as strong or as wise as my mother."

Travis remained silent, feeling his world being torn in two. On the one side, the words appeared as an impenetrable barrier, holding him apart from ever claiming her as his own. A bitter regret clutched at him, urging him to turn away in frustrated anger.

And yet, and yet. There was a second voice, calmer and quieter and easily ignored. One that whispered a beckoning invitation to his heart. As though these strange words made perfect sense on a level far beyond the understanding of his own mind. They kept him standing there beside this young woman, sharing with her a grief and a memory he could not fathom. And gave him the strength to say, "My mother died when I was four."

"Oh," she said, turning to him, her eyes bright with unshed tears for her own mother. "I am so sorry. That must have been very hard for you."

"It was," he agreed, his turn now to turn away and gaze at the endless weaving waves. "I did not have time to grieve for her, though. My two half-brothers had always hated me, and when she was no longer there to protect me, life became very hard."

"I have never met Fabian," Lydia said. "But when my father speaks of him, he becomes very angry."

"Brutus was worse by far. He was older and more like his mother. At least my father says so. I never knew her. She hated the farm. More than that. What is stronger than hate?"

After a pause, Lydia said quietly, "Love." Then stood, watching him.

Travis stared back, unable to speak, his heart inflamed by mysteries and yearnings too strong to contain.

Lydia sensed his flaming heart, and drew him back from the brink by saying, "You were speaking of your father's first wife."

"Yes," he said, the word a sigh of defeat. Eventually he turned back to the sea and continued, "She felt trapped on the estate. She filled her sons with her hatred and bitterness. My father never said, but I do not think he was sorry when she died. But he honored the consul who was both her father—she was the daughter of the consul's favorite concubine—and my father's patron. He treated her as well as he could and gave her sons enough wealth to start them off in the cities of their choosing. Fabian went to Carthage, Brutus to Rome."

"And now you to Constantinople."

"I never wanted to leave the farm. Once my half-brothers were gone, it was a good place to live. A fine place. Rich land and good crops and the sea for a neighbor." His voice turned bitter. "It *was* a good place. Now the client-farmers and freemen are drifting away, and the crops are failing for lack of care. The cost of harvesting what is left is higher than what we are able to earn. All we hide from the government procurers, the tax man steals. Fabian's silver will go some way toward seeing off the money lenders and hiring more help, but I must find a way to free us from these threats. I *must*."

Lydia was silent for a time, then reminded him quietly, "Your mother."

"My father says she was a good woman," Travis said and wondered at the flower of pain that bloomed in his heart. As though Lydia's soft concern offered him the chance to mourn in safety. "He says I look much like her. I remember her laugh. And her eyes. She seemed to drink in the world's joy and find excitement everywhere." Shyly he turned to her, said quietly, "I think she would have liked you."

For Lydia, the ship remained a water-bound prison. Yet the external difficulties were nothing compared to the tumult that raged in her head and heart.

She and her maidservants were relatively comfortable. A portion of the stern deck had been screened off to grant them privacy. Lydia had journeyed with her father before. She knew what it meant to be one of few females among many men, and how to hold herself aloof and reserved. This was a price she had to pay in order to travel. Though she did not like it, she accepted it. And her faith granted her a means by which contact with some of the men could be safely made. Plus she had brought books and scrolls for study, to ease the long hours. No, it was not the cramped quarters and enforced idleness that troubled her so.

It was Travis.

Even with him traveling four out of every five days on other vessels, still he was constantly there, continually in her thoughts. She followed the progress of whichever ship he journeyed in, her heart filled with longing. And always, always her mind returned to her mother's final words, that a lifelong love was best cemented through shared faith.

Lydia was too intelligent and too held by her own faith to disagree with her mother. Arguments and ideas that surfaced were like the brief flashes of desire which flamed up to consume her, then just as swiftly died away, leaving behind only the hollow ache of unanswered yearnings. And fear.

Pylos was to be their second landfall in the Greek provinces. The night before their arrival in Pylos, Lydia found herself unable to sleep. She spent the quiet hours watching out over the stern. Travis' boat was a mere shadow-speck in the distance, its pair of signal torches flickering like golden sea-borne stars. Their own wake shimmered with silver phosphorescent streams. Lydia stared down at this luminous river within the unseen ocean, and knew she could wait no longer. Her emotions were a flood that could not be denied. Either she spoke to him now, or she was lost.

Travis walked the crowded streets of Pylos, and felt the storm rage within him.

Each day's journey drew them closer to Constantinople and the awaiting challenges. The unknown loomed all about him, dangers and opportunities so tightly intertwined that he wondered how he would tell them apart.

Ahead waited the consul's son, the challenge of setting up a new home and the pressures of profitable trading. Behind him, his father and the farm and the poisoning and Carthage and the pirates and the confrontation with Fabian. So much to sort through, so much to prepare for.

Yet all he could think of was Lydia.

She walked alongside him now, her nearness igniting a renewed gale of emotion and desire. He longed to hold her, ignore the crowds and the guards, take her and make her his own. He cursed the fact that they were never alone, never able to know a moment's intimacy, always held apart by custom and the constraints of the voyage.

And her faith.

Her words and those of her father rang continually through his mind. He seemed no closer to understanding than before, yet felt threatened on some deep level by the invitation. And no closer to making a decision. One moment he was ready to go against his father's contempt for all sects and temples, and declare himself. The next, he felt disgusted by his own willingness to change and conform, all for the sake of a woman. A further moment still, and he was sick with love and desire and the sense that the whole world stood in their way.

Lydia chose that moment to stumble, or at least pretend to, for she was lithe and surefooted as a deer. But such playactings were their only chance for contact. Normally the intimacy ignited within him a flame of passion, fueled both by her touch and by the look that passed between them. But this time all he felt was a gnawing ache.

A ripple through the crowd drew him from his reverie. No word was spoken, no warning given, yet the sigh was as clear as a shout of alarm. Travis faltered with the others, spotted the trio, and instinctively drew back.

A line of wizards approached, their robes decorated with the interlocking names of demons under their control. Ornate coned hats declared the temples to which they claimed allegiance— Sabazius, Jupiter of Doliche, Mithra. Servants walked alongside bearing gold shields and diadems, supposed gifts from grateful clients. Some wizards were rumored to purchase such gifts themselves, in order to impress those who sought their services and to justify the prices they charged for casting spells and predicting the future and speaking with the dead.

Travis stepped into the crowd, pressing against the opposite wall, and drew Lydia with him. "Give them room."

"Why?" With an impatient gesture she shook off his hand. Her voice overloud in the sudden hush, she declared, "It's just a bunch of old men."

One of the group turned a lofty stare her way. His long beard was dyed a rich purple. The surrounding people drew a collective breath and pulled away from her. Travis started to do the same.

He felt his skin crawl as the man raised his wand.

Travis did not himself believe in their so-called powers, no, but still there was no sense in tempting fate. Yet Lydia shamed him with her courage. She stood and stared at the purple-bearded man, calm and certain.

The wizard's other hand rose to reveal the *tophets*, or images of power. One was a paper-thin gold band about his wrist carved with runes and signs. This was connected by a slender chain to the golden asp, a snake symbolizing the wizard's might. He shook both the asp and the wand in her direction and hissed words of a spell. The crowd gave a collective shudder.

"Have you ever heard of Simon Magus, old man?" Lydia remained standing there with features set in scornful lines, her hands propped on her hips. "He sought to buy the powers given by the Master Jesus, so that he could sell them."

Perhaps it was his imagination, but Travis had the impression that the old man drew himself back at her words.

She was not finished. Lydia startled all of them, the wizards included, by taking a bold step forward. "The might of the Holy Spirit reached down then, and struck that wizard dead."

The wizard hissed again, this time joined by his fellows. But there was a different tone to the confrontation now, hesitant and frustrated. The largest of the servants moved forward, the golden shield leveled as a battering ram, but he stopped at the sound of Travis drawing his blade.

It was the wizards who gave way, not Lydia. They eased past her, lips drawn and eyes narrowed.

Lydia stood and watched and waited until they were gone. The crowd stepped back into the street, their eyes now on Lydia.

"The Lord Jesus calls us all to turn toward the truth," she said quietly. "His strength and His love and His salvation are there waiting for each and every one of us."

"I must speak with you," Lydia said, her voice low and tremulous.

Travis set his load down at quayside, nodded, and guided her a step away from where the guards were settling their provisions into the rowboat. "I know."

"I thought, well, I don't know what I thought." She gave a wayward strand of raven-dark hair a nervous swipe. It was a totally different Lydia facing him now, hesitant and unsure of herself. "My father has said I must be patient and let you learn the good with the bad, sort through the worldly and seek the eternal truth." Her eyes searched his face. "But I do not have eternity. Not here, not now. I cannot wait any longer, Travis."

He nodded, his heart so swollen the words came out hoarse and shaking. "I can't either."

"I am falling . . ." She stopped, took a very shaky breath. Tension crackled in the air between them. "I should not. Can not."

"Yes, you can," he said, and saw the chasm of indecision shrink to nothingness. "You want me to swear allegiance to your temple. Fine. I will do it."

But her reaction was not what he wanted nor expected. Instead of showing astonished joy, she reacted as though slapped. "What?"

"I have never sworn fealty to a sect or god," he explained. Never had he felt so charitable. "Nor have I ever sought the astrologer's guidance. My father forbade all priests and wizards entry to our estate. I break no oaths, save the unspoken one to my father, and I shall write and ask him to understand."

"I am not asking you," she said, her face flushed a fiery red, "to swear allegiance to a temple."

"Whatever." He gave the air a careless wave. This was not just for her. Twice he had stood stymied by unseen forces, while she and her father had shown a strength beyond his own. "Your father has described how this Jesus god does not demand great sacrifices or gifts of gold and silver, just allegiance. A god who does not show greed or twist the acolyte's life with dominating rules before granting entry into the mysteries is something new. My father will like that."

The fire ignited in her eyes now, sparking in her voice. "So you will go up and swear your allegiance and just go on with your life, is that what you think?"

"It is what your father said."

"No, it is *not* what he said. He has *never* said anything like that."

"He did." Her sudden pushing began to grate. "I stood upon the deck, right there beside him, and asked him the questions at *your* request."

Lydia cocked her hands upon her hips. "And heard not one word of his reply!"

The heat and the frustration had a focus now. Travis ignored the guards' glances, brought his face down closer to hers, offered with fake sweetness, "Perhaps your own understanding of such matters is not as great as you would like to think."

"To even suggest such a thing," she snapped back, "is a perfect indication of your own unbounding stupidity!"

● ● ●

Raffa found Travis heaving sacks of grain from the shore-boat onto one of the vessels. The warrior stood on the gunnel watching his furious effort. When the load was cleared, Raffa slid aboard and motioned for the seamen to climb aloft. Gratefully they scaled the vessel's side and left the pair alone.

Travis stood facing him, his chest heaving. When he could find the breath, he confessed, "Lydia and I quarreled."

Raffa scrubbed the side of his face with a blunted hand, and kept the smile from surfacing. "I doubt anyone within hailing distance of the shore missed that fact."

"We were loud?"

A discreet cough. "Only in stages."

Travis swiped at the grain dust covering his arms and shoulders. "You would not believe what she says I must do."

"I can imagine."

"No, you can not."

"You forget," Raffa said. "I have served with officers who were Christians."

"She wants—" Travis sighed his defeat, lowered himself onto the middle seat, continued to sink until his head was in his hands. "I don't know what to do."

Raffa looked out over the cloudless vista, took a long moment before asking, "How are you feeling these days?"

"What?" Travis raised his head. "Oh, you mean from the poisoning. Fine. I have scarcely thought about it."

Raffa nodded. "Yet only weeks ago, it dominated your world. You were afraid, we all were, that you might never recover. It was a threat so great that you could scarcely see beyond to anything else."

Travis eyed him. "What are you saying?"

"Only that you love her. And she loves you. This much is clear to all who journey with us. Such love is a mighty force, one to be reckoned with."

Travis waved a weary arm in the direction of their main vessel. "I would have to give up my independence to satisfy this crazy god of theirs."

"As to that I have no answer," Raffa replied, reaching for the guide rope and pulling their boat back alongside the larger vessel. "But allegiance always costs a measure of freedom, be it to an army or a temple or a woman. The issue is always to choose rightly before paying the price."

Hannibal eyed his weeping daughter with a mixture of exasperation and real concern. "You could have been harmed, daughter. Even killed. These wizards are not to be trifled with."

"The guards were there." She sniffed, swallowed noisily. "I felt the Spirit's call, and I answered. When the servant started to threaten me, Travis stopped him."

"Travis, yes." Hannibal saw her broken heart in her eyes. "What of my advice?"

She nodded miserably. "I couldn't wait."

"Act in haste, repent in leisure." But his tone was gentled by her anguish. "You have sought to have him run before he could even stand."

"But he treated our faith like a temple sect." A trace of the storm returned. "He thought he could give his pledge, make his sacrifice, then go back to living just as before."

"And so you corrected him," Hannibal countered, "by listing all the rules and all the requirements that would go into making a good Christian. Without acknowledging that none of us can easily grasp these matters, let alone put them into practice. Not even you."

"But he thought . . ." Her chin quivered, her voice gave way to woe. "What am I to do?"

"Pray and be patient," Hannibal said. "The good Lord has a way of working the mightiest of miracles, given time."

But the situation did not improve. Travis avoided the main vessel entirely between their departure from Pylos and their arrival at Pireaus four days later. When she alighted on the Piraeus quayside, Lydia found him watching her with a blend of caution, pain, and old anguish. It left her unable to think beyond the bitterness of loving a man who did not deserve her affection. She returned to the boat heartsore and hollow, not having spoken to him at all.

Their next stop was Chios, where they were held for three days by an early summer squall. Throughout the storm their world remained a uniform bluish gray. The island's mountains were silhouettes cut from the same fabric as the storm-tossed sea, blending easily into the lowering sky. Lydia walked the hills alone save for a single guard, a trusted ally who came no closer than necessary and who would never report about the tears that mingled with the rain.

It did not matter that she was right. Not in these lonely walks. She ached with the loss and the hopelessness of her own pride.

Only when she returned to the inn where they berthed, and looked across the smoky room to the table where Travis sat surrounded by his men and his own gloom, did the stubborn anger resurface, leaving her trapped in the battle against herself.

Their final day in Chios was the Sabbath. The shore-boat made numerous passages ferrying believers from each of the vessels in turn. Lydia waited and hoped against hope, as she had before each of their Sabbath gatherings, and felt another part of her heart melt away when Travis did not appear.

As she stood and gazed out over the gathering, Lydia had a sudden impression that Travis was lost to her. That he would never join with her in faith. That he was never to know the glory of truth. That she would never know the taste of his love. She joined the others in the stern, her face aged, her voice silenced with the grief of knowing her hopes were useless, her cause forlorn.

From Chios they made straight for Gallipoli, and there passed the narrow straits marking the entrance to the Sea of Marmara. From there it was only three days' journey to Constantinople. Three days and the voyage would end, and with it any reason she might have for seeking Travis out, being close to him, trying to solve the problems and ease the barriers that kept them apart. Three days.

CHAPTER IX

Their early-morning arrival in Constantinople was shrouded by water-borne fog. It was a strange haze, hugging the water and drifting up in smoky tendrils to obliterate the world. Overhead, glimpses of rose-tinted heavens came and went between meandering veils. They made their way forward slowly, the oars treading in cautious cadence, less than a boat's length between each ship. A sounder cast the weighted line from each bow, with a second man on watch from each stern.

The diffused morning light grew stronger as the sun rose above the horizon. The mist billowed grand and tall over the water, yet remained bunched ahead of them like frosty mettle upon a giant's fist. They rowed forward, their passage untouched by the faintest breath of wind. Even where the mist parted to reveal the mountain of fog up ahead, still they could not see the water, for there the blanket rested thick and unyielding. The sea remained so quiet and waveless and shrouded that they may well have been transported into the heavens, there to float forever upon an ocean of clouds. Only the oars' steady creak reassured them that they had not entered the ghostly realm.

The sun rose higher still, and reluctantly the dew-laden tendrils began to disperse. First water appeared beneath their bows, then pale forms of other boats through which they steered. Yet still the wall of fog loomed high and vast before them.

A single ray managed to pierce the stubborn mountainous mist, and suddenly the corner of an edifice appeared. Its size drew a gasp from the seamen, then another when the fog parted farther still, and they realized it was not some grand monument that they saw, but a seawall, one corner of one segment of the city's first line of defense. The stone caught the growing light and shone first as amber, then lightest honey, then as solid gold. It towered, a stronghold so mighty as to rise beyond both the might and the imagination of man.

Yet this was only the beginning of discovery. For the giant's misty grip unraveled, each frothy white finger releasing in turn, revealing tier after tier of grand buildings and broad avenues and monuments and statues and gardens and churches and extravagance and riches. This was not a city less than twenty years old. This was a city beyond time. This was indeed a city descended from the very heavens.

The rocky beach where Travis walked was narrow and jammed with boats and nets and fishermen. The stench was vile, both because of the racks of drying fish and because of the wind, which blew from the animal yards positioned just upriver. At

Hannibal's suggestion they had moored in the fisherman's harbor, rather than within the protected inlet known as the Golden Horn. Selecting a cheaper mooring, Hannibal had explained, meant less trouble from customs officials and the valuing of cargo. Hannibal had then left, taking Lydia and some of his men, saying he would see first to lodging and then to locating the customhouse.

Travis walked the rocky beach, putting distance between himself and the laughing, jostling crowd of seamen and Raffa's guards. All save himself were delighted with their landfall, anticipating everything a strange port had to offer. Travis strode angrily along, feeling his thoughts pressing in from all directions, staring at the city wall that rose beside him. Tall fortress towers jutted at regular intervals, dwarfing the highest ship's mast. Guards paced the ramparts, at that height looking like puppets in battle dress.

Travis halted and looked out beyond the harbor mouth to where the sea stretched empty and silent, filled with an eternity of unanswered questions and needs. Longing lanced his self-made barriers. The wound to his heart was a gaping hole, one that he feared would never heal. All ability to deceive himself was lost; he saw the future now for what it was. His only chance for love was gone, not because of any argument or what he had said in a moment's anger, but rather because of who he was. And this he could not change.

Yet the sense of abandonment was a living death, an emptiness so great he felt unable to bear the burden of his own name.

"What are you thinking?"

Travis started and spun about to find Raffa watching him oddly. "What?"

"You've been staring out over the waters as though you seek to pierce the veil of heaven."

"I was thinking," Travis said, then skirted a genuine confession. "I was thinking how good it is not to be alone."

Raffa was not impressed. "Every man is alone, and for all time. He fills his world with friends and family, but still must face the river of solitude some day. I have seen too many mates pass on to think otherwise. In the final moment, we all die alone."

The warrior's sharp tone drew Travis from his own reverie. "What is troubling you?"

"Your moroseness is infecting the men," Raffa replied sharply. "All know there is a time of danger and testing ahead, and yet you show neither will nor direction. No soldier wishes to follow an officer who courts death."

Travis heard the challenge in the old soldier's words. Yet all he could respond with was a confession. "I feel so empty."

"Remember what I said upon the boat, and give this young love a time to heal. As to your emptiness," Raffa shrugged. "Only those with wealth and power can afford the luxury of striving after answers to impossible questions. For the rest of us, we must simply seek to survive. One day at a time. Step by step toward the dark river of eternal night."

"There should be more," Travis said. But what he thought was, I feel wrapped about a void. A heart spilled upon the earth, a vessel emptied of all power and emotion.

"The temples are full of men who claim an answer to that riddle," Raffa snorted. "Their tongues are slippery and their pockets clink with silver they have not earned. But which of them has ever passed across the river of death and returned? Show me that one and I might be willing to listen."

"They say," Travis replied slowly, "their Jesus god did just that."

"I never met the man." Raffa glanced beyond Travis, said, "The first of our challenges now approaches. Can you ready yourself?"

Travis followed the other man's gaze, spotted Hannibal walking toward where their shoreboat was beached, leading a stout man whose oiled hair glistened in the afternoon light. He straightened his shoulders. "I am ready."

"Good," Raffa said, and clapped him on the back. "Such questions are best left for the old women beyond the reach of children and most tomorrows. For myself, I shall fight this day's remaining battle, then fill the final hours with food and wine and perhaps a willing wench. What say you?"

"Not tonight," Travis said, and started toward the waiting pair. A void, he thought. An empty shell. That was all he was. Had it been thus with him always? Travis picked his way across the rocky loam, felt the yearning whisper through his aching emptiness. He knew no answer save one. And she was forbidden to him.

The late afternoon air was dove-gray with dust rising from the city's constant activity. Hannibal Mago stood alongside the customs official, his stony features masking how he had been rocked by what he had found inside the city walls.

Constantinople was a harsh place, brutal in its uncaring haste. The city was literally exploding from the rocky earth. Impatient people stalked its streets, filled with a sense of their own power, restless with desire to draw the future into this very instant.

This was an utterly new city. There was none of Rome's ancient heritage. Yet Constantinople was already grand and filled with imposing structures. The imperial buildings appeared remarkably old, as many were built using stone plundered from more ancient temples and pagan structures, carried to the new city on the backs of slaves. Everywhere there was the dust and noise of further construction.

And the rumors. Already he was beset with snippets of news that concerned him mightily. The innkeeper, the food stalls, even this self-important little official, all were inflated with the power of living at the center of the empire. He could feel its appeal, a tightness in his gut, a magnet drawing him farther and farther away from what he felt were the central forces of his life. And his faith.

They discussed intimate church affairs as though they were gossiping over the emperor's latest concubine. Just to listen left him feeling tainted, his faith somehow dirtied, to see it joined so with affairs of state.

And the name on everyone's lips was Arius.

Hannibal forced his thoughts outwards at Travis' approach. The young man looked racked with anguish. His features were more pinched now than they had been at their first meeting, when he had still been struggling to cast off the poison's effect. Hannibal thought of his own daughter, left sighing by their chamber's single tiny window, staring out at the dust and heat and crowded marketplace, seeing nothing. Travis gave them a single nod, climbed on board the rowing vessel, sat facing the sea, and said not a word. Raffa gave Hannibal a resigned shrug as he steadied the gunnel and waited for the official to clamber on board.

Once under way, Raffa asked him, "What think you of this place?"

"Like nothing I have ever seen before," Hannibal replied, seeing the trace of a self-satisfied smile appear upon the official's pudgy features. "I do not know what I expected to find, but certainly not this. Twenty years ago, this was a Greek village by the name of Byzantium. Now, well, you will soon see for yourself."

"Whoever did the founding had a soldier's eye," Raffa offered. "Bordered on three sides by cliffs and water and a natural harbor. Only one way to launch an attack, only one wall to build and defend."

Hannibal looked at him. "A good place from which to rule an empire, is that what you're saying?"

"Rule is something of which I have no experience," Raffa replied in his soft voice. "But defense is another matter entirely."

"The New Rome," the official announced proudly. His voice was reedy, his manner puffed with conceit. "The new seat of power for a new empire."

"Indeed," Hannibal said dryly, taking in the gold cross that dangled from the official's neck. Crosses were everywhere in the new city, another feature he found both alien and shocking. They adorned pillars and people and buildings and roadsides, even crowning the rooftop of the imperial palace. He had heard of such, but seeing it for the first time was disconcerting. "Let us hope there is truly a change for the better in this new empire, that the corrupt old ways have indeed been eradicated."

Pudgy features settled into sullen lines, and the official remained silent as the boat was rowed up alongside the main vessel. Despite his profession, the official proved ungainly, and had to be helped from above and below when scaling the side. Once erect, however, he swatted away the guard's hand, only to barrel into the man when the ship gave a gentle roll. Hannibal chose discretion, and peered out over the bow until the man had righted himself once more.

The official then started toward the captain, who shook his head and pointed to where Travis stood by the railing. When Travis did not speak, Hannibal offered, "This is Travis, son of Cletus."

"Cynius, imperial customs official," the portly man snapped, clearly disconcerted by Travis' youth and apparent unconcern. "You are master of this vessel?"

"This and the other four gathered about us," Travis replied, his voice overly quiet. "The one there was hired in Syracuse, this one in Africa, the three small vessels are my own." He motioned toward Hannibal. "As for my goods, this man speaks for me."

The young man's lack of interest bewildered the official, which was good. Travis' dull-eyed appearance, however, was not. The customs official glanced about the ship, took in the men's sun-leathered complexions, their salt-encrusted clothing, their modest manner, their choice of port. Clearly there was little here to occupy his time. "Your cargo?"

"Trading goods and wares from both Africa province and Sicily. Spices, wine, oil, cloth."

Beady eyes flickered over the central gunnel, with its ballast of tall clay amphorae. "All of middling quality, no doubt."

Hannibal shot a warning glance at Travis, saw only distant unconcern. "No, actually it is the best. The oil was loaded fresh within a week of pressing."

The official sniffed. Oil and spices and cloth were all items on which the empire had long-established duties. His bribes would thus be lessened by his inability to dicker. "If so, why do you venture so far afield?"

"Because Roman and local Carthaginian officials tax us to death," Hannibal replied, his gaze flat. "We strangle under an odious burden. We seek a new market, where duties are fair and leave enough for a man to live on. We had hoped that affairs might be different in this, the empire's first Christian city. But if we do not find fairness here, we shall move on farther still."

The official spluttered, "But you have anchored."

Slowly Hannibal shook his head. "We have made no permanent landing. Most of our men are still on board. The others can be rounded up in a matter of minutes."

The official reddened, finding himself on the defensive. "This is outrageous."

Hannibal drew a slender leather pouch from his belt, shook it so the coins jingled. "I hear the groves of Ephesus have known a blight this year, and the east has not yet recovered from last year's famine. Perhaps we shall find a welcome there."

The official hesitated, greedy eyes on the purse. "Standard duties plus ten percent."

"Standard plus this purse as a gift from grateful patrons," Hannibal said, his tone brooking no further bartering.

The official hesitated, then jerked a single nod. "I will see to the stamps this very week."

Hannibal tossed the purse to the guard holding the ships' manifests. "Escort our guest back to his chambers. Wait upon him there until the manifests have been stamped, then return with them."

The official reddened, and turned away in angry defeat. Hannibal waited until the corpulent figure had slowly descended to the skiff, then confronted Travis and his flat gaze. "Do you wonder how a Christian could come to lie by omission to an official of the realm? How I might say nothing of your dyestuffs?"

"I wondered nothing of the sort," Travis replied quietly.

"If we were to reveal how ten amphorae contained royal purple dye, it would not only mean a tenfold increase in bribes. We would also be faced with a reassessment of all our goods." Bitterly Hannibal turned to watch the shore-boat row away. "As soon as I saw the man, I knew what we faced. Nothing has changed. The bribes and the corruption and the lies and the injustice, all remain in place. An empire that has been renamed Christian, yet which holds to all that was wrong and corrupt and destructive from before."

"I was only thinking," Travis said, his quiet voice drawing Hannibal back around, "how fortunate I am to have one such as you to call a friend."

Hannibal softened, placed one arm about Travis' shoulders, and drew him to one side. "Sea voyages are unkind to lovers. There is no escape from the confines. On earlier travels I have watched the best of friends become bitter enemies."

Travis shook his head, said in a voice as soft as the wind, "She is gone."

"She is here," Hannibal corrected him. "Give it time."

"What for?" A flash of irritation gave sudden life to his eyes. "Why is it that your sect remains so exclusive?"

"My religion," Hannibal chided gently. "My faith. My life."

"Why must I accept all the rules and regulations, no matter how they threaten to strangle me?"

"Our Scriptures say we should not yoke believer and unbeliever together," Hannibal replied, his tone moderated by the pain in Travis' gaze. "You have run an estate, you know the danger of yoking a stronger beast with a weaker. The stronger animal will either break the neck of the weaker, or slowly choke it. The master must take utmost care to ensure that both animals are of equal strength."

"There is no question who is the stronger here," Travis said bitterly.

Hannibal let that pass. "As to the rules of Christian behavior, all that is required of us is to repent and believe. Yet we are instructed to make an effort to adhere to rightful living, and to do so with love as our mainstay. But it is recognized that we are human, and in being human we shall fail. It is in the power of the Spirit that we find strength to change, and over time grow toward the Master's example."

But Travis was no longer hearing him. "Impossible," he muttered. "She demands of me the impossible, then denies me because I am unwilling to lie. Not to her. I could not."

Hannibal started to reply, saw that his words would be of no help whatsoever, made do with a simple pat on the young man's bowed back and a prayer. One lofted silently upwards, an appeal for them all.

Hanno loved Constantinople. He scurried up the hillside lane and reveled in his freedom. Not even the task ahead could sweep away his joy at being so far from Fabian's household and his normal life of servitude. The city was new and raucous and full to bursting with raw new wealth. Its supposed Christian overmantle troubled Hanno not in the least. Given the chance, he would be delighted to claim Constantinople as his own.

The air was kinder here than in Carthage. The heat was less brutal, the dryness less parched. It was a friendlier place, one filled with the vibrancy of power and new riches. Everything that had been forbidden by the local council was simply moved across the straits to the entirely pagan cities of Chrysopolis and Chalcedon.

In those places, the new Christian churches stood like unwelcome warts, blemishes that embarrassed all but a very few. No, if Hanno had his way, he would gladly spend the rest of his life here.

Except for one thing.

He swept up his multicolored robe and scurried faster, determined to be the first to arrive with the news. His ability to garner information, even here in unfamiliar terrain, was what had kept him free, and not imprisoned within Brutus' household.

The guards at Brutus' front portal made no sign as he rushed past them, save for a knowing smirk. Hanno paid it no mind. Let them think what they would. He was relishing his brief moment of utter freedom, with a purse full enough to grant him the life he had long dreamed of.

Freedom. Hanno had known almost nothing of it. Chosen from a slave's family at an early age because of his pretty face, plucked from what otherwise would have been a short life of drudgery and hard work. Catapulted to the strange, sweet-smelling confines of the main villa, there to be adorned in silks and oils and perfumes, to serve at functions as a prize, a living ornament. He had learned swiftly, and adapted to his new requirements. By the time he had reached puberty, Hanno knew his future lay in using his wiles and his looks and his cunning. When his patrons had shown the first signs of boredom with the boy who was growing into a man and thus was no longer so charming or odd, he had maneuvered his sale to the household and the rising star of Fabian, a man as utterly lacking in morals as himself.

Hanno announced himself to Brutus' manservant, a desiccated shell of a man from whom all life and all interest had long been drained. He settled himself upon the marble bench by the courtyard fountain, straightened the folds of his robe, composed his face into expectant lines, and steeled himself for the ordeal to come.

"Ah, Hanno, my shameless prize."

"Your excellency." Hanno sprang to his feet, trapping all but his feigned excitement down deep, keeping it off his face. "I have come as soon as I heard."

"Please, please, my dear. There is no need to stand upon ceremony with me. Sit yourself down."

"You are too kind," Hanno replied, lowering himself only when Brutus was seated, knowing to do otherwise would have resulted in his being spitted and roasted over a slow fire.

"Have you not been offered refreshment? How shameful. I will have the entire household whipped."

"I could not take a thing, O prince." Knowing too that it was no idle gesture, that Brutus' whims had left their mark on all within reach. Which was one of the reasons he had strived so hard to sleep elsewhere. One of many.

"You must have given more thought by now to my invitation, dear Hanno. Such a sweet child deserves finer lodgings than a noisome inn. And your food. I positively shudder at the thought of you dining on such swill."

"I remain a slave to your kind invitation," Hanno replied, his voice as oiled as his hair. "But I would be of such poor use here, while by remaining out I can be a servant returning with glad tidings."

Brutus stiffened, and with the movement the air of the entire courtyard chilled perceptibly. "You have heard something."

"More than that, sire." The effort of holding to his attitude of servile excitement pressed beads of sweat from his back. They trickled down his spine in torturous leisure. "I have seen it with my own eyes."

Brutus possessed a strong face. Cruelly strong. Wiry dark hair was cropped close to his skull. A jutting forehead was matched by protruding cheekbones and jaw. Anger and aggression had bundled up over the years, pressing out in ferocious force. Yet his voice was as mild as his eyes. They were so incongruous, those two features, as was his slender frame. The body of a lithe and delicate dancer balanced the head of a savage, in which rested the eyes of a dreamer. The effect was unsettling. Terrifying.

Brutus shifted closer to Hanno, took one hand in his own, said, "Tell me everything."

Hanno did so, describing the landfall and the boats and the people, all the while holding to the pretended joy. Constantly fearful Brutus would switch from politeness to one of his legendary rages, and rip out Hanno's polished nails one by one. Sitting there and talking so excitedly and allowing his hand to be softly fondled was excruciating.

"Five boats," Brutus mused when he was done. "Yet you said they left Carthage with only four."

"It is true, O sire, I swear it. I stood and watched their departure from the bow of the boat that brought me here."

"Of course you would not lie to me," Brutus said, turning the hand over, probing deep, locating each pressure point in turn, stopping just short of real pain. "You are my loyal servant."

"They must have hired or bought the fifth boat along the way," Hanno said, knowing he was babbling, unable to stop or drag his eyes away from the probing fingers. "It is a large boat, and arrived as full as the others."

"And this merchant and his daughter, the ones who traveled with my dear brother. What of them?"

"They have taken lodging at the Inn of the Loaves and Fishes."

"Christians. How very interesting."

"Yes, sire, it is as I told you. Hannibal Mago is renowned throughout all Africa province for his adherence to the Christian sect. And for his power as a merchant."

"My brother, he is there also?"

"He, I, that is," Hanno gently slipped his hand free, breathed a great silent sigh of relief, searched in his folds for a linen napkin with which to wipe his forehead. "Forgive me, sire, the heat. No, he and his men are busy searching the waterfront for rooms and storage space."

"Which means he intends to stay."

"Perhaps I could help you with further information," Hanno offered eagerly, wanting more than anything else in his life to simply be away. "The servant who is not known to be of your clan."

"My clan. Yes. Indeed. You may have your uses after all, residing apart from my household."

"I am your willing slave," Hanno replied, slippery with relief.

The soft eyes with their nightmarish glaze smiled slightly. "It must be so very expensive for you, this living and dining and traipsing about the city."

"I have a bit of savings of my own," Hanno replied delicately, "which of course I lay in offering at your feet."

"Of course." Brutus slipped a doeskin pouch from his girdle, settled it with a soft clink into Hanno's cupped hands. "Allow me to assist you along your way."

"My prince—"

"Information," the gray voice purred. "Everything you can find. Especially any weakness in this circle of his cursed men. And swiftly, do you hear? We must act with all possible speed."

CHAPTER X

Hannibal walked the market streets, alone save for two unobtrusive guards. Lydia he had sent to listen and learn within the churches, a task he had found to be utterly beyond him. Two days in Constantinople, and already he was disgusted by the maneuverings and the politics that echoed through the supposed holy chambers. Lydia had accepted her task with the same silent submission with which she had greeted all life since landfall.

Travis was no better. Hannibal had assigned him the task of locating suitable warehouse space, and the young man had done so with lightning speed. The only problem was that the building Travis found contained no living space for Hannibal and Lydia. Only later, when reflecting upon the young man's quiet sorrow, had Hannibal decided that Travis had made the proper choice after all.

Hannibal followed the road's course and entered the largest of Constantinople's several market areas. The street remained paved, a rarity for markets, and was lined by great columns. Between them rose the shops, their wares displayed in front like human lures.

He turned onto another road, muddy this time, lined by shops for leather workers. The local freemen were distinguished by swarthy features and tall, stiff caps. They stopped and stared at his passing, calling to one another in a dialect he could not understand. Hannibal met their dark looks, took in the leather aprons and the cluttered benches.

He felt eyes upon him everywhere, yet was not overly troubled. He was a trader, he knew the way of such markets. Word of him and his boats and his wares would have spread like wildfire, whipped to a frenzy by newsmongers seeking to earn the silver coin. Hannibal remained stoic, greeting the market's familiar clamor with stern-faced silence.

Dogs foraged amidst the feet of passersby. Horses waited with heads bowed patiently as goods were loaded or unstrapped. A lance of sunlight pierced the dust clouds, transforming the air into shimmering veils of gold. There was much noise and smell and heat. Hannibal felt himself growing a second skin of soot, and wished for a breath of wind.

The market teemed with life and with avarice. It was a merchant's theater, full of mock anger and casual desire. The only true emotion here was greed, all else was a charade. Sunlight and shadow sliced the lanes into jagged blocks of action. Strident voices bounced and echoed and mingled one with the other. Heat and dust formed the backdrop. Strolling musicians and overthin acrobats filled the courtyards with forced gaiety.

Tribal visitors entered the market with all the excitement of children. Their ways he knew, for his own home markets teemed with their comings and goings. They bore coins called small cash, tied in kerchiefs and saved in the packed earth beneath their beds. Brilliantly colored woven tapestries, the work of nimble fingers over a thousand afternoons and more, were carried on eager shoulders. Brass goods hammered into designs and polished until they shone like golden urns, great bundles of finest goat's hair, stinking piles of salted hides, reed baskets of spices and herbs, these goods and more were brought to the city's main market in search of a buyer. All day would be spent exploring the market, bartering over goods both brought and desired, escaping the worst of the heat in tents where sweet tea was sold. The braver ones would take a longer walk to the city's center, and gawk at an alien world of big buildings and bustling people.

The market stalls were passed from father to eldest son. Those who ran them were called blessed by whichever gods they worshipped, and known to be owners of great fortune. Travelers eyed the wealth on display with great envy, and complained bitterly over prices paid and offered. The stall proprietors shrugged with studied carelessness and hid shrewd eyes beneath heavy brows and darting glances. Life is hard for us all, they would say for the thousandth time this day. The fates bestow upon us meager portions, and the government seeks to take what is left. My babies cry from hunger as do yours, and the moneylender owns all that you see here. If you seek more than I offer for your goods, go to the Church of the Apostles and make the prayer of the hopeless, because sure as the sun has risen today and will do so again tomorrow, you will not find such riches here.

"Sire, sire, this way, please."

Hannibal started at the tug on his robe, motioned as the guard stepped forward to fend off the youngster. "Eh, what's that?"

"You are invited, sire. My honored father awaits you."

Hannibal smiled. He had himself spent many of his young days hawking for customers. "You mistake me for a man of substance."

"Oh, no, sire." The youth was of perhaps nine years, sharp featured and bright of eye. "You are the prince from Africa. You come with five ships. Three are of a form not seen here before, a mingling of fishing vessel with trading craft. All the sea folk say it is a craft from the ancient legends, and mark you as one who holds to ways now forgotten."

Hannibal leaned closer to the young face and demanded, "How do you come to know all this?"

"My honored father has instructed me to tell you he knows of your warehouse. That he recognizes you as one who will take care, and not deal in haste. That he wishes to show he too is a man of caution, and shall pave the way between you with what you seek that is not in coin."

Though he knew the patter, the giving that ignites hunger for more, still Hannibal was shaken by the speed with which his deeds were known. "And what is it I seek?"

Again the impatient tug on his robe. "My father awaits, great prince. Please, come with me."

"I am not a prince," Hannibal replied, but signaled the boy to go. Instantly his sleeve was gripped and pulled. Hannibal allowed himself to be led through an arched alcove. This opened into a small courtyard paved in mosaics so ancient they flowed like shallow waves. Hannibal looked around him, saw buildings that spoke of great age. He tried to orient himself, and decided here was the border between the market and the old Greek village. The courtyard's relative quiet was shatteringly powerful after the market's cacophony.

"Welcome, great prince, welcome." A lean-featured man whose beard was more gray than dark emerged from the shadows and bowed. "You do my humble dwelling honor."

"I am not a prince," he repeated quietly, bowing in return. "Hannibal Mago, late of Carthage."

"Nathaniel Tobias, at your service." He smiled fondly at the boy who came over to stand at his side. "And this is Gabriel, my only son."

"A promising lad," Hannibal said. "How—"

"Please, please, allow me to offer you the hospitality of my humble establishment." With a sweeping gesture he bowed Hannibal inside.

Hannibal motioned his guards to step into the shade, then entered the portal. The shop's interior was cool and inviting, carpeted in soft layers, with leather cushions lining the tapestry-covered walls. A single brass table adorned the center of the small chamber. He swept his gaze about the room, knew instantly that here was a man of worth. No goods were visible, which meant he either dealt in jewels and silver and gold, or in mass quantities, or both. "It is I who am honored."

"You will take refreshment? A tea perhaps?"

Hannibal nodded, taking in the largest tapestry's central marking. It was the *Chi-Rho* symbol, a joining of the first two Greek letters of Christ's name. The emblem had become the Emperor Constantine's chosen symbol of faith, after it had appeared in the second of his famous visions, silhouetted against the sun. On the tapestry, the emblem was surrounded by an intricately woven series of fish. The work was beautiful, depicting symbols of both Christianity's era in the catacombs and the moment of its freedom.

Yet his time here had already shown Hannibal that not all who adorned themselves with Christian symbols shared his faith. So all he said was, "Interesting work."

"Indeed." The trader walked to the tapestry's side, lifted it, and revealed a narrow passage. "Perhaps you would find this even more so."

There was little he could do but accept, though the movement away from his guards and the doorway was worrisome. Everything here was new, alien, scented with risk. Reluctantly Hannibal allowed himself to be led forward. But when he saw the stairs and the mosaics fronting the first step, his concern vanished. "Remarkable."

"You may enter if you wish," Nathaniel offered.

Suddenly breathless, he descended the narrow stairs. It was exactly as he expected. Exactly. A chamber measuring a mere four paces wide and six long. A nave the size of a stone crib. Walls and floor tiled in symbols both Christian and commonplace—a dove, a fish, a lamb—and designs that could have been a cross, or could have been something else entirely.

The cellar harkened back to the time when the act of Christian worship was a crime punishable by torture and death. Back when chapels were either in caves or tombs or underground cellars, kept small because only people each worshipper knew intimately were admitted. Back when would-be believers underwent two full years of instruction before baptism. It was indeed so like the chapel where Hannibal had worshipped as a child that it brought tears to his eyes.

He turned in a slow circle, filled with the still and silent wonder of decades of prayer, until Hannibal faced the merchant's own measuring gaze. He sighed the world back into focus. "I thank you, Nathaniel Tobias. This was indeed a gift."

"My grandfather built this chamber," his host said, the words captured by the stone-lined cellar, echoing tightly about the cramped space. "It served those of the Greek city who dared to go against the emperor's edicts."

"My own family knew just such a place," Hannibal said, and found himself filled with longing, for his home and his wife, and for what was no longer, the sense of simple faith that this city had stolen from him. He did another slow turn, asked quietly, "What has happened to us?"

"We have grown, and the world has tainted us," the trader replied. "Or some of us. Shall we return upstairs?"

Once they had reclined and been served tea, Nathaniel continued, "I was told of a new trader from Carthage. Four ships."

"Five, Papa," corrected his son.

Nathaniel gave the boy a proud look, then turned back to Hannibal. "Ships filled with every manner of goods. A warehouse now rented. And a daughter, an unmarried beauty, who goes to one church after another. She speaks with the priests, she prays. She is quiet, reserved, almost as a woman bereaved. Yet her manner draws attention as one for whom faith is genuine."

"I and my father before me, and his before him," Hannibal countered. "All have been merchants. I am thus trained in the art of being the first with information. I also know that many would tempt me with tidbits, seeking to learn if intrigue and information could save them from opening their purses."

195

"I do not seek to lower price or postpone payment," Nathaniel replied. "On that you have my word."

"Then what?"

Thoughtfully the trader sipped from his vase-shaped glass. "This is your first trip to Constantinople?"

"You know that it is."

"And will it be your last?"

"Ah," Hannibal said, nodding. "I think I see."

"What would be better for both of us," Nathaniel went on, "to make a larger profit on one voyage, or make a fair return on many such journeys over many years?"

"I will reflect," Hannibal replied carefully, "on what you say."

"I could ask for nothing more." Yet the trader did not rise to signify an end to the discussion as Hannibal expected. Instead, dark eyes flickered toward his son. "He is still with us?"

"At the courtyard entrance," the boy confirmed.

"Tell me," Nathaniel said, turning his attention back to Hannibal, "does the name Titus Octavian mean anything to you?"

"It is somehow familiar," Hannibal replied, then recalled Lydia telling him of her conversation with Travis, and the estate's problems. "Ah. He is a consul's son?"

"He is now a prelate in his own right." The tone grew more guarded. "You have had dealings with him?"

"No." Hannibal hesitated. "I have a friend, a possible partner, whose father manages a family estate."

"A young man who has busied himself with locating warehouse space and stowing your goods?"

"Your sources," Hannibal replied, "are nothing less than amazing."

"Might one ask what is in the large clay amphorae that were so carefully guarded at every step of the move?"

"Oil," Hannibal replied succinctly. "For the moment."

"I understand." Dark eyes became piercing. "There are problems with this family estate?"

"It is not his family's, but rather the prelate's. His father is manager only. And it is not my story to tell. Why do you ask?"

"You are being followed by one of the prelate's spies. Rather, by one of his follower's spies. And the young man also has a watcher, a stranger, one of fine robes and oiled skin and coiffured hair." Nathaniel sipped once more, weighing his thoughts carefully, before continuing, "Before his death, the Emperor Constantine offered positions of honor to many who would come out from Rome. He sought to reinforce Constantinople's position by drawing from the old Senate and other power structures. Some came, mostly families who had been secretly Christian. But there were others. People motivated by baser means."

"Profit," Hannibal said. "And this prelate is one such?"

"Not only him, but those who have gathered about him. They are a dangerous group. Inciting trouble, insinuating themselves into both the court and the church, with no interest other than their own gain."

Hannibal felt the walls constrict about him. Politics within the church. Or the church active in politics. "I thank you," he said solemnly, "for this gift of information."

"You should tell your young friend to take great care. These are dangerous people. Ruthless." Nathaniel stopped, said carefully, "I offer this and all else that I might be able to supply without charge or obligation. Call it a gift among believers."

Hannibal started to reply with formal thanks, then stopped. Truly there would be no better place than here to begin. "Tell me. Who is this man I hear spoken of everywhere, the one they call Arius, and this group they call the Arians?"

It was a quiet dawn. A pair of fishing boats glided by, so close together their grayish-white sails seemed joined, a pair of square billowing wings for a single overlong craft. Travis stood upon the rooftop terrace and waited for the light to strengthen. At such times he was glad he had chosen this house, though the rent was staggering. He did not belong in the newer Roman city. No matter what they might say of a location in the older Greek sector, he needed this sense of freedom. When the newness and the strangeness of Constantinople became too much, he could return here and look out over the vast blueness and quiet green islands, and know a sense of peace. A sense of belonging. Even here.

The house was three-storied and built on a rise. Because it abutted a low point in the seawall, his second floor was level with the guards on the ramparts. His third floor rose well above the city wall and its confines.

The ground floor contained the warehouse as well as dwellings for servants and clients. The second floor held offices, kitchens, and public rooms. The third was smaller and contained only two rooms. One was his private chamber. The other remained empty, the windows shuttered, the door barred. He tried to think of it as his father's future room, and to ignore the hollow feeling he felt whenever his attention turned in that direction.

Such times before sunrise were soft, luminous, scented with flowers and the sea. He often climbed the ladder to stand on his rooftop and peer out over the city. It gave him respite when his inner turmoil made sleep a memory, and granted him a means of closing the door on the night and preparing for the day ahead.

Close at hand that morning, all remained dark and mostly silent. In an unseen alley, curs growled and fought over a bit of offal. A set of fearful footsteps tap-tapped hastily down the cobblestoned way. All other sounds remained trapped behind stout doors and shuttered windows.

Up the hill behind his house shimmered tiny fragments of beckoning life. An inn with a tree-lined courtyard, lamps swinging from the branches. Dawn patrols. Wealthy folk with servants before and guards behind. A torchlit early-morning procession winding its way around one of the Christian churches. Travis watched the flickering lights, and wondered if perhaps Lydia was among them. He turned away, stifled by his loneliness, and wondered how he had ever been convinced of the rightness of traveling from his home in the first place.

He remembered his father then. Stern and silent and trapped by a world he could neither control nor change. A man who had risen far, held much back, endured even more. A good man by his own measure. Travis examined himself from that viewpoint, wondered at how his father had ever managed to endure a loveless marriage, vowed he would remain single for the rest of his days.

Raffa's careful tread scraped across the floor below, then the ladder creaked under his weight. "The men are ready."

"You'll be with them this first day," Travis said.

"Aye." He dropped his forearms upon the roofwall beside Travis. "It's a good plan, and the men like it. But still I am worried."

"I'll be fine." Time after time, while the boats were being unloaded, merchants and others had approached them, asking to hire the vessels for transport across the narrow channel to Chalcedon and Chrysopolis. Considering the distance, a voyage there and back requiring less than a day, the money offered had been substantial. Travis had asked around the waterfront, learned that most vessels of any size were already gone, off on more profitable summer voyages to distant lands. The only boats remaining were punts too narrow to transport goods or many people, or fishing boats whose pungent odor put off all but the most desperate.

Yet warehouse space in the two cities across the narrow straits cost a tenth of that in Constantinople. Besides that, pagan temples and all of the pleasures banned by the Christian city had been relocated there. So besides the traders, nervous matrons sought the old gods' help with undisclosed crises, and eager crowds of young men traveled to taste forbidden delights. In the space of yesterday afternoon alone, the three longboats had been booked for weeks to come.

"Two men to watch the warehouse, two for you, it's not enough," Raffa groused in his quiet voice. "But I'd have a riot on my hands if more were pulled from the first day's journey. This city and its Christian ways are not to the men's liking."

"I am going to the market," Travis replied. "Starting on the search for some way to fulfill my father's desire for a new base here."

"And you shall take care," Raffa said, watching him. "And not deliver the letter to the consul's son until we return."

"Four days we've been here. No one has approached us, nor shown the first sign of threat."

"And what of the trader's warning to Hannibal?"

"Who knows what was behind the man and his words? I will take care, I tell you." Travis hesitated, then confessed, "I had thought of visiting one of the Christian temples as well."

That brought a start. "For what purpose?"

"I hear tales," Travis said slowly, "of miracles beyond explanation."

Raffa was not impressed. "You haven't traveled as I have. All gods lay claim to the invisible realms. Sabazius, Jupiter of Doliche, Mithra—their followers all have stories of great wonders wrought by their powers. Most people are weak by nature, lad. They seek comfort in what cannot be explained or seen or understood. Stories of such wonders are fuel for their fires of belief, nothing more or less."

"So you think they're all lies?"

"What matters how I believe? I live by what I see and feel and touch. I believe in what I can lay my hands upon. It has served me well."

"And the night in the pirate's village," Travis pressed. "What was it we faced there?"

Raffa showed a moment's hesitation, then shrugged. "For that, as for much in life, I have no answer."

Yet it is answers I seek, Travis said to himself, turning back to the rose-tinted horizon. There must be some way I can cast off this pall to my heart. There must be.

When Travis did not speak, Raffa shifted himself erect. "I must go. We are pledged to sail at first light. Take care, lad. I smell danger on the wind."

● ● ●

Each market street had its own flavor. The most silent were the gold and silver lanes, heavily guarded and ominous. The most beautiful was the street of mosaics, where much of the street and all the walls and columns were decorated with multicolored samples of the clay painters' art. The lanes leading to the weavers' market were roofed with bales of dyed yarn, racked and hung to dry. They shaded the passages with hues of red and orange and blue and gold. And occasionally there was a display of thread dyed with the rare royal purple color.

A rich merchant's wife declared her family's wealth with swaths of semiprecious stones sewn into her veil. They captured the light and sent flickering lances toward all who passed. A bevy of armed servants hovered, ensuring her isolated safety.

Travis walked and drank in the sights and sounds, made careful note of all who dealt in the purple dye and yarns, and ached with longing to share it all with Lydia. It was not the same without her. The sun still shone from a cloudless sky. The air still carried the heat and the dust and the sea's salty perfume. Yet all was empty now, without a center. Travis felt as though his heart had been replaced by a great unmoving stone. But he would not give in to grief. Not then. There was too much newness, too much challenge. He would hold his loss within, and take it out when the earth was once again stable beneath his feet.

He turned his attention outwards, listened to the constant chorus surrounding him. Welcome, welcome, sir, madam, may the heavens grant you long life, prosperity and many sons. A tea, perhaps? A hot day requires refreshment and patience in equal measures. But sit, sit, you grace my humble establishment. How might I be of service?

Children of the stall holders hung by their respective pillars, their piping voices a continual chorus. Enter, please, kind sirs. Delight yourselves with the finest wares from Thrace, Numidia, the mysterious lands beyond the great seas. Travis walked, felt eyes upon him everywhere, wondered if he had done right in refusing Hannibal's assistance with this matter as well. Yet a part of him said the only way his heart could heal was by placing as much distance as possible between him and that pair.

He turned to one of the guards, the man Damon. Like all who did not work the chartered boats this day, he was a Christian. "Do you know where I could find the Christian temple?"

"They are called churches, sire, and they are everywhere." He seemed awed himself by the news. "There are sixteen already within the city walls, and five more being built."

"Where is one?"

Damon pointed to where a cross rose above the crowded lanes and the cramped buildings and the dust. "There is the sign."

The church was a grand structure, tall and long and built from ancient stone. Travis climbed the stairs, found himself surrounded by a crowd more confined than in the market. He scanned the people, saw tribal dress from a myriad of lands and races. Yet there was no sense of danger. Not even the guards seemed threatened by the press. Instead there was a festival air, a harvest of smiles, a sense of shared anticipation. Travis allowed himself to be swept up and along, pausing only to deposit his arms with the attendant waiting over a pile of staffs and knives and other implements, before passing through the great portals.

The vast antechamber was in itself one of the largest halls he had ever seen. Great stretches of the walls were covered with

203

mosaics, a common enough feature in themselves. Yet here the basics of life were being transformed.

Mosaics and statues were everywhere a part of Roman life, most often dedicated to the body culture and the satisfying of various appetites. In pagan families, household gods were also depicted; the more hedonistic the household or temple, the more graphic and lurid the scenes represented.

Here all was different, the Roman world turned on its head. Travis stood before the largest mosaic and did not bother to mask his astonishment. It depicted freemen and nobles and slaves working together as equals, an unheard-of act, building a church. Overhead, angels served as invisible celestial helpers, bringing them strength and food. As Travis stood and watched, he saw one group after another come and stop, some to pray, some to study. Many were of the lower classes, some even slaves. They stood wide-eyed and awed before a vision portrayed, one beyond their wildest dreams.

One man pointed to the design of a vase held by angels, readying to pour out a shimmering light-filled liquid upon the workers. "Teacher, what is that?"

"The water of life," the gray-bearded guide replied. "The gift of heaven to all brethren."

They could not read, Travis realized. They had no education, yet they yearned to hear and understand. He searched the faces about him, saw this was the truth. They *hungered* to learn what was here on display.

A murmured chant rose from within the main hall, and immediately the mingling throng became an urgent crush pressing through the inner portals. Travis waved to his guards and allowed himself to be pressed forward. He was carried through the doors and into a hall whose huge spaces seemed an imitation of the very outdoors. His gasps joined with the others as he took in the ceiling so high it was lost in the smoke of a thousand candles. The flickering light gave shimmering life to the mosaics on the walls, these far grander than those outside, and all depicting a single man. A stranger. One mosaic portrayed his brow wreathed in thorns, another showed ribbons of blood streaming from his back and arms, another still depicted him nailed to a cross. Yet his face remained serene throughout. Distant from all that was done to him, as though joined to, yet not truly a part of, his own agony.

"Glory to God the Father and the Son and the Holy Spirit, now and forevermore. Amen."

The music was a slow and steady chant, a lesson taught in song, given in slow and measured cadence, so that all might understand.

"Blessed is the kingdom of the Father, now and forever and unto the ages and the ages. Amen."

The priest approached through the same door as all the others, clothed in garments for the outside world, simply another common man save for the gilded shepherd's crook he bore. The crowd parted steadily before him.

"Lord, O Lord, look down from heaven and behold this vine that You have planted. Amen."

Before the altar he stopped, dropped his outer robe to the floor, and accepted from an acolyte the priestly robes. With them he took on an otherworldly dignity. A man as all others, brought

205

to the high post not as one separate, but one as others. As the glittering robe was fastened to his shoulders, the voices droning from the balcony began a different chant, one taken up by voices throughout the great throng. Travis heard men and women, slave and freemen and noble alike, begin to sing from every side.

> *"Of the Father's heart begotten,*
> *Ere the world from chaos rose,*
> *He is Alpha, from that Fountain*
> *All that is and hath been flows;*
> *He is Omega, of all things*
> *Yet to come the mystic Close,*
> *Evermore and evermore."*

Travis understood that even the priest's entry and vestments were a lesson beyond words. These were not his robes, his crown, his authority, proclaimed his acts. He came and accepted his task, served, and departed. Arriving and leaving a common man, like all men.

> *"Sing ye heights of heaven, His praises;*
> *Angels and archangels, sing!*
> *Wheresoever ye be, ye faithful,*
> *Let your joyous anthems ring,*
> *Every tongue His name confessing,*
> *Countless voices answering,*
> *Evermore and evermore."*

The words were utterly free of fear and pain. Anger had no place in this dwelling, nor secrecy. All was openness. All was joined. Travis looked about the great hall, trying to identify what he felt building within his heart. He searched the features of those near him, and beheld an ecstasy of praise and joy and love.

CHAPTER XI

After the service, Travis and his guards ambled along the sloping cobblestone passage in companionable silence. Constantinople was erected upon seven hills to match those of Rome, and much of the building land had been hewn like giant steps from the rugged earth. From their vantage point, they could see how the city was situated on a peninsula and surrounded by water on three sides. Sea and ever more sea, and in the distance, great hills rose on the strait's other side like dreams on the border of dawn.

The builders of Constantinople had followed Roman traditions. Main thoroughfares were straight and lined with statues and columns. Churches were established at the places of honor, marking the central plazas, the forum, and other points of power, taking the places traditionally held by the temples.

Constantinople was also a vast melting pot. Roman dress and

the honorary toga were in a distinct minority. Every manner of tribe and race and culture strode the streets and filled the air with their cacophony.

Then suddenly the air was pierced by a different clamor.

Perhaps because of the church's lingering peace, perhaps because of the tumult from unanswered questions; whatever the reason, Travis did not even see the attackers until they were upon them.

It was a desperate move, a daylight assault on a city street. There were four of them, and they made the mistake of targeting three at Travis. They came with swords at the ready, the steel glinting an alert. He reacted without thinking, flinging himself *toward* the nearest man, rather than away. Travis gripped the attacker's raised sword arm, then twisted the man's body so it became a shield between him and the other two. A sword thrust meant to slice Travis' rib cage instead pierced the first attacker's side. The man howled and loosed his weapon. Travis tore the sword from his grasp, then flung the now-limp body at one foe and hacked at the other. But the adversary was too swift, parrying Travis' blow as his companion slumped moaning to the stones.

"Alarm!" Damon sidestepped a thrust, managed to unleash his own blade, parried the second thrust, ripped upward and just missed slicing through the man's face. "Alarm!"

Travis ducked a swinging blow, came up from beneath before the man could recover, and stabbed. He was still scarcely at the ready, and it was a poor blow, missing its mark and barely scoring a flesh wound across the shoulder. Yet the man did not parry and attack again; instead, he looked at Travis in dumbfounded shock before toppling forward. The other guard's sword was buried in his back.

Travis spun about in time to see the two remaining attackers stumble away, turn a corner, and vanish. When Damon moved to follow and press the offensive, Travis cried, "Hold!"

Reluctantly Damon resisted the urge to follow. Travis went on, "They know the city and we do not."

"Best not to become separated," agreed his other guard, a gnarled and knotted veteran called Manlius. He wiped his blade and sheathed it, muttered, "Strange how thieves would attack in broad daylight."

"My gut says they were not thieves," Travis responded, his knees shaking with aftershock. Now that there was time to think, he felt lucky to be alive. "Nor just a random attack."

"Raffa was right to worry over our numbers," Damon offered.

"I think . . ." Travis' voice trailed off as he caught sight of a dark smudge rising from the Greek city down below. A faint flicker of flame shot through an upper-story window that looked surprisingly familiar, and he stiffened with renewed alarm. The attacker's sword clattered to the cobblestones as he pelted down the lane.

"Sire!"

"By me!" He did not waste breath with further words. Travis raced down the increasingly narrow lane, dodged an overloaded feed cart, spun at the first turn, and saw that Damon had almost caught up with him. Another turn, and a final, and he saw the crowd gathered outside his house. Smoke had already spread a dark stain around the top windows.

Travis spun and caught Damon as he was about to fling himself at the doors. "Wait!"

"It may not be too late, sire, we must—"

"Wait, I tell you." Travis released the guard and turned to the crowd. "Five silver pieces for any willing to help clear the house of goods!"

The crowd surged forward with greedy eagerness. Five silver pieces were more than many had held at one time in their lives. Travis pointed at Manlius. "Stay here and guard what they bring out. Make sure none depart without being searched." To the crowd, "No one is paid until all are out!"

He turned and together with a dozen willing arms heaved at the doors. Smoke billowed through the courtyard, giving pause to the faintest of hearts. Travis strode forward, saw through the gray veil the form of one guard sprawled by the far wall. Then the other appeared, a cloth tied across his face, a weal purpling the side of his head, his arms holding a box of spices as he staggered forward.

"Sire, they came, I don't know how many—"

"No time!" Travis ripped the box from his hands, flung it toward the first person behind him, pointed at two others, cried, "Take the fallen man outside!" To Damon he said, "Take as many as you need, form a line, bring out all you can manage." He spun and pointed without seeing. "Six of you, follow me!"

"Sire, the flames—"

"The amphorae!" Travis flung the words back over his shoulder. "We must save the amphorae!"

◗ ◗ ◗

Lydia climbed the stairs to their rooms, glad that the heat of the day held most of the other guests quietly indoors. She had no interest in trading pleasantries with anyone. The inn being Christian, it was more orderly and somewhat cleaner than most public houses. The hostel was also one of the city's finest, situated along the main thoroughfare from the emperor's palace and the central church, called Holy Wisdom, or Haga Sophia. But the rooms were cramped, the stairs too narrow, the top landing scarcely large enough for herself and her guard. And too often the landlord waited with oily words and a request for more money.

She pushed the door open, promising herself that the next day they would begin the search for more comfortable housing. Then she saw Hannibal seated by the window, staring blindly at the heat-drenched city. "Father!" She rushed over. "What is it?"

His face was drawn and haggard. "They say another investiture contest is underway."

Investiture contest was the name society had given to the struggle over succession. "Then it is war," Lydia said.

Hannibal stared at his daughter. "These sons of Constantine are Christians. How is such a thing possible?"

Lydia settled down beside him. "Tell me what you have learned."

Hannibal made a visible effort to sort through his tumultuous thoughts. "All the rumors we heard before our departure are true, those and more. The empire was divided among Constantine's three sons. The generals refused to accept the risk of power being divided among others. They chose to see others as threats." He turned a tragic gaze toward his daughter. "They have murdered them all. Every male relative of Constantine, save the three sons and two infants, Gallus and Julian. All are dead."

"This can't be," Lydia breathed.

"But it is. Constantine, the eldest son, is to rule the western provinces, Constantius the eastern, and Constans Italy and Africa. Already they are quarreling. The generals are choosing sides, drawing legions away from their posts, preparing for civil war."

Lydia turned her face to the window. "It is horrible," she mused. "Yet it gives credence to what I have heard over the past days."

"Such as?"

"Some of the larger churches are being drawn into political conflicts." She gave him a stricken look. "I did not want to tell you. You have been so distressed these days."

"Not just me." He inspected Lydia. "You should go to him, daughter."

Lydia's headshake was little more than a tense shiver, a pushing away what could not be. "He will not change. He has told me that himself. It is over. I was a fool."

"You are many things," Hannibal said quietly, "but a fool is not one of them."

She clenched her jaw, suppressed the struggle yet again, refocused on the matter at hand. "Within some of the larger churches, elders and priests are claiming allegiance to one political ideal or another."

"This I had heard traces of as well," Hannibal confirmed grimly.

"They battle one another in the emperor's court. They call each other apostates. Outcasts of God. Heretics. Not true believers."

"You have heard this for yourself?"

"Yes, but there is more. Nonbelievers have bought and connived their way into positions as elders or deacons of those churches involved in politics. They do this not through love of God and a life of service, but because it gives them political clout. They use their church position to gain entry into the emperor's court."

"Who has told you this?"

"Women," she said, and faltered, unsure how to describe what she had seen. "There are groups, men and women alike, who rebel against this. I met such a group yesterday, and again this morning. The women wear white scarves bound about their heads at times of worship, some all the day long. They avoid the churches who have taken up politics." She looked at her father, trying to gauge his reaction. "They do not say being involved in politics is wrong. Some are actually members of the imperial court. But they object to the *churches'* involvement. They congregate in other churches, or meet in small groups and study the Scriptures together."

But Hannibal was no longer listening. "Corruption in the church," he muttered. "Quarreling among ourselves. Accusing believers of a lack of faith, judging each other publicly. What sort of beacon have we become?"

Lydia opened her mouth, closed it, unsure of what to say. She found herself vaguely embarrassed by how deeply those women had touched her. Their gentle ways, their wisdom, their strength of faith, all had called to something very deep within her. They came to their chosen church not to worship, but rather to worship *publicly*. Their worship was a daily act, a constant communion. Others grew increasingly removed from the outside world. Cloistered, they had called their way of living. Separating themselves from all that was tainted by the world. Seeking to both understand and live the words, "And the pure in heart shall see God."

Word was returning to the city of men's movements as well. Hermits, they were called. Recluses. Cappodoceans. The Desert Fathers. Seeking secluded places and establishing homes for all who wished to come and dwell with them, dedicating their lives to worship. A worship held utterly apart from what was entering into some of the city churches.

The women had spoken of such a place of their own, a community of believers within a walled compound, some two days' journey from Constantinople. They had spoken of it not as a prison, but rather as a release. An attainment. A goal toward which they worked, seeking in their home groups to learn the holy Word, to join in hours of prayer, and to prepare themselves for this wondrous step. When widowhood or age freed them from their responsibilities and their mates, they would go. Younger women were not discouraged from marrying, yet were shown this as an alternative. The ascetic life was a concept based upon one segment of Paul's teachings. Lydia had found herself drinking in the news, feeling for the first time that here was a release from the loneliness and pain and sorrow. A new reason for living. A *better* reason.

"Father," Lydia began. "The women, they have invited me—"

But before she could continue, the door burst open to admit one of Raffa's men. His chest heaved beneath a heavy coating of dust and sweat and soot. A trail of blood streaked one cheek from a cut across his forehead. "You must come!"

Hannibal's chair clattered to the floor as he stood in alarm. "What is it?"

"Disaster!" The word was choked and hoarse. "Make haste!"

●●●

Travis was far too exhausted to rise at Hannibal's approach. And too proud. He sat where he was, his back to the wall across from his warehouse's burned-out hulk, and savored the astonishment that spread across Hannibal's features. The street was blocked from side to side, end to end, with goods. Behind them sprawled a blackened, coughing, muttering crowd.

"I have promised them payment in money I do not have," Travis said in greeting. He waved a weary arm over the exhausted gathering. "They have earned it. Each and every one of them."

Hannibal nodded slowly, taking it all in. "How much?"

"Five silver pieces, twenty-three helpers in all." Travis blinked eyes made gritty with fatigue and soot. "It has cost us our profit for the voyage, but we are not wiped out."

Hannibal motioned to one of his guards, who turned and ran off. His departure revealed Lydia, who stood back and somewhat removed from the others. Travis struggled to his feet, then stood where he was, uncertain what to do.

But Hannibal did not notice the look that passed between Travis and his daughter. His own gaze traveled from the mammoth pile of goods to the smoldering ruins that had been their warehouse, then back again. "You saved it all?"

"All we could lay our hands on," Travis said, his eyes not leaving Lydia's face. "The vandals were in too much of a hurry, whoever they were. My men put up a fierce struggle, more than they expected from two men, I suppose. The fire was set in only one place."

"Injuries?"

"One with a head wound, another badly bruised, some of our helpers with burns. The healer is seeing to them." Travis could not take his eyes from Lydia. It was the first time he had seen her since their arrival, and he drank in the beauty of her like an elixir. She responded with the silent open gaze of a trapped gazelle, caught by forces she could not fathom, until suddenly she surrendered, opened her heart, showed him the agony that held her. And the love.

Travis started forward, not realizing he had moved until Hannibal stopped him with a hand on his arm. "Go," he said quietly. "To the baths with you and your men. We will stand guard. When are the others due to return?"

"Before sunset. But I—"

"Go, I say. You are exhausted. We will still be here when you return."

Reluctantly Travis turned away, lifted his men from their tired slouch, and started down the cluttered way, feeling Lydia's gaze upon his back. He turned at the corner, saw she was still standing there, still watching him, still frozen in the captivity of impossible passion.

The main public baths were located near the entrance to the old Greek city, and competed in size and splendor with the finest of the forum structures. The two entrances were surrounded by taverns and inns. Travis wearily entered through the main arches, paid the attendant, and accepted both towel and wrapping-cloth. The four guards, as exhausted as he, stumbled along in silence.

He passed the portal leading to the gymnasium, with its sweating wrestlers and lounging gamblers. Stairs took him up from the disrobing antechamber into the steam room. The room was long and low and windowless and hot. Achingly hot. Beneath the stone floor, bath slaves tended long furrows of slow-burning coals night and day. Their life span was said to be shorter than all but the miners of sandstone in the hills. Travis and the others took places on the stone benches and breathed the spice-laden air in short gasps. He could feel the damp heat seeping into his very bones.

When he could bear the heat no longer, he passed through the next portal and lay on one of the many marble tables. He dozed in languid contentment until an attendant arrived and began to scrape his body with an ivory trowel. Then he was soaped, using a sponge roughened with volcanic dust. The intention was not just to clean away all dirt, but to slough away his upper layer of skin. That completed, rough hands oiled and massaged him to a groaning pulp.

The centerpoint to Roman culture was the body. Clothes, sport, baths, food, even many of the temple rites, all designed to accent and deify this first of their gods. Throughout the empire, all such baths followed the ancient traditions; mornings were reserved for the men, afternoons for the women. In some pagan towns, the evenings were mixed and given over to licentiousness. In such baths, the mosaics were usually of Bacchus, god of wine and sensual pleasure. Beneath the waters he flowed seductively into portrayals of Venus, goddess of love. With flickering torches for light, the figures appeared to writhe in lurid ecstasy at every disturbance of the water's surface.

When he could stand again, he entered the baths. There were three with different temperatures—the frigidarium, tepidarium, and caldarium. Each was a full fifty paces long. Travis lay in the more comfortable tepidarium, one arm flung over the side, floating and dozing and reflecting on the day.

When Travis finally pushed himself from the waters, the four guards reluctantly followed. There had scarcely been a dozen words between them since the fire. Yet when the bath attendant came rushing up, the others instantly drew in around Travis, all taut and ready for danger.

"Master, forgive me, there are soldiers outside who would speak with you."

Travis shrugged off the hand. "Soon."

The hand was nervously replaced. "A thousand pardons, but they say now. It was," the attendant swallowed apprehensively, "a command."

Reluctantly Travis allowed himself to be pulled forward. "Soldiers, you say?"

"Six of them. They say you must either come now, or they shall force entry." The attendant was clearly petrified. "Please, sire, we wish for no trouble here."

"I will come."

Swiftly he dressed, his skin repelled by the filthy clothes. But there were no others. Everything else had been destroyed in the fire. Travis walked outside, his four guards in close attendance. The soldiers waited just beyond the entrance. "You wish to speak with me?"

"You are Travis son of Cletus, late of Carthage?"

"I am."

"You are to come with us."

"Brothers," Damon said, stepping forward. A swift hand-sign was given, half hidden by the folds of his garment. "You can see from the state of our dress that we have had a ruinous day. Whether your purpose is to inquire about the street attack or the fire, could we not deal with it here?"

"I know nothing of either," the senior guard replied. His five-man squad remained at the ready. Instead of a spear, each carried a stout stave, a more effective and less deadly instrument for keeping the peace. Their helmets were simple bronze domes, save for the metal flap descending over the left ear, the side turned toward oncoming trouble. Armor covering the left shoulder was polished metal; the remaining breastplate and other side-gear was more supple leather. The short-swords' leather scabbard flapped comfortably upon their thighs. The officer hesitated, his gaze flickering over Travis' guards. "I was ordered to say nothing, give no explanation. Just to bring the man in. Alone."

"Alone!" Manlius stepped between Travis and the soldiers. "You are arresting him? Why?"

Damon stopped him with a warning look, then turned back to the soldiers and insisted quietly, "We will say nothing, you have a soldier's word. A boon. One comrade to another. What is behind this?"

The soldier checked in both directions, said softly, "All I know is that he is to be arrested. The charge I have not been told. Nothing more, except that if he resisted at all, I was to cut him down, him and all his fellows."

For a brief instant Travis was tempted to give the cry, unsheathe his sword and fling himself onto the soldiers. But they watched him with the steady alertness of those ready for trouble. Any such move would be suicide for him and his men. Besides which, his body felt made of rubber. "Where are you taking me?"

"A city jail." Another hesitation, another checking of the ways. "From what I heard, for this night only."

"And then?"

"You must come," the soldier replied grimly. "Now."

CHAPTER XII

Travis greeted the dawn in a fight for his life. He knew it was morning because a gray shadow-light streamed in through the barred opening far overhead. The scene it illuminated was grim. The straw-littered dungeon was fetid with unwashed bodies, and with doom. Travis knew it lay beneath some massive official building, he had seen that much as he had been shepherded along the evening before. But his knowledge of Constantinople was too limited for him to identify the palace or its location.

Nor had he much cared. He had allowed himself to be directed onwards, knowing at least one of his guards was dogging their steps, unable to think far beyond the next moment. He had been struck by too much, too fast. Only when he was herded down the steep stone stairs, and the stout dungeon door was thrown open, and he breathed the first taste of foul captivity, did he try to struggle. But the soldiers had been ready, and with sharp raps of their staves had sent him sprawling.

His arrival caused little reaction. A single torch burned resentfully, smudging the wall and distant ceiling with great streams of pungent smoke. The floor was dotted with moaning and snoring straw-topped bundles, the walls lined with others chained in place. Travis crawled to an empty corner and lay there for long hours, listening to the groans and hawking coughs and muttered cries, before sleep stole up and captured him as well.

He woke to the sensation that his skin was alive and crawling.

With a strangled yell he leaped from his covering of straw, then spent frantic moments trying to rid his garments of unwanted vermin. He stopped, his chest heaving, at the sound of coarse chuckling. Travis turned, saw his antics were being watched by those already awake. One of the men, a hulking barbarian with one eye turned milky and blind, pursed his lips between a scraggly beard and made smacking sounds.

The door's bolt was thrown with a rusty clang, and the portal opened to admit a pair of soldiers. They stood guard as two lackeys set a cauldron down by the entrance. One lackey ducked in a ladle, filled a bowl, and offered it to the first prisoner already standing in line. His mate took bowls to those chained to the wall.

Travis joined the line, then tensed when the burly man moved up behind him. He felt his skin crawl as the smacking sounds were repeated.

When the rough hand tried to grab him through his garment, he was ready. He whipped an elbow up and about in one motion, striking the man across his jaw and sending him sprawling.

The man rose with a roar of fury. Travis glanced toward the door, found no help there. The guards stood and watched with bored amusement. The others in line reacted by shuffling closer to the wall, where they were both farther from the fight and better able to watch.

Travis turned back in time to meet the man's rush. The hairy giant was a head taller and almost twice his weight. But Travis had spent hours of every day since his tenth year being trained by Rome's finest. He was the product of an empire where wrestling was considered an essential element of every young man's education.

He did not try to check the rush, but rather fell back, drawing the man with him. He rolled onto his back, planted his feet in the man's chest, and sent him soaring overhead. Travis spun to his feet, then slipped on the straw and the filth and went down on a knee and a hand. The man blasted out a curse and came up churning. An unaimed blow caught Travis in the shoulder as he was rising, shooting him against the side wall and numbing him from wrist to neck. The man had the strength of a bull.

Travis backed away in frantic haste, shaking his arm to restore feeling, but the man was as fast as he was big. With a roar of triumph he wrapped great arms around Travis, pinning his hands to his sides. He lifted Travis and began to squeeze.

His ribs creaked under the strain, as his vision began to go red at the edges. Knowing he had to act before losing consciousness, Travis leaned his head as far back as he could manage, then shot it forward with all his strength, cracking the man's nose with his forehead.

With a cry of real pain the man dropped Travis, grabbed his nose, stepped back. His hands came away red, his face now halved, the lower portion sheathed in blood, the upper half a mask of rage. His lips drew back from bloodstained teeth.

He started forward, but this time Travis was ready. Travis slipped under one swipe that would have broken his neck if it had connected, then shot up, all his strength focused upon a blow that he sent charging into the giant's larynx.

Choking, the man dropped to his knees. Travis took a half-step back, aimed, and shot a single heel-kick to the center of his opponent's forehead. The giant went down like a felled ox.

Travis was still standing over the fallen man, his limbs trembling, when a guard stepped up beside him. "Such talent should keep you alive and well. For a time, at least."

Travis turned to the soldier, tried to control his breathing enough to gasp, "Has anyone asked for me?"

"There are always people hanging about the gates," the guard replied, without concern. "Their cries are like the ravens, raucous and tiresome. Come along or be dragged."

"Why are you doing this?"

"Because I am so ordered."

"But I am accused of no crime," Travis protested. "Nor have I been tried!"

Impassively the soldier motioned with his stave. "Take your bowl, you can eat while the lackey fits you with leg-irons for the journey."

The line of prisoners and their guards left the city by the Aemilianus Gate. They walked a path between the cliffs lining the Marmara Sea and the township of hovels springing up outside the city walls. Famine had devastated many eastern provinces, forcing the poorest freemen to flee to the new capital, where Constantine had instituted a program of grain distribution. Their tents and brushwood lean-tos stretched across the hard-scrabble hills. Life in such unofficial towns was precarious. Bandits roamed at will. There were neither sewers nor fresh water. Few infants lived to see their second birthday, and many who did were sold into slavery to feed the remaining mouths. A few of the dwellers emerged from their shanties of wood and brush to watch the prisoners shamble by, their eyes deadened and uncaring.

Travis shuffled along, chained to a line of forty or so prisoners. Already his ankles were raw with the iron's chafing grip. He followed the others' example, in his left hand holding the lead-chain, in his right the one connecting to the prisoner behind. Thus chance stumbles or tugs would not trip him. He kept his eyes pointed down, as they all did, watching carefully for tripfalls or jinks in the path. A burning thirst seared his throat.

As he walked, Travis felt the power of thought drain from him. He was bereft, a stray bit of cord and muscle strung together by the nothingness of chance, swept along by the chaos that surrounded him. He was consumed by the struggle to vanquish this moment, then the next, then the one after. That was all there was, and ever would be.

Just before midday they stopped at an inn's rock-lined well. Travis squatted with the others, the well's ridge offering scant shade for the fortunate few. The guards settled beneath the inn's straw awning to wait out the worst of the heat.

Travis accepted his share of bread and water, kept his eyes directed over the cliffside and out to sea. The water was so blue as to appear an earthbound sky, with soft green islands for clouds. Still and clear and empty. As inviting as death.

Steps trod over and stopped beside him. A shadow passed over his head as a familiar voice asked, "Did I ever tell you of the jail I frequented in Gaul?"

His relief at finding Raffa squatting beside him was so great he lost his ability to speak. Travis huffed a moment, then said hoarsely, "I feared I had been given up for lost."

"None of our little band has slept this night," Raffa replied, and rubbed a dusty hand down one bearded cheek. His eyes were sunken with exhaustion. "Half of the city's officialdom has had their sleep disturbed by the alarm being raised outside their gates."

Travis swallowed for control, managed, "I had almost given up."

"Easy to do when the world turns against you." Hastily Raffa dropped a leather bag into Travis' lap, then opened a ceramic jar and began rubbing a greasy salve inside Travis' leg-irons. "I only have a moment, and could only do it here away from the city's prying eyes."

"You were following me?"

"Damon has remained stationed outside the jail since your arrest." Eyes shone with fatigue and concern. "I bring food and hope. And assurance that we will not rest until you are freed."

Travis fumbled at the sack's drawstring with numb fingers. "Why is this happening?"

"That I cannot say, nor who is behind it. Not yet. But we will find out." Raffa cast a grim smile. "You should see Hannibal. He is a man gone berserk."

Travis asked because he had to, though it cost him. "And Lydia?"

Raffa hesitated, then replied honestly, "I have not seen her. Best you keep your mind on what is ahead." He motioned at the sack. "You must eat, and quickly. My silver bought us a few moments only, and I must take this back with me."

Travis raised the drinking skin, spilled as much as he drank of the cool sweetened wine. He lowered the skin, saw the hungry hopelessness in the eyes of the man beside him, passed it over. He withdrew fresh bread and cheese from the sack, tore off chunks and shared that as well with the men to either side. He said to Raffa, "I have little appetite."

"Eat while you can. There is hardship awaiting."

Travis tried to force bread down an overly dry throat. "I am being sent to the mines?"

Again the hesitation, then Raffa surrendered a nod. "Yes, and even that information cost us much time and more coin. Whoever is behind this has planned and bribed well. And has the power to hold people silent." He pointed at Travis' scalp. "Did a guard do that?"

Travis touched his forehead, drew back a finger sticky with congealed blood. He had not even noticed. "I was in a fight this morning."

"With another prisoner," the man beside him offered, tearing off hunks of bread and cheese with ferretlike teeth. "A great brute of a man. Walloped him good, the lad did."

Raffa was not amused. "There is rumor of a price on your head. Be on the lookout for others who seek quarrels for no reason." He glanced behind him. "They are coming. I must go."

He raised Travis with him, grimaced at the sound of the chains clinking, drew him into a fierce embrace. Raffa slipped a smaller pouch into his hand and whispered swiftly, "Hide this well."

Before Travis could respond, Raffa drew back, clasped his shoulders with meaty hands, said fiercely, "Were I able, I would stand in your place."

"I am grateful," Travis said, lowering his hand and the pouch it now held to his side, "for everything."

"Enough," a soldier snapped. The pair moved forward with hands on sword-hilts. "I risk my rank for this chatter."

"Guard your back," Raffa said, stepping away. "And know we will not rest until you are once again with us."

Travis stood and watched the gray-headed man stride off. As he reached the first curve, Raffa turned and waved once. Travis called out, "You are a friend!"

"Little good that will do you, where you're headed," the soldier rasped, running hard fingers over Travis' form. When he came to the clenched fist, he said, "Open it, or I will break the fingers one by one."

Travis let the pouch fall to the earth. The soldier kicked it away, kept guard over Travis while his mate bent over and hefted it. "Sit back down."

"I will remember this," Travis said, lowering himself so his haunches rested where Raffa had sat.

The soldier sneered as he moved away. "The mines have a way of shortening one's memory permanently."

"Here," the ferret-faced man said, when the soldiers had retreated to the inn's shade. "You'll not find bread like this where we're headed."

Travis accepted the piece, occupied himself with eating what he could not taste. "I thank you."

"It is I who am obliged," the man said merrily. "Your meal has restored me. The name is Nasrud."

"Travis, son of Cletus."

"An odd name, Travis. You are of Gaul?"

"Near Carthage. But my father was from the province of Britain."

"Ah. Evil barbarians, the lot, from what I've heard. Never had the pleasure of travel, myself." Nasrud nodded cheerfully. "Your food has placed a debt on me, barbarian. You a Christian?"

Travis started to deny it, then stopped. There was something in the overly casual tone that gave him pause. He gave a half-nod, half-shrug in reply.

"Thought so. If what your friend has said about a price on your head is true, you'll do well to search out your companions at the mine. No man can watch his own back all the time."

"On your feet, the lot of you," the soldiers barked, moving forward and prodding the men with sheathed blades. Travis swallowed the last of his bread, rose with the others, kept his head down. He grasped the chains and fell into step.

The path turned and jinked, following the cliffline. The sun blasted them from above; the stones rising to either side of the path roasted them with reflected heat. The water and wine he had drunk at the well soon became a memory as faint as the shimmering horizon. Dust caked him from head to toe, sweat streamed and stung his eyes, breath came in gasping heaves. The only sounds were the snarled curses of the soldiers, the clinking of their chains, the moans of the weaker prisoners, and the occasional cry of a lonely seabird. Twice they stopped and stepped aside, allowing passage to donkey caravans coming the other way, the crude carts heavily laden with reddish-gray stone. The carters did not even look their way.

Toward late afternoon faint sounds rose in the distance. The noise worked its way through Travis' exhaustion only because it suggested an end to the agony of walking chained in line. He passed around a final outcrop to face red sandstone cliffs that dropped

231

into the sea, sharp angry shapes carved by eons of wind and storm and rain. The sandstone mines were the stuff of fables, the prison of last resort, the final earthly home to Romans considered beyond hope or correction.

Their manner made rougher by fatigue, the soldiers snarled them into close formation. A lackey bent and scurried as he pulled free the connecting chain, but left the leg-irons in place. Whip-bearing guards walked up and began prodding them forward, wasting few words on the new men.

They were led down winding sandstone stairs to where a handmade cave was cleft from the dusty rock. The men were pressed forward and into the cavern. Travis turned for an instant, caught a final glimpse of light and blue and sea and freedom before a cursing guard hammered a whip handle into his kidney, hurtling him into the shadows.

CHAPTER XIII

"Christians? Any Christians among you?"

He was poorly put together, that little man. No two of his parts seemed meant for the same body. One leg was shorter than the other, his body was bent to permanently favor the longer limb, and his head was far too big for his stunted frame. Yet Travis felt instantly drawn to him. He raised his hand and called out, "Here."

"Another one, may God have mercy on us all." He motioned to the whip-toting guard, who nodded once. "Anyone else? No? Come along then, this way."

The limping old man led him down curving stairs, and beneath an outcropping that forced even him to duck down and under. Beyond opened another chamber filled with dust and hammering men and the stale smell of sweaty doom. "My name is Inigo. And yours?"

"Travis, son of Cletus."

"We give no heritage here, my son, we hold no rank. Nor do we ask another of his past or his crime." He led Travis through chamber after chamber, all carved from the soft red sandstone. Prisoners dressed in rags and rusting chains labored at the walls, carving out blocks of stone, then prying them free. Others were busy in the center spaces, shaping the blocks into dressed stone. Few glances were cast their way. "We are all the same here, all sinners, all one in God's eyes."

Illumination came from open squares overhead, through which the stone was lifted. Underfoot the sand was soft and fine as dust, the result of decades of mining and shaping stone. "I have been accused of no crime."

"That doesn't matter. You are here, and from this place there is but one escape. One eternal rest. As from all worldly existence." The old man stopped, huffed a breath, said, "But while you are here, work and you shall be fed. Shirk your duties, and we all suffer. Therefore you must work. Will you give me your word on that?"

"I do."

"Come along, then." He limped down a final set of curving stairs and passed under an alcove so low Travis went onto his knees to enter. The old man watched him rise, and said, "A silent reminder of the attitude one must maintain toward the Maker of All."

Travis looked about, saw fifty or sixty men and women busy working at the walls. Many wore bits of rags tied tightly over mouth and nose. The light was cool and softly pink. The dust was thick and coated every surface. High overhead, a single square showed a small patch of sky. "I have entered Hades."

"No, my son. Out there," Inigo pointed back beyond the overhang, into which was carved a great cross, "those prisoners who do not know our Lord, they dwell in darkness, as much of their own making as the Romans'. Whatever you hear at night, whatever cries and pleas might spring from desperate lips, do not be tempted to enter the other caverns. None who have left here have ever returned." He limped forward, motioning Travis along. "And now to work."

Lydia walked with her father and the trader Nathaniel back from the Law Courts. Though his face was drawn with strain and fatigue, Hannibal remained intent upon Nathaniel's explanation. Lydia could not bother to listen any further. Her feet hurt and her head spun from the oily words of countless officials, all of whom had promised much and delivered nothing. Everywhere she had faced hands outreached for silver and eyes greedily measuring the size of Hannibal's purse. Her very spirit felt as though it panted for breath and a shred of hope.

The *Mesó*, or Honorary Way, was grand and colonnaded, with statues adorning most corners and many small plazas. The avenue was lined with parks and palaces and government buildings. The largest columns flanked great marble placards, their uppermost friezes carved into a series of laurel wreaths. Each was a notice that some official had either offered or been forced to accept responsibility for a massive public project.

Hannibal stopped beneath a placard announcing that a certain legate had committed to buy grain for the city's poor, and demanded of her, "How can you know such things?"

She did not need to ask of what he spoke. "All the believers of Carthage are aware of this, Father."

"Not I."

She glanced at the sun, calculated she had less than an hour before she was expected at the secret meeting. "You are known for honesty and the straightforwardness of your faith. Why do you think the bishop asked you to come? Anyone else would be driven to anger and battle by what he saw here."

"And I, I am driven to madness." He refused to allow his daughter to lead him onward. "This Arius had the gall to claim that our Savior was not truly one with the Father?"

"That is not so troubling as how many are willing to agree with him," Nathaniel pointed out. The trader acted as both host and guide, as he had done since the night of the fire and Travis' arrest. "Or that the new leaders have sided with this movement."

Hannibal directed them toward a stone bench fronting a bank of blooming flowers. "Here, here, I must rest and have you two tell me what else I do not know."

"Father." Lydia sighed her protest. "We are all tired. You have been up since before dawn, we have spent the entire morning arguing with officials of the courts, surely we would all be better off—"

"Here I stay," he replied stubbornly, fatigue etched deeply into his craggy features, "until I have received some answers."

Nathaniel nodded to her, urging Lydia to sit down on her father's other side. The guards spread out to cover them from all sides. Since the taking of Travis, they went nowhere without heavy surveillance. "There are many questions for which we have no answers at all," Nathaniel said, his voice a call for peace among them all, "including why it has proved so hard to find someone willing to address this issue of Travis' capture. Someone with power is behind this, mark my words. And something is at issue far beyond the detention of just one young man."

"But he knows no one here," Lydia protested, "save the Prelate Titus Octavian. And they have never even met."

"The prelate, yes, there is an interesting puzzle." Nathaniel scanned the crowded lane, ensuring that none paid them overmuch attention. "He is resisting my entreaties for an audience. More than would appear reasonable."

"I was speaking," Hannibal said stubbornly, "of this one called Arius."

"His ideas are no longer a matter of the church," Nathaniel replied. "They have become a matter of politics and intrigue throughout the empire."

"That is impossible."

"That is fact," Nathaniel corrected. "Constantius has moved his headquarters to the west, where he is preparing for war against his brothers."

"I speak of faith," Hannibal protested. "You speak of war and politics."

"Listen to me, and you shall understand. Constantius is determined to set his own imprint upon the empire. Where the father Constantine continually set his Christian faith in direct opposition to the old pagan beliefs, Constantius seeks a compromise. Arius has granted him just that. The Greeks have no trouble with the concept of one supreme deity above all the other gods. Constantine himself worshipped the Unconquered Sun before becoming a Christian. But the idea of a single God who revealed Himself in the form of a mortal Son? That to the pagans is a scandal."

"And so they changed the concept of our Savior to suit their whim?"

"To suit their ambitions," Nathaniel corrected. "Constantius is facing civil war. Already there are inquiries and disputes and the call for generals to declare their allegiance. The last thing Constantius wants or needs is squabbling among the people over religion. Many of the churches already had people who agreed with Arius, and this suited his plans. He would accept this, and use it as a means of spreading oil over the troubled waters. In truth, I do not think such issues matter to him at all. What he wants is to rule a unified Roman Empire."

Hannibal dragged hands over tired and sweaty features. "This I can neither believe nor accept."

"Father, I must go." Lydia rose to her feet, addressed Nathaniel. "Will you see him home?"

"Yes, but it is not safe—"

"I will be well guarded." She turned and fled before either could raise another protest, signaling for three of the guards to follow.

Lydia hurried down the steep cobblestone way, reflecting that perhaps it was just as well her father was so preoccupied. Something told her he would not approve of what she was doing. But she had no choice. The direct channels and their meetings with all the petty officials had taken them nowhere. And Travis had to be saved.

The entire city was filled with pilgrims. Church courtyards and basilica were large and usually overflowing. Men and women alike clustered and sang or knelt and prayed or walked with the measured gait of penitents around the cross or the tombs of martyrs. The air was filled with incense and the murmur of a hundred voices speaking a dozen different tongues. Lydia passed through one such crowd, saw the ecstasy of faith on a multitude of faces, and offered a swift prayer of her own. Her father felt swamped with troubles, she realized, and failed to see the incredible upsurge of faith which was also taking place. But it was there, all around them, strong and vibrant and alive with joy.

Only for the soldiers did the crowds reluctantly give way. The legionnaires tramped through at regular intervals, coming from and going to duty at any of numerous towers and stations along the city walls. Occasionally tired-looking contingents would parade through, spears held high, followed by wagons bearing their wounded. These were always followed by merchants and rumor-mongers and mothers, all seeking the latest news from one of a dozen different conflicts.

Lydia entered a cobblestone courtyard with occasional spaces for fountains and blossoming trees. Like most squares, it was adorned by a church at one end, lofty and large with tall windows and doors meant to copy the entrance to the kingdom of God— high and broad and always open. She approached a villa gate to one side of the church, knocked, and when the face-gate opened, announced herself.

The matron and her daughter who received her were stiff with absolute correctness. Both had carefully coiffured hair and perfectly rouged faces. Both wore garments of finest cut and hues. Both wore jewelry, their crucifixes formed of gold and gems. The daughter wore a bright scarf upon her curls, the matron a jeweled veil.

Lydia pressed her hands together, feeling clumsy and awkward and ugly. This was the other face of the church's growth, the side with which she could never feel comfortable. They were both so poised. They held themselves impossibly erect. They wore their riches with such a regal air, without the first shred of self-doubt. "Thank you for seeing me like this."

"Nonsense," the matron replied with frosty condescension. "It is such a pleasantry, offering refreshments to newcomers. Will you take mulled wine?"

"Thank you, no. I was wondering—"

"Let me see." The matron's eyes were slightly slanted, large, and so black they appeared as twin pools of liquid night. Giving nothing away but polite disdain. "Carthage is your home, is it not?"

"Yes." Lydia willed herself to be patient. "That is correct."

"I fear my family no longer has holdings in Africa. They were all sold in the time of Diocletian. Perhaps you have heard of my farming relative, Licinius Maximus?"

"No, I'm afraid not."

"Oh, surely you must have," the daughter complained. She strived to imitate her mother's air, but was too inexperienced. Her attempts at regal aloofness came off as a sniffish whine. "They held the largest estate in the Dougga valley."

"After the emperor, of course," the matron added.

Lydia said, "My family had no land."

They were both shocked at the news. "What? None at all?"

"My family are merchants."

"Ah, traders." Mother and daughter exchanged glances. "How positively enchanting. With barbarian caravans arriving from mysterious hinterlands, no doubt."

"Yes," Lydia agreed miserably.

Their stations firmly established, the matron deigned to be more forthcoming. "So what is it that I might do for you, my dear?"

Lydia sat up straighter. "I was told by Priscilla, a woman I have met at the church, that your husband has recently been appointed one of the city's chief magistrates."

"Yes, well, we must all accept our share of onerous duties." The lofty gaze inspected her. "Priscilla is one of the ascetics, is she not? No, that is not the name they prefer any longer. What is it now? Oh, this head of mine, so many things to keep track of these days."

"Cloistered," Lydia replied. "She—"

"Yes, that is it exactly. Thank you so much, my dear. Cloistered. After the places they are setting up, I believe. Cloisters where one may retire to pray and contemplate." She raised her gaze to the ceiling. "Oh, what a wondrous life that must be. Alas, I will have to forgo that pleasure, much as it calls to me. You have no idea what burdens I am forced to carry, this household, my husband's career, my daughter's placement in society."

"I have a friend who has been unjustly imprisoned and sent to the mines," Lydia said, forcing herself to hold to a calm she did not feel. "He was neither charged with a crime nor given a trial."

The dark gaze turned keen. "He is special to you, this young man?"

"He is a Roman citizen," Lydia persisted. "His father is manager of a large estate near Carthage."

The matron gave a frosty smile of understanding. "Oh, my dear, the tragedies of this world. The caesar is away, and all about us are factions tearing each other to pieces. No doubt your young man has become embroiled in affairs of state that would have been better off left alone."

"He arrived just three days before his kidnapping," Lydia replied, her voice grating from the strain of not leaping to her feet, slashing at the matron and her frosty superiority, screaming at them for help. "It was his first journey ever outside Africa."

The matron regarded her for a long moment, something new flickering in those cold dark eyes. "Indeed a mystery," she murmured. "His name?"

"Travis son of Cletus. I beseech you, my lady—"

"I will see what can be learned." The matron cut her off by rising and offering a regal hand. "So good of you to stop by, my dear. Forgive me for rushing off, but so much requires my urgent attention. I am sure you understand."

CHAPTER XIV

Travis labored as never before. The work was hard, harder than anything he had faced on the estate, only the lack of proper food made it almost impossible.

Mornings he awoke and accepted his wooden bowl of watery gruel with the others. What food they were given was lowered by rope-sling from the opening high overhead. As he ate, he heard screams and wails rising from neighboring caverns, same as the noises that pierced his nights. By the third morning, he no longer paid them any mind.

In times of crisis, discipline within the cavern was loosely maintained by all. When, on the fourth morning, a band from a neighboring cavern tried to steal their morning cauldron of gruel, all acted as one to expel them. Otherwise, when they were left alone, all authority rested with Inigo. He was permanently cheerful, a comical little man with a wild fringe of white hair and a twisted shape, who bustled about continually giving light to the gloom.

"Oh, I am too honest for my own good," he was in the habit of saying. "And far too talkative. Oh my yes. I could be one or the other and still live in safety and comfort. But not both. Never both. It was not honesty that was my downfall, you see. Nor my tongue. No, it was the combination of the two."

The priest was far too old to do much work. Normally he sat in the center of the cavern, tapping away at the stones, doing little good, but insisting on holding the hammer and chisel and at least making an attempt to help dress the blocks. "It was my insistence on telling the royal court what I thought, you see. I felt compelled to say publicly that it was a sin to murder the male offspring of Constantine's relatives in order to assure the transfer of power. *Earthly* power. The same power that was working its way into some of God's houses. Power and intrigue and dissension and jealousy. And I, talkative and honest priest that I was, insisted on telling all and sundry how these certain churches were being corrupted."

Few of the prisoners understood anything of what the old man said. It did not matter. It was enough to have him there, guiding, shepherding, bringing a semblance of peace to the horror. Travis paid his words as little mind as the others at first, working and waiting with all the patience he could muster for his rescuers. He kept his mind occupied with thoughts of freedom, of solving the mystery, of revenge.

And of Lydia. He spent agonized hours filling the dusty chamber with his memories. How her almond eyes were formed by high cheekbones, with drops of sunlight gathered within soft brown depths. How her hair was long and collected into a single tress, gathered and sent cascading over one shoulder, there to be touched and stroked when she was still and listening, or pressed to her mouth when she laughed. It was a child's action, this hiding behind her hair, and remembering its unconscious simplicity seized Travis' chest with such force that it threatened to crush his fragile heart.

Then three events occurred that almost broke him.

The first was listening to an overseer beat a man to death. The sound of the whip and the answering wails were common enough, though the overseer seldom did more than check in their cavern. They worked well, they were silent, they did not cause trouble, they stayed to their position, and something more. For some reason the guards and overseers seemed a bit in awe of the diminutive Inigo. They permitted him to greet each line of new prisoners with his call for Christians. But the overseers and their whips were never far away. The lash was a terrifying sound in their cramped hole, echoing back and forth with the force of a lightning bolt. This day, in the chamber just beyond their own, a hapless prisoner was caught at some offense, or perhaps was simply chosen to die. Whatever the cause, the overseer lashed and lashed until the screams died to whimpers and then to silence, the final strikes sounding wet and pulpy in the utter quiet.

When it was over, Travis joined the others in pretending to work, but he could not stop himself from shaking. The blows had seemed aimed for his own heart, tearing away the final vestiges of hope.

Later that same day, one of their own had died. He had been ill for a time, nursed with the little care Inigo could muster, granted rest while the others worked, his face bathed, his body prayed over, with each of the others giving him one extra spoon of their own gruel. But in the end he died, and as his body was lifted up like a parcel of stones, up and through the opening far overhead, Travis stood with the others and listened to Inigo intone a prayer, and saw himself being lifted up one day soon, his own arm dangling loose in lifeless defeat.

He returned to his work, feeling trapped and crushed and caught in currents beyond his control, beyond his understanding. Nothing he could do or say or even think offered a way from the morass. He was trapped. And he was sinking.

He saw it then, as clearly as anything he had ever seen with his earthly eyes. He had lived his life as a fighter. His intelligence had been honed to a cunning, his anger so tightly concealed it was masked even from his own awareness most of the time. But a fighter just the same. Angry just the same. Hard and aware and focused and tight, a shield in one fist and a sword in the other. And at heart level, another shield, just as strong, just as fiercely protective, ever ready to fight. To strive. To win.

For once, just this once, the shield shifted a fraction, enough for a brief glimpse of what lay beneath. The memories were there. All of them. Of his father's absence. Of the mother who left when he needed her most. Of his brothers' cruelty. Of the servants' fearful neutrality. Each memory bared in a flickering of the shield, a tiny glimpse of all he had fiercely kept down away from himself. Yet the memories and the pain had always remained, there to be drawn out in a finely focused beam of hate and anger and hurt, channeled to do his bidding.

The wounds became visible then, the tightly bound cords of emotion unraveling bit by bit, revealing the ravaged flesh of his own heart. Pain. Pain and loneliness. Anger at the world, at fate, at family, at himself.

"Are you all right, my son?"

"What?" Travis turned in numb surprise.

"You have been standing here staring at the wall for such a time." Inigo watched with genuine concern. "Do you feel ill?"

"No, I—" Travis raised a hand to swipe at the dust covering his face, realized he still held the hammer, looked at it dumbly, for a moment unable to recall what it was.

A gentle hand guided him toward the cavern's center. "Here, you can sit with me for a time and work the cut stone. We can spare you an extra bit of water, yes? Of course we can. Here, my son, drink."

Travis drank, then stumbled over to where the unfinished blocks were piled, and collapsed. "Lost," he mumbled. "All lost."

The old man squatted beside him, waited a long moment, then said, "You are not a believer, are you, my son?"

He was nothing. A hollow gourd through which blew the winds of time, swept away by the futility of all effort, all strife, all hope. "No."

Instead of the order to depart, to leave the group and enter the final abyss, Inigo waited a moment, then said gently, "Sometimes a man can only know the light by first knowing the darkness."

Travis raised his head to the tiny patch of blue overhead, saw not freedom nor the sky, but rather his own body again being raised. The only escape he would ever know. "I do not know what you mean."

"No," Inigo agreed, not the least troubled by the news. "But if you listen, then with God's help I will explain."

● ● ●

The slave Hanno entered the inner courtyard to find the beast uncaged.

"Three times he has slipped through my grasp! Three times!" Brutus clenched the air before him, strangling the invisible forces arrayed against him. "Four men attack three, only two manage to escape unharmed, while Travis and his men remain unscathed. Not a scratch upon the cursed lot!"

Hanno made himself as small as possible, shoulders hunched, head bowed, hands clasped fearfully before him. Small wonder the place was silent as a tomb. Brutus' rages were legendary, often ending with a need to restaff his entire household.

The man paced the walled courtyard with the lithe grace of an infuriated panther. "Four more are sent to burn him out, reduce his and his partner's wealth to ashes. And what happens? They are chased out by two men. Two! And the fire does nothing but make Travis a hero of the entire Greek city."

Five silver pieces per man. It was a master stroke. Declaring to all the world that here were men of both substance and wealth. Who met disaster with lightning brilliance. Who had both their own injured men and the strangers enlisted to help treated by the city's best healer. Who paid their debts instantly, without quibbling, once the disaster was passed. It was said that when they heard of the arrest, the men who had helped in rescuing the goods then carted them across town to their new dwelling place for no charge. And none tried to steal in the process. Despite himself, Hanno felt a grudging admiration for Travis.

"At great cost and greater risk, I not only have him arrested, I arrange for his death. Again! A known killer, promised his freedom if he succeeded. Twice the size of that blasted youth."

Brutus wheeled about, his hands clenching and unclenching in unheeded spasm. "Twice, do you hear me?"

"I hear, O great lord."

"And what happens?" Brutus spun about, spotted the blunt practice sword propped in one corner, and in one frenzied motion leaped and hefted and spun and sent the blade crashing down on the nearest marble bench. The blade shrieked and sparks flew with the stone chips. "Does he perish? No!" Another wild swing. More chips flew about the plaza. "Is he sent in the secrecy I paid for to the mines? No!" Another crashing blow. Hanno tried not to flinch as stones flew all about him. "And now can he be destroyed as I order? No! And why not?" A great two-handed blow split the bench and shattered the blade. He flung the hilt up and over the courtyard wall, and shouted at the sky, "Because my cursed brother has taken refuge with a Christian priest imprisoned by the emperor! The same cursed emperor who has placed this same cursed priest under his cursed imperial protection!" He wheeled about, screamed, "Is this a conspiracy planted by the gods against me?"

"I think not, my lord," Hanno replied quietly.

Brutus stood silent and heaving, watching the slave from beneath his knotted brow. Finally he growled, "You know something."

"Perhaps."

"Do not play coy with me." But the snarl lacked real threat. The chance of an opening was suddenly too real. "I do not have time for a slave's games. That cursed trader Hannibal is scouring the city, offering to press his silver into any palm who would dare act against my will. A puny lad from the backwoods of Africa suddenly has the power to threaten me!" With the speed of a striking snake, Brutus crossed the courtyard to breath heavily upon

Hanno's downturned face. "So speak while you still have a tongue in your mouth, slave, and pray I do not turn my ire against you."

Hanno did not move, gave no sign of his quaking heart. He kept his tone quiet, calm, definite. "I think not."

"You what?" The effrontery startled Brutus from his rage. He stepped back a half pace, his eyes widening as though to take in what he only now was seeing. "You what?"

"I have found the answer." Not a possibility. *The* answer. For the first time Hanno raised his gaze, showed the confidence he had nurtured since the idea came to him in the middle of the night. "With one fell swoop you shall stop them all."

Despite himself, Brutus was intrigued. "The trader, the warriors who hunt their master's culprit, the clamor demanding I release this scullion?"

"All of them. Travis as well."

"If what you say is true, you shall be granted your freedom."

Hanno forced himself to meet the gaze head-on. It was the hardest struggle of his life, but more than his life depended upon doing it, and doing it well. "Freedom is such a costly state, my lord."

Gray eyes so light they appeared almost to have no coloring at all widened at the slave's audacity. "You tread a hair's breadth away from a slow and painful death."

"What I have is worth the risk," Hanno replied, no longer able to hold the tremor from his voice. "And more."

Brutus crossed his arms, nodded once. "Very well. Give me what you promise, and you shall have both freedom and the silver with which to enjoy it. Displease me, and I will grant you a death which lasts longer than you ever thought possible."

Hanno released the sigh he had been holding since conceiving his idea. "My plan shall not fail, my lord. It can not."

CHAPTER XV

"O ur blessed Christianity has grown by leaps and bounds," Inigo declared cheerfully. "Oftentimes it spread along avenues established by the Hellenistic culture. Even in the heart of Latin Rome, the first converts were Greek. The church's first liturgy and prayers and songs were all in Greek. Only with Constantine did this begin to change."

"He was a general, and not an educated man," Travis offered, remembering his lessons. "And spoke no Greek."

The little priest nodded approval. "Every Roman province has its own society and history and gods. If there has been any unifying culture throughout the empire and the ages, it has not been Roman at all, but rather the Hellenism of Alexander the Great. Greek was its language, Platonism its way of thought. Spreading from Athens to Alexandria and beyond, it did not strip away other cultures, but lay a glossy veneer over whatever was there already. It offered a common tongue of culture.

"To be called Hellenized meant the same, be the person Gaul or African or Jew. Even 'city' is a Greek concept. Because Christianity moved along these Hellenistic patterns, our faith spread from city to city. Thus even today, the countryside remains almost totally pagan, while most cities are as much as one-fifth Christian."

These times with Inigo had become the centerpiece of Travis' life, his sanity. In late afternoon arrived the second and final meal, more of the same watery gruel, sometimes flavored with a bit of meat, more often not. Eating was preceded by a simple blessing from Inigo, and was followed by the silence of exhaustion.

At dusk the cavern walls began to shrink. They closed in as light dimmed, growing tighter and tighter still, until even drawing breath grew difficult. Most responded by giving in to wearied sleep. Travis fought slumber because of his dreams. Every day that passed without word from the outside left him more afraid that word would never come. Sleep closed in with endless nightmares of being buried alive, left underground to struggle forever, trapped and suffocating and—

"It is a two-edged sword, this passage of the Christian message through these Greek channels. Oh my, yes. You see, the Greeks were positively obsessed with what they liked to call the mystery religions. All good Stoics and Platonists saw initiation into some such temple as the final goal toward which honorable men should aim. Sacrifices and feast days and the like were all simply parts of biding time. When the demands of the outer life were met, and the person was ready, he set the world aside and took up the ascetic life. They began to learn the hidden mysteries, which gradually would raise man from his earthly mire and grant him entry into the world of the gods."

Travis listened because he had to, though he understood only one word in three. Inigo taught because it was his life's passion. The old man grew alive in such times, his voice gaining strength and fervor. When the darkness was fully upon them, and the priest was spent and could go no further, Travis was able then to lie back, somehow comforted by these half-understood words, and know that the dreams would be kept at bay. For a time. "This is bad?"

"Of course not. But like all other religions with a semblance of positive elements, these mystery religions seek to *better* man. By his own efforts, guided by the secrets entrusted to the temple, man *raises himself* to meet a higher power."

The others within the chamber treated Travis differently now. He was seen as Inigo's favored, an acolyte taking instruction from the master. Few tried to listen to what the old man said. They were by and large simple folk, their faith a simple faith. They bowed their heads and accepted the blessings said over food and each new day with the same quiet humility with which they accepted their fate. Travis found himself watching them more with each passing day, sensing without understanding that there was much he could learn from them, though their attitude challenged the very basis upon which his life had been formed.

"Thus many of these Greek-trained messengers not only *carried* the message of Christ, they *changed* it. They sought to bring the straightforward message of God-made-man into line with what they had previously learned. But this does not work, you see. Oh no. God has done away with the need for such secret mysteries, and all with one utterly simple, utterly powerful gift. All that was hidden has now been revealed."

Inigo raised his face toward unseen heavens, his eyes shining in the cavern's gloom. "And here is the uniqueness of Christianity. The wonder of wonders. God chose to enter the close and narrow confines of human form. From boundless power and timeless light, to a tiny, frail, and utterly human existence. By doing so, by taking all our frailties and mistakes and sinful nature upon Himself and then dying upon the altar of the cross, God *erases* these demands and laws and mysteries. He *lowers* His divine and holy being to the level of fallen man and says, 'Here am I, where you struggle and live. Here am I. I have come, and lived, and died, and been raised from the dead. Accept the gift. Walk the bridge that I have built. And come unto Me.'"

Hannibal entered the church courtyard, less than comfortable with the grand structure. And the crowds. Where did all these believers come from? Why were they gathered? For faith? Or personal gain? He searched the faces about him, fearing he would find only the same avarice and cruel search for power that he had seen stalking the royal courts.

But it was not so. Quite to the contrary, the courtyard and church steps and surrounding passages resounded with the sounds of singing and praying and unbridled joy. Hannibal sighed, knowing that his own faith had been struck telling blows by all he had seen and heard.

He entered the church and stood with the others, watched the priest enter and don his robes and intone the blessings with rich and rolling voice. He heard the grand liturgies, joined in singing so strong it filled the vast chamber to overflowing. But it touched him not. For the first time in living memory, he stood amidst other believers for the Sabbath ceremony with a heart as spiritless as dust in the wind.

The Church of the Holy Apostles was built upon the crest of a hill, and commanded a view of all Constantinople. The entire interior was walled with slabs of multicolored marble, which shimmered and flowed with each passing cloud. The tomb of Constantine rose to Hannibal's right, the emperor's own robe cast across its base.

The holy book was brought out and shown to the church. Ignoring the crush about him, Hannibal forced his way to the front. He stared at the marvel, remembering the story. How the Emperor Constantine himself had ordered his friend and priest, a man named Eusebius, to inscribe one for each of the fifty churches Constantine himself had founded. Each book had been written in the finest hand, set upon carefully matched elk and antelope hides—pages worth a hundred times their weight in gold. And here it was. All books of the Bible brought together and bound as one volume. All the mysteries of the holy spoken Word revealed at once. A marvelous feat, one known throughout the empire as a new sign and wonder. Hannibal was determined to take such a volume back with him for his home church.

Home. Hannibal was carried away by his longing. It held him through the rest of the service, and carried him out into the brilliant summer sunlight.

Behind him, the church's solid bronze dome shone like a crown above the city. He had no eyes for it, nor for the great expanse of blue stretching out in three directions. Without thinking he followed the crowd, his feet meandering forward as though of their own accord. He felt drained of energy, even of the will to think, to plan, to use the abilities that had always served him so well.

Hannibal found himself standing at the edge of a plaza. At the center of the courtyard rose a giant statue. For some reason, the power of that sculpture granted him a means of drawing the moment and the day into focus.

Hannibal turned, saw how his guards were hanging back, giving him room. He returned his gaze to the sculpture. It was unlike anything he had ever seen. The marble was so pure as to appear to be frozen milk. It depicted a tall, muscled warrior facing a pair of lions with nothing but a legionnaire's shield and spear. The lions were taller than the man, their talons long as his hand, their teeth half the length of the sword hanging at his side. But the warrior showed no fear. His clean-shaven features were stern but strangely stoic, as though he did not care whether he lived or died. Meeting this challenge well was all that mattered.

Hannibal gazed long and hard, lost to the crowds sweeping about him. The Roman world was filled with statues, giving form to legends and gods and distant rulers. But this statue was utterly different.

He turned, saw another man standing not far away. He walked over, found his voice with difficulty. "This is Constantine, is it not?"

The stranger nodded. "Commissioned it himself not long before his death. Never tired of viewing it."

"No," Hannibal agreed, turning back around. "I can well understand that."

The stranger moved off. Hannibal scarcely noticed his departure. Finally, finally, he felt he had come to grips with who this man, this Christian emperor named Constantine, truly was. The ruler had spent his life battling two great foes, one within, the other without. Never knowing if he could win the quest, yet facing his opponents with single-minded courage. A human, full of a human's faults and frailties, yet trying just the same. Hannibal felt awed by the man who was no longer there.

"Oh, there you are."

Hannibal turned to find his daughter rushing toward him. She hurried over, grasped his hand, then started back in the direction from which she had arrived. "Come, we can't keep the prelate waiting."

Reluctantly he allowed himself to be turned away. Halfway around he stopped, looked back at the statue, and said quietly, "You are much stronger than I."

"What was that, Father?"

"Nothing." He glanced at his daughter. Hard, she was taking this very hard. Her face was daily becoming more pale, more drawn. Yet there was not an air of defeat about her, rather one of an otherworldliness. He felt his heart clutched by a new fear. "Are you unwell?"

"Me? Why on earth do you ask such a question?"

"Answer me."

"I am fine, Father." Her voice was toneless, as though mentally she was scarcely beside him at all.

"It is bad to lie, daughter, doubly so to speak an untruth on the Sabbath."

Her gaze turned to him then, the depths and pain wrenching him. "There is no cure for a broken heart, Father." She turned away. "At least, not one to be found in this world."

They stopped before a great portal. At Lydia's hand signal the guard rapped loudly. Hannibal demanded, "You are not thinking of committing," he stopped, finished, "an utterly sinful act?"

"Rest easy, Father." She stood with the regal calm of one who had already removed herself from this earth. "I serve the one true Lord. It is all I have left."

"Except your family," he reminded her.

"Yes," she said quietly, facing the door with chin held high. "I will always have that."

The door was opened by a massive guard, one who barred the portal with his own bulk, permitting entry only to Hannibal and his daughter. Hannibal stopped his guard's protest with a swift hand motion, then led his daughter forward and through the gate.

The palace was grandiose in a hastily constructed fashion. Constantinople was filled with such structures. In the previous days, Hannibal had visited many of them. Too many. There were said to be over three hundred court buildings and four thousand villas already completed within the city walls, with dozens more being thrown up everywhere. Already the most hastily built were showing signs of shoddy construction, with cracks in the walls and bits of plaster falling from distant ceilings. Hannibal followed his daughter through one great room after another, blind to all but his worries.

Titus Octavian was seated upon a gilded chair resembling a small royal throne. He did not rise at their approach. His face was lean and bony, his clean-shaven features held the bluish tint of ill health. He waved a short gilded stave, as though beckoning them forward. "So you are the friends of my late father's faithful servant."

Hannibal did as was expected, and gave a deep bow. "Of Cletus' son, my lord. A young man named Travis. It has never been my honor to meet the father."

"Honor, yes." A flicker toward where Lydia stood in ethereal silence, then an equally swift dismissal. "You have a letter for me."

"Alas," Hannibal said. "It was burned in the same fire that almost consumed my livelihood."

"A fire. How tragic." The prelate fingered the jewel-encrusted cross that dangled from a heavy gold chain about his neck. "And yet you survived unscathed."

"I and my goods both, thanks to the heroic efforts of your servant's son. Travis now suffers the injustice of slaving in the sandstone mines—"

"Travis, yes, I have heard that name somewhere before. Remarkable how the old legionnaire would select such a strange-sounding name for his heir." He had eyes the color of mud. His smile came and went with the speed of a lizard's tongue, never rising to his eyes. Nothing touched his eyes, no light, no recognition, no concern. They peered out in calculating emptiness, framed by a face as spirited as a death mask. "He is the designated heir of Cletus, I presume."

"Lord, I do not know," Hannibal stammered, caught off guard by the question. "But as I was saying—"

"The mines, yes, I heard you. It is indeed a tragedy. If what you say is true, of course." The voice droned flat and uncaring. "I will have my own men check into this immediately."

"But I have brought evidence with me—"

"Come back the day after tomorrow," he said, waving the stave in dismissal. "No, too soon, too soon. Three days hence. Or perhaps four. Better still, I will send word. Where are you staying?"

"With the trader Nathaniel Tobias."

A faint flicker within those lifeless eyes, then, "Word shall be sent to you as soon as I have learned anything."

But Hannibal was not so easily dismissed. Not now. "Sire, you are our last hope. I have spent days scurrying about the law courts and the palaces, begging audiences, speaking with hundreds of officials, spending money as if it were water. All this for the son of a man who has served your family faithfully for—"

"Guards," intoned the dull voice. Instantly Hannibal was surrounded. His arms were grasped in grips like iron shackles. Titus Octavian waved them away. "Good day to you, merchant."

The guards dragged him protesting bitterly across the court-yard, then literally flung him through the portal and into the arms of his own men. He righted himself with fury, started for the door just as it was slammed in his face. "A curse—"

"Don't."

His daughter's arm stopped his raised fist. And something in her voice. He turned to her, the anger ebbing. She looked up at him in tragic calmness. Lydia demanded quietly, "Did you ever expect anything else? After a week and more of trying to see him?"

His shoulders slumped in defeat. "No. I suppose not."

"Father . . ." Lydia hesitated, for once the calm isolation failing her. Her chin quivered before she straightened herself with visible effort. She dragged in a deep breath, said in tragic solemnity, "You are the finest man I have ever known. The very finest. Now listen to me." Another breath. "Know that I love you and Mother with all my heart. Know that whatever happens, it is of my own will."

Alarm raised his hackles. "What are you saying?"

"Just that you must trust me, and remain who you are." The steady gaze belonged to someone else, and not his daughter. A woman who had moved beyond time and age, and entered into a realm ever beyond his reach. Lydia went on, "Do not let them destroy your goodness. Do not come to doubt yourself. Too many rely on your strength."

Before he could recover enough to respond, she hugged him once, holding him with a fierceness that frightened him as much as her words. Then she turned and fled.

Hannibal stared dumbfounded at one guard after the other. "What in God's name is this?"

"Sire, I—"

"After her, don't let her get away!"

They turned, confused, surrounded by milling crowds and a dozen different passages. Two held close to Hannibal while the others fanned out, disappearing down lanes. One by one they returned, checked to see if by some chance she had reappeared, then left again. With each passing moment Hannibal's heart swelled, the thuds rising in his ears like tolling doom.

CHAPTER XVI

From the very start, Lydia's favorite church was the first one built in Constantinople, the Church of God's Holy Peace, or Haga Eirene. It was far overshadowed by the newer and larger Haga Sophia, or Church of Holy Wisdom, just across the huge central plaza. As a result, Haga Eirene, or Saint Irene as the locals now called it, had become something of a backwater, visited mostly by pilgrims. Few of the imperial courtiers who gathered upon the Sophia's outer steps would dream of entering there. Which suited Lydia perfectly.

The interior smelled a bit stale and stuffy, the carpets upon which the believers knelt in prayer a bit frayed. But there was an air of fervent worship within the great hall, shared by all from the highest priest to the lowest commoner, a sense of joy upon entering God's hallowed home.

After fervent prayer, Lydia left the church at the appointed hour and flew down the stairs, her heart tripping faster than her footsteps. She passed through an opening in the old Byzantine wall, and approached the *Milion*, or First Milestone. The plaza was square, the sides consisting of four great triumphal arches. The entire space was roofed by a gigantic cupola, said to hold at its very peak a fragment of the True Cross. Already the plaza was being referred to as the center of the known world, with all distances about the empire given from this point.

It was a gathering place for ascetics, a center of pilgrimages for those who sought to cast off the cares and temptations of this world. Cowled figures passed with measured steps, crosses dangling from ornamental chains attached to wrist or neck or robe. Their hoods were pulled down far enough to shield their faces from view. They held themselves apart, as though seeking to pass through the din of life unscathed. Women moved like ghosts in the afternoon light, their entire bodies lost within gray folds.

"You are Lydia, daughter of the trader Hannibal Mago?"

"Of Carthage," she agreed, giving the response as the coiffured man with the strange lisping voice had directed. The same one who had presented her with the ultimatum. She offered the note, the one she had been instructed to bring with her. "You are from the cloister?"

"I have never been there," the older woman replied. "Few who have seen it are ever seen again, which is as it should be. I for one have no desire ever to return here. You are ready?"

Lydia swallowed, and said quietly, "I am ready."

The cowled woman accepted the note, then unfolded a second gray robe, raised it and let it cascade down over Lydia, covering her from head to toe. "Then let us be gone from this foul place," the cowled woman said, and glanced a question her way. "There are guards beyond the square's perimeter who are charged with our safety. Whoever your patron is, he must have great power."

Lydia kept her head bowed and said nothing. The woman took her silence as an answer and turned away. Lydia followed, passing through yet another line of acolytes, and walked from the plaza. Yes, it was indeed a foul world. And if she could not have Travis, then she wanted nothing more to do with it.

Hannibal half-walked, half-ran the length of the colonnaded Mesé thoroughfare, the message crumpled in his fist. His guards hastened to keep up, but dared not speak for the fire that flashed in his eyes.

He crossed the forum, the oval plaza fully five hundred paces wide and tiled entirely in polished marble slabs, and passed the rose-tinted column from Heliopolis. They sprinted to pass before a contingent of praetorian guards and *clibanari*, mail-clad soldiers bearing the heavy weapons adapted from Persian forces. He turned down the road leading south past the Trojan Palladium, the great palace that Constantine had ordered dismantled and carted hundreds of leagues to be rebuilt here. He did not grant it a single passing glance.

The hippodrome stood at the end of a long road turned golden in the harsh afternoon light. By the time Hannibal arrived, he could taste the dust in his mouth. He turned abruptly, checked behind him, saw that no one had followed. In the afternoon the city seemed to float upon the shimmering air. For once, it had truly become a city of angels, a place joined more to the trembling heavens than to the rocky, indistinct earth. Hannibal wheeled about and entered the great arena.

The stands were empty tiers of stone, steeply graded and split by broad stairs. Great shelves jutted out at regular intervals. During races and annual celebrations of the city's founding, soldiers in full dress regalia stood and sweltered upon these viewing platforms. Their armed presence was far more than just ornamentation; several emperors had come close to losing the throne during the frenzied excitement of celebratory games.

Hannibal passed down the empty connecting corridor, climbed the chest-high stone barrier, and strode across the dusty soil to the stadium's center. There rose the Serpent Column, a vast triangular structure taken from the Temple of Apollo in Delphi. As he approached, a strange-looking man appeared, with carefully coiffured hair and multicolored robes. He stepped away from the column's base and called out, "Dismiss your men."

"Where is my daughter?" Hannibal grated, barely able to hold himself back from wringing the man's scrawny perfumed neck.

"Dismiss your men," he cried shrilly, backing away in haste, "or you shall have no daughter to ask about."

The group froze at the words. Hannibal recovered first, said, "Wait for me at the entrance."

"But, sire—"

"Go, I tell you." When they were alone, Hannibal said, "Tell me now, and tell me swiftly, while you still have the breath left to speak."

Arrogantly the man drew himself up. "You shall be well advised to drop your threats, Hannibal Mago. For it is I who hold the keys to your daughter's future."

He checked his forward movement with effort. "Who has sent you?"

"It does not matter, and if you seek to learn, it is your daughter who shall pay for your curiosity with her life," the man snapped. "She has joined a cloister. And done so of her own free will. It was her choice, I suppose she told you. She was ordered to speak with you about this before she left."

The news slammed into him with the force of a thrust spear. "This can't be."

"It is, and it is done." The coiffured head tossed back triumphantly. "You are to cease with your meddling, Hannibal Mago, and return to Carthage. You and your men and that detestable Travis, son of Cletus, who is to be released this very day. Take him and leave, or your daughter shall suffer."

Hannibal had to struggle to form the words, "And Lydia."

"She has made her choice, I tell you. The cloister is well guarded, set upon private lands well removed from this place. You shall never see her again. That is all."

"I don't believe you!"

"Believe this, then." He flipped out a note, letting it fall upon the sand between them. "For the sake of your daughter's life, take this Travis and all your rabble and depart these lands, never to return." The man wheeled about, his robes swirling grandly, and stalked off.

Hannibal reached down a trembling hand, picked up the paper, cried aloud when he recognized his daughter's handwriting.

And the words. There could be no question who had written them. They formed his wife's favorite part of the Sabbath liturgy. A scroll bearing this inscription was set above her bed.

The note read, "Sorrowful yet always rejoicing, dying and yet we live."

Hannibal crushed the note to his chest, dropped to his knees in the arena sand, and wept.

CHAPTER XVII

I own nothing, not even my name," Inigo murmured cheerfully. In the final moments of another day, the chamber was almost lost to the gathering of night shadows. All around them were the sounds of sleep and fatigue and quiet despair. "I was converted by a traveling missionary at the age of sixteen from a despicable religion. One so horrid I do not care even to describe it."

Travis thought of another night and the pirate village and the dance of masks. "I can imagine."

But Inigo was too caught up in the winds of memory to hear. "When I was called to serve our Lord as a priest, I chose the name of a bishop from Antioch. One who lived soon after the Master's death, one known for the strength and purity of his faith and walk. I have tried to live with his example ever before me."

"If I am ever freed," Travis said fervently, "I will fight for your discharge. This do I swear."

"My son," Inigo replied fondly. "I release you from your vow."

"You cannot."

"But I must. You see, it was the emperor himself who sent me here."

"Constantine? Why?"

"No, his son, Constantius. He is a follower of Arius, you see. It is part of his rebellion, casting out his father's name and memory, placing his own mark upon the empire. I stated publicly that Arius' teachings were false. There are many who follow the emperor's lead, in matters religious as well as temporal. I felt I had to speak, if not for the emperor's sake, then for the sake of his followers. The emperor condemned me to the mines. But he also set an injunction upon those responsible, that if I were hurt in any way, they would join me here. It was not the emperor's intention to make another martyr, rather to make me retract my statement." A pause, then, "You have heard of Arius?"

"No."

"He was quite a good man, from the sounds of things." A more eager note entered the old priest's voice. There was nothing he loved more than to teach. "A bit of a dreamer. Nothing wrong with that, of course. The world is always in need of people who seek to point the way with ideals beyond the grasp of most. But he was also a heretic. Constantine's bishop, a man called Eusebius, has said that a heretic is one whose love of change is stronger than his love for the truth. I fear this happened with Arius. Heresy is not total falsehood, you know. If it were, people should instantly call it a lie and turn away. No, heresy is dangerous because it is *partial* truth. The word itself comes from *heiro*, you know, which means to pick and choose. A heretic takes a half-truth, then stretches it into a false extreme." He stopped. "Where was I?"

"Arius."

"Ah, yes. He was well trained, by the Greeks of course, and his readings took him nearer and nearer to the ancient source of heresy, a group known as the Gnostics. In truth they were not a single group at all, but rather a whole realm of sects, some holding fast to a kernel of truth, others beyond the ability of any sane man to fathom."

Once again Travis understood only a fraction of what he heard, but he did not try and stop the old man with questions. He dared not even shift position, for fear that it would halt the flow. The old man tended to ramble, and spoke as though he were addressing a class of acolytes, but Travis did not mind. He loved the voice as much as the lesson, and clung to the sense of sharing a passion and a hope.

"There is no way, of course, to know whether or not Arius fell under the Gnostic spell. But one thing is certain. What he declared, and what some Gnostics had been saying back soon after our Lord returned to heaven, are very similar indeed."

The old priest pulled himself farther up the wall until he was sitting upright and had both hands free to mold the growing darkness. "Arius and his followers, who were first called Meletians and are now known as Arians, said that God the Father and Jesus the Son were not one and the same. They could not be. God was holy, divine, above this sinful and tainted earth. There had to be some point when the Father created the Son, and thus the Son was not, as they put it, coeternal. He was God's instrument of salvation, and although a perfect man, still human in nature, not divine."

271

The old man looked at Travis, his eyes two bright pinpricks in the darkness that sought to swallow them whole. "The answer came most strongly from one whose teachings I follow, a fellow priest by the name of Athanasius. He was the former bishop of Alexandria and has been forced into exile, just like me. What Athanasius said I agree with, with all my heart and mind and soul. He replied to the Arians thusly, that God and Jesus the Christ were and shall remain eternally one and the same. In the form of our blessed Savior, the divine Word was made human. God was born upon this earth. God knew hunger. God thirsted. God was tempted. God was beaten bloody, then nailed to a cross. God suffered. And God died a human death. The Son was truly man, you see, and truly God. That is the glorious mystery of the Incarnation."

Slowly Travis raised himself, using the darkness to mask his quiet movements, drawing himself up so his face was only inches from the old man's. He wanted to hold fast to those eyes, strain to keep sight of their eternal vision, hold to the hope that burned so brightly, even here.

"Through the Word is the world created. So it is right for the Word to re-create us, to restore us. We were created in the image and the likeness of the Word. Like the first Son, the true Son, we were shaped to worship the Father. It is thus the Son's responsibility to make us anew in the Father's holy incorruptibility. By becoming one of us, Jesus sanctifies all of us. His life, His death, and His resurrection all form the impossible bridge across the immeasurable chasm. The Cross becomes the key by which we may all enter the gates of eternal life."

Travis waited until he was sure the priest would speak no more on his own, then started, "How—"

A voice boomed out from beyond the cavern's entrance, "Travis, son of Cletus!"

He was on his feet before he realized he had even moved. A flickering glimmer brightened gradually, dispelling the cavern's shadows and transforming everything to hues of orange and gold. A pair of torches and their bearers ducked beneath the overhang and entered their chamber. A guard repeated, "Travis, son of Cletus!"

"Here." The air was not there for him to speak loudly, or even draw the breath his lungs were crying out for. He reached out, felt his arm grasped by the old priest who had risen to stand beside him. "I am here."

"You are to come with us."

"But he has done nothing!" The priest stepped forward, his words a querulous cry that echoed back and forth through the chamber. "He is a good worker!"

"He is also free, old man." The first soldier bent back down to depart. "Now come along."

Travis found his legs unable to move. His lungs heaved, yet no air came in. His hands gripped, yet felt nothing. He turned to the priest, but could not identify the old man. He truly saw, truly felt, truly heard only one word. Free.

Inigo moved his face closer until Travis' roving gaze was able to fasten and hold. "Remember what you have learned here," he said, the eyes filled with loss.

The old man's sadness caused him to focus. "Inigo, this I swear to you—"

"Go with God," the old man responded, his grip turning as fierce as his voice. "And *remember*."

CHAPTER XVIII

Constantinople's original Greek center was still intact, minus the Acropolis and other temples. Beyond the port and the fortified seawall, a maze of narrow lanes extended like a cobblestone web. The newer Roman city ran inland from the crumbling Greek town wall. It rose in regular stages up the hillsides, the stolid Roman architecture stamped indelibly upon the rocky terrain.

Within the older Greek village, the house walls were white and tall and offered only armored doors or narrow windows to the street. Overhead ran connecting passages, their undersides formed into curved tunnels. The tunnels, the ornamental posts, the doors, and the alcoves into which statues of local deities had formerly been placed, were all painted palest blue. Many of the lanes were so narrow that Travis' sword scraped along the left wall, his right shoulder touching the other.

For Travis, the passageways bore an early-morning look of fresh mysteries and new beginnings. He walked behind a strangely subdued Raffa; the warrior had remained quiet and reserved since embracing Travis upon his release, then leading him to where Gaven and Damon waited with horses. Their return had been silent and steady, except for two brief halts for food and water. The guards had remained at careful watch throughout their return, saying little. Travis had not challenged their silence. He had been far too grateful for the chance to drink in a world extending beyond one rock-walled cavern. He had followed Raffa's horse through the moonlit night, reveling in the wonder of it all.

Raffa stopped and pounded on a tall, nail-studded door. A crone opened the face-portal, peered through in sullen suspicion. Raffa leaned closer and spoke a single half-heard word. The woman shuffled back and pulled the door with her.

Inside, the tiny courtyard was fresh and airy and shone from recent scrubbing. A fountain tinkled musically in one corner, its curved edges holding baskets of blooming flowers. Travis seated himself upon the stone bench opposite and inhaled their fragrance.

He was so tired he felt old. His bones ached, as though the weeks of imprisonment had been etched into his very marrow. He closed his eyes, the grit scratching beneath his lids. The morning continued to strengthen, bringing dawn up and over the wall opposite where he sat. Sunlight played against his shoulders, a warm, soothing presence. He lifted his face, basking in the light. Such a simple thing, sunlight. So normal, so common. So precious.

There came a moment of floating between sleep and wakefulness. Travis' face remained upwards, his body still, yet there was a sense of the golden power lifting him away. He drifted on a river of light, rising from his fatigue and his pains. He knew where he sat, knew what was to be done in the coming moments, yet for the moment nothing mattered save the gift of freedom. He felt words form somewhere so deep within his drifting mind they might actually have come from outside himself. Thank You, he said within his heart of hearts, and watched through closed eyes as the words were formed and released into the light that bathed him within and without, Thank You for this gift of freedom. For teaching me what it means to truly live.

There came a scraping footstep, a signal of someone else's presence in the courtyard. Travis felt the flowing peace and light return him to himself. So gentle and natural that while it lasted he felt it would stay with him for all his days. Yet he knew it was not so, that this was not a gift he could control, that it would come and go at its own choosing, and not his own. And yet even when it was not there, still it would remain, a part of who he was for all the days left to him. And beyond.

He opened his eyes.

A dark and bearded man stared down at him. "You are the one Hannibal has spoken of, the prisoner?"

"I am Travis, son of Cletus," he replied, the moment's peace still resonating in his voice. "And a prisoner no longer."

The man's robes trailed across the stones as he stepped around the fountain and came to sit across from Travis. He was tall with lined face and hair streaked with gray. "I have watched you. Were you praying? Did not Hannibal tell me you are a pagan?"

Travis opened his mouth to reply, knew he could not, so simply said, "I have traveled all night and am very tired."

"I know what I have seen," the man persisted.

Travis knew it was both too precious and too new to explain, so did not try. He took in a deep breath, tasted the oppressive silence surrounding the place, asked, "Where is Lydia?"

"She is . . . away." The man sighed, his shoulders slumping. "Forgive me. I am Nathaniel Tobias, and this is my home. Hannibal Mago and his daughter have been my guests since the fire. My warehouses hold your goods along with theirs." He gave a seated bow. "You are of course welcome. Again I must beg your forgiveness. It has been a harsh time for us all."

Travis nodded, not understanding, not wanting to know. Not then. "And Hannibal?"

The subdued note deepened in his features and his voice. "He too is away."

Knowing it was only a half-truth, knowing whatever remained concealed was behind Raffa's silence, knowing too he could face nothing more without food and rest. "I have eaten only gruel for days."

"Food is being prepared. And a bath." Nathaniel rose to his feet, the air of defeated confusion following him. "I will show you to your room."

He awoke to night shadows and the blessings of a flickering lamp. Travis pushed back the coverlets and sat up, his eyes never leaving the ruddy flame. After a time there was the sound of shifting from the room's opposite side, and a sleepy Raffa emerged from his own pallet. Travis remained intently silent for a time, before saying, "I never knew what a glorious thing light was, until it was taken from me."

Raffa stood, stretched, walked to the table by the door, lifted a cloth to reveal yet another plate of food. "Hungry?"

"I feel that I could eat forever and still not be filled," Travis replied.

"Take it slowly," Raffa advised, walking over and setting down the plate. He pulled over a chair, sat and watched as Travis devoured the food.

When he could not eat another bite, Travis leaned back against the wall, cradled the goblet, looked into the luminous depths, confessed, "I had almost lost all hope."

"And I," agreed the quiet man.

Travis took a swallow, knew there was no use in avoiding it further. "There is an air of desolation to this house." He looked up at Raffa. "Is it Lydia?"

Raffa hesitated, then confessed, "Were it anything else, I would say wait and hear what must be said when you are stronger."

"So," he said, the word a slow sigh of acceptance. "And Hannibal?"

"He has taken it hard."

Another swallow, then forcing the words through a throat suddenly closed with fear. "She is dead?"

"For us," Raffa replied slowly, "she might as well be."

"The emperor is away," Nathaniel was saying. "Our enemies act with impunity."

Travis tore his gaze away from where Hannibal sat slumped at the table's far corner. He was a mere shell, hollowed by the same torment that cried silently from his dull gaze. "Who are they?"

"A loose contingent of people who wish for a return to the old ways," Nathaniel replied. "They seek a Roman Empire ruled by pagan gods. They are determined to strip away all they consider both alien and overly restrictive."

"The Christian-based laws," Travis guessed.

"Anything that holds them from living and doing exactly as they please," Nathaniel agreed. "They accept the Arian movement as a compromise only because it is a step in the desired direction, which is the total and utter destruction of all things Christian."

"Religion and politics," Hannibal moaned, speaking for the first time since the meal had begun. "We should curse the day they were first joined."

"My dear friend, the key is not for Christian believers to abhor earthly power," Nathaniel replied, his gaze compassionate, yet his voice firm. "The Israelite kings were not told to refuse their task of ruling the nation. The key is to maintain not a separation between faith and power, but rather a division between the church as a body, and politics as an act."

Nathaniel stopped and waited, searching Hannibal's face, pushing with his silence as well as with his words for a response, a rise, a return of his friend's spirit. When Hannibal refused to respond, he continued to press forward with, "By all means, rulers should be Christian. Yet even so, they will be human, and liable to err, to fail, to sin, to fall into the temptation of wielding power for power's sake. The church must be seen to stand at a distance. Otherwise the people will view acts of these rulers as what it means to be Christian. They will see the flaws as a chasm, demands to which they cannot agree, and forget that Christ did not tell them to pledge their allegiance to any particular group or power. No!

Christ said to *believe*. *This* is the act of faith. All that follows is man's imperfect attempt to walk and act as God leads."

But it was as though Hannibal were incapable of hearing. "I should never have come to Constantinople. Never."

Travis stood, bowed to his host, raised Raffa with his gaze. Once in the courtyard, he said quietly, "I must try to get her back. I cannot ask you to come, nor any of the others. But try I must."

"I beg you not to do this," said a voice behind them. Travis turned to see Nathaniel pass through the portal and join them. "It will be dangerous, not just for you, but for all of us."

"Our men are soldiers," Raffa replied, paying Nathaniel no mind whatsoever. "They chafe at this boat work and carting people about, when an attack is under way. They feel a need to strike back at whoever is causing us such strife and woe."

Causing *us*. "All are welcome," Travis said, "all who truly wish to come."

"I beg you," Nathaniel protested.

"The men grow weary of rowing and sailing," Raffa replied. "Hannibal's men shall wish to join us as well. They pine for their bright-eyed nymph." Raffa glanced back toward the dining hall. "And for the man."

Nathaniel looked from one hard face to the other, sighed, "I see there is nothing I can say to change your minds."

"I must try," Travis said, addressing his host for the first time.

"And I," Raffa agreed. "Too much has happened. Too much has been lost."

"You could help us," Travis said, "by telling us anything you know as to where they might have taken Lydia."

Dark eyes darted worriedly from one to the other. "How am I to believe that this is anything more than a blind and headlong rush for vengeance?"

It was Travis' turn to pause and ponder. He then turned to Raffa and demanded, "What of my amphorae?"

"They are stored here."

"Show me." To Nathaniel, "Come with us, please."

The chest-high clay vessels lined one wall of a crowded inner storeroom. Travis waited until the two men had slid in alongside him, then broke the first jar's seal with the hilt of his sword. He cut through the ropes and pried back the salt-stiffened leather top. Nathaniel sniffed, his nose wrinkling at the residual smell of the little sea animals.

"Dip in your finger," Travis instructed.

Hesitantly the trader did so. He drew out his digit, held it up to the torchlight, and his eyes widened to dark moons. "Can this be?"

"Ten amphorae of royal purple dye," Travis confirmed. "If Hannibal chooses to trust you, then so will I. I wish for you to find me not a buyer, but an opportunity. A basis upon which we could start a new life. That was what my father charged me with, when he sent me here. These amphorae represent all we have left. The estate he managed for so many years has been drained by tax syndicates and confiscation of our produce."

"The estate has been devoured," Raffa murmured.

"This was not just some random act, which came and left us able to repair and continue," Travis went on. "This was deliberate destruction."

"And when that did not drive them from the land," Raffa added, "they tried poison."

"Of this I have heard," Nathaniel said, looking from one to the other. "You think it is all connected?"

"Why was I imprisoned? Why are we being forced to return to Carthage, leaving Lydia hostage? What is the purpose behind these continued attacks?"

Distractedly Nathaniel lifted the hem of his cloak and wiped his finger clean. Finally he raised his head, said in quiet decision, "I will see what I can discover."

CHAPTER XIX

The hillside was verdant in a dry and dusty manner. Palms rattled their fan-shaped branches in the wind. Slender firs weaved like graceful green fingers, tracing the clouds' passage across the sky. The air was fresh and cool for a change, spiced with the flavor of coming rain.

They halted under a stand of old olive trees, the trunks gnarled and twisted. Many branches were bare save for a few silver leaves, lingering like the last threads of hair on an old man's head, trembling in the wind.

Their goal rose up ahead, a community of baths around ancient natural springs. The thermal springs were a half-day's hard ride, or two days' leisurely trek, from Constantinople, mostly uphill. Their usage by royalty meant the road was well-maintained and fairly secure.

Their movements were swift and silent, the sense of impending danger tightening them into a well-defined unit. Travis undressed and bathed in the nearby stream. Two men watered, fed, and curried his horse. Both his clothes and their steeds were gifts of Nathaniel, who had seen them off with urgings that speed and more speed was their only hope of averting disaster. Travis' robes had been treated with dye from his own amphorae, their color now befitting a royal messenger.

Travis looked across the narrow valley separating them from the baths. The cluster of palaces shimmered in the dusty distance, their marble facades reflecting the afternoon light like multicolored mirrors. "Everything looks quiet."

"Aye," muttered Raffa, grimacing as one of the men tightened the brace to his leather chest guard, adjusted the folds of his overmantle, then fitted silver bracelets to his wrists. Beside him Damon submitted to similar grooming. Their finery was also taken from stock Nathaniel supplied to the royal garrison. "They're all inside plotting the destruction of more innocents."

"You always were morose before battle," Travis said, grateful for a reason to grin.

"I feel like a powdered courtier," the man quietly grumbled, and stomped off to his waiting mount. Damon followed and mounted, then adjusted his crimson robe with the ease of one long used to the dress of royal parades.

Travis swung into the saddle, said to the others, "Give us an hour. Then ride over and wait by the food stalls, in clear sight of whichever entrance we use."

The trio took the road along the valley's southern lip, then down toward the thermal baths. The closer they came, the grander and more imposing grew the central edifices.

The baths were surrounded by stalls selling fruit, sherbet, wine, and food, all at vastly inflated prices. The former temple to Venus had been made roofless, the goddess' statues headless. The open cupola was now the entrance to the grand structures beyond.

The bath dwellings were actually carved from the cliffside. Their facades copied the now roofless temple—grand and bordered by rows of fine columns. Travis asked directions, was pointed to one of the central structures.

They dismounted, handed their steeds to an attendant, climbed the broad stairs lined with lurid statues of clearly pagan design. At the top Travis turned and pretended to admire the view, his eyes upon the distant grove. A series of quick flashes burned his vision, reflections from a carefully aimed blade. He turned and followed the attendant inside.

Nathaniel's hasty investigations had netted two finds. The first was, as an act of piety, the newly converted Titus Octavian had given an old fortress on land owned by his family to women seeking a place of spiritual refuge. A cloister, the place was now called, a new term intended to denote a house closed to all but its occupants, a haven given over to prayer and study. But the rumors did not end there.

According to whispered comment, Titus himself issued invitations to women of good families, even scaling the barriers of royalty itself. Yet passage onto these lands was next to impossible without either a royal decree or written admission from Titus himself. With the ruler and his entourage away preparing for war, entry was virtually impossible. The estate was patrolled by far more armed guards than were required to watch over farmland and a villa of cloistered women.

The second item of interest was that, despite Titus' supposed Christian faith, he spent most Sabbaths out at his villa in the baths. It was, according to his own statement, due to ill health. Still, the baths were renowned as a gathering point for those who found a Christian city in Sabbath devotion to be a stifling experience.

The interiors were dressed in local marble and wildly painted designs. Travis stood in the inner alcove, surrounded by more wealth on display than he had ever thought existed. Grander statues were mirrored by smaller works of exquisite artistry, carved from what appeared to be solid gold.

The first of several baths was in a chamber to his left. A single glance explained why these dwellings were carved from the mountainside. Steaming waters poured from fissures, spouting fountains of sulfurous water so hot it would strip skin from bone. The current ran through carefully maintained channels, cooling as it flowed, spilling into the great marble baths, then rejoining downstream and eventually pouring into the neighboring river.

Perfumed braziers wafted up great billowing clouds of cloying scent, seeking to override the bath's pungent odor. The wall hangings were of rarest cloth and intricate design, the floor mosaics appeared to use semiprecious stones. It was a place for people with so much wealth they did not need to ever think of money.

"The master is unaccustomed to any interruptions whatsoever upon his day of rest," announced a frosty voice.

Travis turned to confront another servant, this one older, rail thin, and as erect as a general on parade. He grasped his robe just below the silver shoulder-clasp and swept a disdainful gaze over Travis, lifting his nose in the process.

"Forgive the intrusion," Travis replied, and brandished the scroll Nathaniel had supplied. It was one the trader had received from the emperor's household several years before, and bore the silver banner of a royal decree. The seal had been hastily repaired, and was kept turned away from the servant's gaze. "I carry urgent news from the city."

"Very well," the servant replied, extending his hand. "I will take it."

Travis withdrew the scroll. "It is intended for the hand of Titus Octavian himself. Those are my orders."

The servant gave him another inspection, his glance flitting over Raffa's centurion dress and back. "Wait here," he snapped.

His pulse racing, Travis nodded to Raffa, who turned and walked to the main entrance. From there a single hand signal was flashed to where Damon stood attending the horses.

The servant reappeared. "Come along, then."

They walked past one grand hall after another, each more luxuriously appointed than the last. Their way took them into the central courtyard, where a group of onlookers cheered a pair of wrestlers. Even the servants and household guards were caught up by the revelry, craning and jostling each other for a better view. The oiled bodies grappled and writhed in the brilliant sunlight. As his eyes adjusted to the radiance, Travis felt his heart freeze solid. He jerked back into the shadows, drawing Raffa with him.

The soldier breathed, "Do my eyes deceive me?"

"No." It was impossible, but it was true. There in the courtyard, writhing in furious intent, was his half-brother, Brutus. Despite the years since their last meeting, the misshapen head placed upon such a perfectly lithe form was unmistakable.

"Well?" The servant returned crossly to where they stood in the shadows. "Are you coming?"

"We will wait here," Travis replied, gathering himself in a rush. "Our mission is intended as confidential."

"Oh, very well." The servant wheeled about. Travis took another step back, Raffa moving with him, until both the shadows and the portal protected them from view. He turned his attention back to the courtyard. Brutus. The sight of that loathsome face contorted in furious concentration brought back a flood of memories and emotion.

"Yes?" An aging slender man with a bluish tint to his features stepped forward, a robe gathered and flung about his body. He still dripped with sweat from the baths. "You wish to see me?"

"Forgive the intrusion," Travis said, keeping his voice low, backing up another pace, drawing the prelate with him. "There is a certain matron of the royal family, one Pherenice, who resides at a cloister upon your domain."

"What if there is?" The prelate's voice was clipped, irritated, as he followed Travis back another step.

Travis raised the scroll, said as they had planned with Nathaniel, "I am ordered to deliver this to her. And to return with her reply. I have been ordered to make all haste, and must therefore request passage across your lands."

"Give me the message," the prelate commanded. "I will have my men deliver it personally."

"I am not allowed to do that, sire," Travis replied, his voice tensing as he heard a cheer signaling the wrestling match's end. Instantly the senior servant left his master's side and scurried into the sunlit passage, clapping his hands and ordering the attendants back to duty. Travis focused his attention upon the now solitary prelate. "Please, this is most urgent."

"This is ridiculous, is what it is," the prelate snapped. "Who has the audacity to suggest that I and my men are not worthy to pass on a message, royal or not?"

Travis' reply was cut short by the crowd of men pressing toward the entrance, his brother in the lead. Arms reached out to slap Brutus' shoulder in congratulation. Another three steps and they would enter the shadows, and the chance would be lost.

Reacting instinctively, Travis flipped the scroll about and backhanded the prelate across the temple. His knees crumpled, but Raffa was there to catch him. With the prelate on Raffa's shoulder, they turned and fled for the entrance.

The single guard on duty was so startled at the sight that he had scarcely gripped his sword before Travis' fist clobbered the side of his head, sending him sprawling. Down the stairs, tossing the prelate across the front of Damon's horse, mounting and spurring their steeds forward, down the street, and collecting their men with a shout, beyond the stalls and the people before the first cries wafted up behind them.

Green fields lay baking under an empty sky. Behind rose looming thunderclouds, yet ahead all was blue and dust and heat. The highlands they traversed were like a great earthen sea. Vast open plains rushed toward the dikes of jagged mountains. One moment all was flat and cultivated, a land subdued by man. The next moment nature retook control, with rocky crags and sheer cliffs and unwelcome faces.

They flew past signs of cultivation, patchwork stretches of green struggling to rise from the rocky earth, and the faint sounds of sheep bleating beyond the horizon. Cactus were planted as natural barriers against predators, growing into walls taller than a man. The pounding of their hoofs, and the sight of two dozen armed and grim-faced men riding with their robes streaming in the wind, was enough to halt work at every farm they passed.

Titus Octavian was handed from one rider to the next at each halt, when the horses were granted a brief time to blow and drink sparsely from nearby wells. A knife to his ribs kept the prelate from speaking. His tied wrists were hidden beneath the folds of a robe unraveled and redraped about his arms. He was not weathering the ride well, his unhealthy pallor growing bluer at each stop. As little attention was paid to his comfort as to his feeble protests.

By dusk the mountains were upon them. The pass was guarded by a great watch-fortress, set firmly upon a flattened hill. The stones had been ripped from the crown, shaped, and set down again so precisely that no mortar was required to hold them in place. The six sides were spaced unevenly, so that the fortress covered every bit of level terrain. Thus an invading force would find no ground between the cliff and the fortress walls to gather and prepare for an attack.

They paused beneath the stone crown at Raffa's suggestion. What band of marauders, he argued, would stop below a Roman fortress to water their horses? They stood in clear sight of the guards upon the walls, and ate a sparse meal of hard bread and cheese. Titus Octavian ate with little trembling movements, dribbling crumbs about him, casting frantic glances at the phalanx of men that pressed close about. His whimpered queries and pleas were met with hissed orders and the sharp end of a blade pricked against his ribs. None had spoken to him since their departure from the baths.

They arrived at the prelate's domain with the final light of day. The outpost was a crude collection of farm buildings and a larger series of guard huts and stables.

"Just as the trader said," Raffa muttered, drawing up alongside Travis. "Far too many guards stationed to protect a covey of religious women and some barns."

Travis wheeled his mount about, trotted over to where Titus sat slumped upon the neck of Damon's horse. Clearly this was the hardest sport the man had experienced in years. Travis gripped a fistful of the man's dusty robe and dragged him upright. "How much do you value your life?"

"Please, I beg you—"

"You have much to atone for," Travis hissed. "A ruined estate, my father's unanswered pleas for help, a poisoning that almost killed me, a kidnapping, threats against the woman I love. Your life hangs by a thread."

The eyes gaped, the mouth worked, finally the words emerged, "You are the son of Cletus?"

"That and more." Travis reined himself close enough to snarl directly into the prelate's face. "One wrong step and I am your judge and executioner."

Sweat dampened the dusty brow. "Anything," he whimpered. "Tell me what you want."

"Fresh mounts, for a start." Travis pointed down at the stables. "We will go down there, and you shall order them for us. One word, one sign, one false move, and you might stop us, but know that the first blade will be aimed for your heart." Travis waited until he was sure the message was clearly received, then went on, "Now this is exactly what you are going to say. This and nothing more."

CHAPTER XX

They rode through the darkness, guided by a pair of guards—all whom Titus Octavian had permitted to accompany them. The prelate had followed Travis' instructions to the letter, his voice dull but firm, his loyalty reassured by the closeness of his own death. His other guards had been ordered to saddle and scour the domain's borders, as there were rumors of marauders on the loose. Guards who had seldom seen their leader face to face had armed themselves and mounted with the speed of men spurred to show their skills, gathering into well-disciplined groups and vanishing into the night.

Travis and his team made good time, following as they were guards who knew the route. The treacherous track wound about half-seen obstacles and drops down caverns as dark as doom. Travis struggled to hold his mind to the challenges at hand, but fatigue was a club that pummeled his head and shoulders. The more exhausted he became, the more his half-brother's face swam before his eyes. Brutus as he was before, cruel and vicious in games meant to maim and terrify. Brutus as he was now, surrounded by cheering friends in the house of Travis' enemy. The implications were staggering. Travis glanced over to where Titus Octavian drooped in his saddle, flanked by Raffa and Damon. The pair rode with drawn swords laid across their pommels, a constant reminder to the prelate and his tongue. Yes, there was indeed much to be learned from Titus, even more for which the prelate had to answer.

The cloister appeared without warning. One moment they were wending their way about a jagged rock outcrop, the next they confronted an ancient walled compound. As they continued about the long stone wall, it became clear that once this had housed an entire farming community. Numerous rooftops appeared beyond the wall, all set far enough apart to grant space for vegetable gardens and animal pens.

When a corner separated them from the two advance guards, Travis sidled up next to Titus Octavian's horse and hissed, "When we arrive, send away the guards. Tell them this is a confidential mission, and they are to join their fellows in the search for marauders."

The prelate did not answer. In the shadows Travis could see his jaw hanging slack in exhaustion. He reached over and shook the man roughly. "Say it!"

"Confidential," the prelate managed.

Travis exchanged glances with Raffa and wheeled away. It would have to do.

As they approached the main gates, he sidled up close to the guards, their sword arms occupied with torches, and waited as they shouted, waited, shouted again. Finally a querulous voice rose from within, "Who dares disturb our peace?"

"Your master, Titus Octavian."

"We recognize but one master, and Titus is not He."

"Open up, I say!"

As the bolts rasped back, Raffa moved forward, drawing Titus and the other guards with him. A rough nudge prompted him to straighten somewhat and say to the guards, "You have dispatched your duty. Join the others in the search of my perimeters."

"But sire—"

Raffa raised his blade slightly, so it caught the torchlight and reflected it back into the prelate's eyes. "Do as I say!" The voice rose to a reedy screech. "This is a confidential mission, on orders of the emperor!"

As the guards wheeled away, the great portal opened to reveal a regal gray-robed woman who looked up at Titus and said with derision, "The emperor indeed. Certainly nothing less would cause the great Titus Octavian to finally respond to my many messages." She glanced about the gathering with the haughty command of one born to rule. "And who might these others be?"

"Friends," Travis replied quietly.

"If you travel with Titus Octavian," she snapped back, "I most seriously doubt it."

Travis glanced back, saw the pair of retreating torches, leaned over his horse's flank and said, "He has been persuaded with a bared blade to join us, milady. I beg you, grant us leave to enter."

The lofty gaze turned on him. "And just who, pray tell, might you be?"

"Travis, son of Cletus, here on the most urgent of business. And your name?"

"Pherenice, niece to the emperor Constantine, cousin to Constantius." The woman's gaze flickered once, a barely perceptible cleft in the noble countenance. "Do I have your word that no harm will come to the ladies in my charge?"

"Upon my life and honor."

Another imperceptible pause, then she stepped back. "Very well. If for no other reason than to have this man answer to my charges."

"He will first," Travis said, riding forward, "answer to mine."

"There is only one way on and off this rocky hinterland," Pherenice was saying. "Titus Octavian has effectively sealed us in. I am certain none of my missives to Constantius have arrived, if for no other reason than there has been no response. Not one."

Travis rubbed a weary hand across his neck. The hall where they stood was stone-walled and unadorned, save for the simple wooden cross affixed above each door. All the chambers he had seen were plain to the point of austere, lacking any vestige of luxury or ease. The emperor's cousin was dressed in a simple gray robe, washed until the fabric was frayed. Her bearing held to regal aloofness, yet her gaze was direct, calm, searching. It was a disconcerting combination. "The emperor is away."

"The *emperor* is dead. The *augustus* is away," she corrected. "No one was ever intended to become overall ruler again, which was perhaps the greatest error Constantine ever made. He saw for himself how difficult it was for one man to rule the empire. Yet he forgot how tantalizing the desire for absolute power could prove. Mark my words, the brothers' quarrel will soon come to war."

"My lady, forgive me." Now that he was here, the pressing need for answers was matched only by his desire to see Lydia, and to sleep. "There is one among you whom I would dearly like to see."

"No doubt." For an instant a different woman showed through, one of warmth and humor and sympathy. "Yet a decision upon that must be delayed a bit longer."

"For what reason?"

"For me to take the measure of him who asks." She gestured at the door. "You said this could not wait, not even for you to garner the rest you and your men clearly need. I suggest we begin."

Seeing that argument was useless, Travis pushed through the door to find Titus Octavian seated at a long refectory table, flanked by a bevy of menacing guards. Those standing had the soldiers' experience of living with fatigue and sore muscles. Not the prelate. He remained awake only because they forced him, barking commands to each nod of his head.

"Titus Octavian," Travis rapped out, willing himself to show no weakness. Yet fatigue gripped him, turning his body into one huge ache, and applying a layer of grit under each eyelid. "You have much to answer for."

"Rest," the slack-featured prelate moaned. "I must sleep."

"When you have told us what we need to know," Travis said, deigning not to sit beside the princess, though his neck and shoulders and back cried a protest against any further exertion. His time in prison remained a millstone of weariness bound to his body and spirit. "Why did you level such an attack at my father?" Travis ignored the questioning glance from Pherenice. "He was your loyal servant. The estate was one of the best managed in all

Africa, clearly a great source of income. Why did you seek his destruction?"

"Not I," came the moaned reply. "I have done nothing."

"Of course," Travis said. Boring in. Knowing he had to fight to gain what was required while the man remained weak and off balance. "It was my dear half-brother Brutus. We all know that. But he would not have acted without your permission. He is your man, is he not?"

"You shall have to ask him."

"Nonsense," the gray-frocked princess snapped. "For once you shall answer me directly. Why have I and my charges been imprisoned here?"

"Why should I do such a thing? I gave you the very manor where we now sit, did I not?"

"You are holding them as hostage," Travis guessed. "Hoping the three brothers would all destroy themselves in the battle for Constantine's throne. Or at least leave them so weak that pressure could be applied, and another placed in power. Who was that to be, you?"

"Not I." Defeated now. Slumped over in more than exhaustion. "But one who felt as we did."

Pherenice turned to Travis, a blaze of triumph upon her features. She rose and walked to the door, said to the matron waiting, "Bring pen and paper."

"Food," mumbled Titus. "Rest."

"Water now, food and rest when we have spoken," Travis replied, and faltered. Fatigue passed before his eyes like the shadow of death's wing. He caught himself from falling by leaning forward, planting his fists upon the table. Squinting, drawing the blue-jowled prelate in focus, demanding, "Why did you attack my family?"

A gentle hand rested upon his shoulder. Travis turned with an effort, saw the princess watching him gravely. "Leave two of your men. Take the others, follow the matron to chambers made ready for you."

"But I—"

"Go," she said, quiet yet firm. "I know what must be done." She looked across the table, her face now cold. "He will stay and he will write the answers we desire in his own hand, sealed with his own ring."

CHAPTER XXI

He awoke to a soft hand brushing gently across his forehead. Over and over, a feather-stroke that both cooled and inflamed. Travis lay with eyes closed, reveling in the gentle caress.

"I know you are awake," she whispered.

"No, I still sleep," he replied, his suddenly thundering heart far louder to his ears than his words. "And shall slumber for ever more, unless I know the touch of a fair young maiden's lips."

The caress stopped, and all was still, and for an instant he knew the heart-wrenching fear of rejection. Then she lowered herself with a sigh, a gentle wind that warmed his face as she bent over him, lower still, until he tasted her.

An instant, an eternity, a joining, a beginning. Lydia raised herself back up, whispered, "Why, oh why did you come?"

Travis opened his eyes then. Drank in the sight of her, the beauty and the distress and the love. "Because I have something to tell, something to give, something to ask."

A trace of the former Lydia returned, a simple movement, a cocking of her head to one side, the hint of a smile, which was almost overshadowed by the pain in her eyes. But not quite. "A riddle? You come and destroy the fragile peace I am building, and offer in return a riddle?"

"That and more," he whispered. "Much more."

Something in his gaze ignited the light in those dark eyes. Her fear, though great, was not great enough to extinguish the spark of excited hope. He met the jewel-like gaze, and felt as though he passed through the portals to enter her innermost being. Her voice trembled as she said, "Tell me."

"I have been through much," he said, and swung up to sit alongside her, and told her of his captivity, and of his own fears, and of his meeting the one known as Inigo, and through him the man also known as God. The God. Telling her all. Holding nothing back. Sharing the darkness of his night, the depth of his fear, the loss of all but the memory of her. She listened and she cried, her fingers laced among his own, so the tears fell unhindered and her shoulders trembled with sobs she kept quiet only because she did not want to miss a single word.

"The lessons are too new, too different, still too un-learned," he went on, leaning forward now, tasting one cheek and the saltiness of her joy. "I am a novice, entered into a world that is alien to me. I need a teacher, a friend," stopping now, breathing hard, trying to hold his own voice level, though his heart swelled to fill his chest and threatened to cut off his ability to speak, to whisper, to say the words singing through his being.

"I need a wife. One who can help me with what I need to learn. All my days."

CHAPTER XXII

Travis left the old Greek town and walked the maze of narrow ways connecting the market to the newer Roman city. Smoke rose in well-defined funnels from man-made caves set along the city walls. Slaves tended fires that heated water for both wealthy households and for the baths. In the winter, further fires would be set to funnel hot air through vents beneath the stone floors of public buildings and villas.

"He will fight with no care given to rules," Raffa warned, his ever-quiet voice laced with worry. "Expect the hidden blade, the poisoned tip, the feint within a feint."

In the port beyond the city wall, freemen unloaded inbound vessels, moving in timed cadence like links in a sweating human chain. Their groaning chant of hei-yo, hei-yo, paced the movements. Their eyes did not rise unless the water boy was close, and then only for the instant permitted by the lash-carrying overseer.

"He will seek to wound, to harry," Raffa went on. "To wear you down, prepare you for the kill."

"If I did not know this to be the optimism you take into every battle," Travis replied, "I would be worried."

"Better worried than dead," Raffa said morosely. "I still think you should let me handle this one."

"And me," Damon agreed from behind them. "Such rabble should not be permitted to place you at risk, sire."

"Especially when you are still weak from the mines," Raffa added.

"I am all right, I tell you." Despite the danger that lay ahead, Travis found it difficult to concentrate, to prepare. He took great draughts of the dry mid-morning air, liberty coursing through his veins. The crowded streets, the sights and smells and sounds, the animals and vendors and dust and heat and sun—it was already a part of him, this city.

He passed women carrying water in the ancient fashion, great vessels settled carefully upon their heads. Men balanced impossibly huge loads of woven baskets on their heads and shoulders, shouting reedy cries as they hawked their wares and wobbled forward. Whenever someone raised a hand, the hawker stopped and feebly permitted the load to come to earth. Straightening was slow and gradual, a testing of each joint in turn. Few who witnessed the effort had the heart to argue long over the price.

A donkey trotted along the corridor, its hoofs an echoing drumbeat. The load of clay cooking pots clattered and chuckled at all the oaths tossed by those forced to shrink into doorways at its passage. The old man held its reins from behind, deaf to all shouted his way, allowing the donkey to clear his way for him. Travis swung in alongside the old man, smiling as the rheumy eyes widened in surprise.

"This is the place," Raffa said, drawing him back, starting toward a portal shaded within a broad verandah.

"Wait." For the first time that day, Travis felt a sense of tightening, his senses focusing upon the moment. A half-seen shadow within the alcove drew his attention. He stepped forward quietly, cautiously.

The doorkeeper was normally some elderly relative, there to hail servants and bow through arriving guests. Here, however, Travis found a half-familiar face. One so beaten down he did not even bother to raise his head when Travis stepped forward to stand directly overhead. Travis leaned to one side, saw the metal collar protruding from the torn and filthy robe, inspected the face half-hidden between drooping shoulders, and declared, "I know you."

The man's gaze shifted upwards. He caught sight of Travis, gave a squeal of pure terror, and bolted to his feet. But his headlong rush for the door was stopped by the short span of heavy chain bolted between his leg-irons. He tripped and sprawled into Raffa's strong grasp. He gave another cry of horror, and drew back as though retreating from a bed of snakes. "Do with me what you will!" Terror drove the voice up to girlish heights. "Do your worst!"

"You're Fabian's servant," Travis said. "The one he dispatched upstairs for the silver."

"I have no life left to me!" The voice was theatrically shrill, the gestures wild. "I am forced to lie sprawled in the dust at your feet, awaiting your bloody sword."

Travis ignored the curious glances being cast their way from both the street and the chambers within. The pieces were falling into place. "Fabian sent you here to Brutus, didn't he. You were the one who approached Lydia about the monastery and then sent the message to Hannibal."

"Nothing could be worse than the fate I already know!" A thin hand lifted to reveal yet another heavy band of iron fitted to his wrist. The connecting chain rattled as he struck a bony chest. "I am doomed! Doomed!"

Damon stepped through the portal and by his presence held the onlookers from coming closer. Raffa remained at the entrance, looking back and forth between Travis and the chained slave in utter consternation. "Fabian's slave? Here?"

"I'm sure of it," Travis said, and reached forward. The skinny man shrieked in terror. "Be still," Travis commanded, pulling down the birdlike arms, forcing the man to sit back upon his little stool. He then turned to the gathered faces, said, "You may return to your gaming. The spectacle is over."

The slave sat with back jammed against the wall, his fists raised in anticipation of blows to come. Travis demanded, "What is your name?"

A moment's hesitation, a swallow, then, "Hanno."

"Yes, that's right, I remember now."

Raffa squinted at the bruised and terrified form, asked, "What is he doing here?"

"Seeking to do us harm," Travis replied. "Spying for my two half-brothers."

"Let me wring his scrawny little neck."

The wails commenced again, only to be cut off abruptly by Travis barking, "Stop it, the both of you."

310

The crowd, seeing no blood was to be spilt, lost interest and began to disperse. Travis waited until attention had turned elsewhere, then demanded, "Brutus owns this place?"

Hanno dropped his arms a notch, calmed slightly by Travis' tone. "Yes."

Travis inspected the chained and manacled slave, tried to hate him for having plotted and spied against him, found it impossible. No longer was he the colorful oddity. The slave was gray and beaten, waiting in terrified public submission for his doom, like a trembling mouse caught in the cat's claws. The beast would soon tire of his game, and then would come the slow and painful end.

"Brutus," Travis demanded quietly. "Is he here?"

"Not yet." The terror diminished another notch. "Never before the noon bells."

Travis searched through the open portal, saw nothing that called him to enter. Such teahouses were always full. Merchants and sons of princes gambled at the tables and spun yarns and traded shards of gossip with hangers-on at the emperor's court. Women plied their ancient trade, swishing from table to table until one was called over, pretending to be offended by the lurid offer. Rooms overhead were rented by the hour. "Tell him a man has come seeking him, one who now holds his very life and that of Titus Octavian in the balance."

A trace of the old Hanno resurfaced. "And if I do?"

Raffa leaned forward, said quietly, "Then I might let you live."

Travis stilled him with a glance, said, "A way might be found to free you of your chains, and return you to Carthage."

"Not to Fabian," Hanno pleaded. "He would take orders from his brother and roast me over a very hot fire."

311

"I do not see," Raffa muttered, "how you have much room for barter."

Travis raised his hand for silence, said, "I have a man who is starting a new trade, one that requires a man who knows how to listen and report what he hears."

"Septimus?" Raffa looked at him in utter astonishment. "You would team the likes of this one up with Septimus?"

Travis paid him no mind. "Bring Brutus to the Thieves' Market. The hour past noon, when all is quietest. Do so and we shall see if a better fate than this can be arranged."

CHAPTER XXIII

Once away from the teahouse, Travis followed Nathaniel's directions to the weavers' market. To either side of the dusty lane, tailors sat on tiny stools, their place adjusted to catch the best light. Women stood about them, berating the little men loudly over price, over quality, over the time they took to complete a garment. Arm and needle rose and fell in continuous gyrations, the tailor's reply swinging up and down in cadence. It was a time-honored ritual.

They stopped before a derelict building. A head poked through a great chink in the wall, caught sight of them, and disappeared just as swiftly. Travis checked Nathaniel's instructions once more, said, "This cannot be the place."

"If it is," Raffa said doubtfully, "then I shall be forced to have second thoughts as to the trader's honest intentions."

Damon cocked his head, demanded, "What is that infernal sound?"

A man dressed in elegant robe and slippers threaded with gold hustled from the tumbledown structure. "Welcome, *effendi*, you are most welcome to my humble abode."

"Humble is most correct," Raffa muttered.

Travis eyed the strangely dressed man, with his clipped pointed beard and fawning manner, asked doubtfully, "You are Zeno?"

"Indeed, indeed. And you are Travis, son of Cletus, late of Carthage, friend of Nathaniel, known as the one who has narrowly escaped the clutches of imprisonment and death." Hastily the man took hold of Travis' arm and pulled him toward the building. "I know, I know, my humble abode appears as nothing, but all my money has gone into my weaving."

The closer he came to the doorway, the louder grew the strange clacking. "What is that noise?"

"Come, *effendi*, all shall be made known to you."

Within the doorway, the air was crowded with familiar scents—cotton and wool dust, dyes, sweat. But the scene itself was utterly alien. Men and women sat before hand-guided wheels, spinning thread. The concept was known to him, as smaller spindles had been used by local spinners for generations. But these wheels were far greater, and the attachments far more elaborate. A series of interlocking bone and wooden components produced a super-fine thread. And did so swiftly. The speed at which they worked made his head swirl.

Yet what came next was the marvel. Threads were set like a triangular veil upon a great upright frame. The weaver then took up a short wooden spear, one of many plucked from the side of the frame, each holding a different colored thread. The spear was then shot through a central opening in the interlaced pattern, sweeping from one side to the other. After each transition, a wooden blade was slammed down hard, tightening the thread into place and causing the clacking sound. On and on it went. The weaving created a multicolored fabric faster and cleaner than anything he had ever seen.

Travis faced the strange man and his proud dark gaze.

"Why are you showing me this?"

"The merchant Nathaniel calls you honest. Trustworthy."

"You have been asking about me?"

"A man arrives from Carthage. He bests the customs officials, who are known to strangle silver from the mouths of camels. He is then betrayed by corrupt men, sent to the mines, only to return and be feted as a hero." The man smiled. "Would you not ask over such a one as this?"

Travis returned his attention to the workers. "This is beyond anything I have ever heard of or imagined."

Zeno took in the room and the workers with a great sweep of his berobed arm. "I am Persian, from the land beyond the great eastern hills. My people developed this form of weaving in the time beyond time."

"The war," Raffa said. "I have heard of a war against the Persians."

"I came in the time of peace. I am Christian, and my land is ruled by Zoroasters, the worshippers of fire. One of my own household informed on me. I and my family were condemned to death. I sought sanctuary here. Now I seek wealth." Another grandiose gesture. "All the cloth you see being made is already purchased. Yet my attempts to find a partner, a *trustworthy* partner who will grant me the money to expand and find better quarters, all has come to nought."

"They are a closed lot, these merchants," Travis guessed.

"They seek only to shoulder me aside," Zeno agreed. "Spies come disguised as investors, wanting my machines, not my aid. Yet these are not as simple as they look. It has taken many centuries for my people to work out the system, and the secret of their construction is held by only a few."

Today was not a time for lengthy deliberations, nor a time for caution and doubt. Travis gave the room another long sweeping look, and decided. "I have ten amphorae of royal purple dye."

"Ten amphorae!" The weaver did not seek to mask his shock. A hand clutched the robe over his heart. "I could sell eight, and with that both acquire space and build a dozen more machines. With the other two I could prepare cloth worthy of the emperor himself." Dark eyes clouded over. "What check do you place upon such an offer?"

"Only that you treat me as you have sought to be treated yourself," Travis replied. "I am no merchant, but I am ready to learn."

West of the Lycus River harbor, beyond the city gate closest to the central market and at the opposite end of the plain from the tribal tents, stood a lonely well. Stretching out like a fan from the well were the animals and corrals of the market stallholders. The area was laid out thusly because the tribesmen were known to be men of nimble fingers, who held no respect for the laws of ownership. A tribesman caught within the corrals was killed on the spot, night or day. A corpse found within the animal compound was all the evidence the law required.

Beyond the animal compound was a patch of dry and dusty earth a hundred paces to a side. There was a second well at its center, but it had not held water for over three centuries. The place was known as Thieves' Market. During the day, the square remained empty. After dark, legionnaires patrolled here in squads of five. Surrounding structures were flimsy, the air fetid.

"Madness," Raffa declared gloomily, his eyes quartering the dusty square. "A meeting such as this should be in the light of all the world, the center of the forum, at the steps of the capitol, where none would dare strike a blow."

"My only hope," Travis replied quietly, "is to do this where public shame does not tip the balance."

Raffa was silent then, knowing further argument was useless. They had traveled the same lines numerous times since Travis had described his intentions, and then limited the guard to just three men. Raffa turned and walked to where Gaven stood at the square's opposite side, sword unleashed, body poised for battle. Travis leaned against the crumbling stone border-wall. Damon walked over and squatted down in the wall's shade.

"You are taking a great risk," Damon said quietly, "meeting Brutus like this."

Travis nodded, felt the need to explain, could not. "Despite all that is, all that he has done, still he is my brother."

Damon looked up at him. He had a sharp-bladed build, tall and broad-shouldered. He spoke little, and when he did, the words emerged with toneless reluctance. His eyes were steel points driven home with a warrior's force. "You have changed."

Travis did not try to deny it. "There was a priest among the prisoners at the mine."

Damon's gaze was careful. "He touched your heart?"

"His words," Travis replied slowly, "were all that saved me."

Damon was silent a long moment, his gaze searching the shimmering heat. "My father's people were called the Salassi. You have heard of them?"

"No." Travis hunkered down alongside the warrior. Such occasional tales deserved his full attention, as these fragments were often all they had of name and heritage, and thus were guarded jealously.

"Our people ruled mountain valleys north of Italy, or so the story was told to me. Our rite of passage was a successful raid on passing caravans. Then the Roman armies came, I don't know when. Before I was born. They warred with us, one village at a time, one valley after another. My father and my mother were rounded up with the other survivors and sold into slavery. He was trained as a blacksmith, my father, and after many years of hard labor earned his freedom. He worked as supplier to the local legion, and they took me on."

"So you became a soldier."

Damon nodded. "There was a general, a man of worth. One of the Praetorian Guard, who had earned his title through valor and not with a full purse. He was a friend of Constantine, and yet sought to be a friend to his men as well. I marveled at this, and at his desire to tell us of what this Christianity meant to him." Damon looked over at Travis. "You have heard the story of the centurion who met Jesus on the road and asked for a healing for his child?"

"No."

"Then I shall share it with you," Damon said, rising to full height. "When this danger is behind us."

Travis followed the warrior's gaze, felt his gut tighten at the sight of Brutus stepping into the hazy sunlight. The chained and bedraggled Hanno tugging at his sleeve spotted Travis, and pointed. The reaction was instantaneous.

With a gesture as swift as lightening, Hanno was tossed aside. Loathing and rage and shock raced across Brutus' features. Travis stepped forward to meet him.

"You." The jutting forehead fell to a nose pointed downwards like a plumb line. Sensuous lips were offset by the chin of a fighter, aggressively strong. Yet the voice was as soft as the eyes. "I should have known."

"Hello, brother." Of all the encounters Travis had dreamed of, nothing could have prepared him for this. Yet his sense of calm remained both powerful and all-pervading. The danger was real and here and stalking him, yet kept at a distance by some impenetrable shield.

The lithe body lowered into the wrestler's crouch, the feet beginning a softly tracking dance. "You have come with a contingent of guards, a bevy of watchers." The gray eyes flitted, fastened upon Raffa. "Yes, of course, there is your little friend now."

"Only three, I have come with only three," Travis replied, refusing to give in to the urge to crouch himself, and thus begin the wary dance of death. "I have something for you."

"Yes, and I for you." Brutus slapped the long-bladed knife strapped to his hip. "You and I will depart this earth together."

Travis dipped into his robe, came out with the unsealed letter, tossed it into the dirt at his brother's feet. "Read it."

The gesture caught Brutus off guard. "What form of ruse is this?"

"A confession. Written by your friend Titus Octavian, and in his own hand. This is a copy, one for you to keep. I have others." When Brutus made no move, his tone sharpened. "Read!"

Reluctantly his brother lowered a hand, picked it up, backed up a pace, warned, "There are a dozen men about this plaza, brother. Legionnaires under my orders. Here to arrest the kidnapper of the prelate Titus Octavian. A false move, and your end shall rush up to meet you."

"That is the last threat," Travis replied quietly, "you shall ever deliver."

Disconcerted by the calm, Brutus unfolded the skin. A feral snarl drew back his teeth as he read. Furiously he cast the letter aside. "Lies!"

"Go back to Rome," Travis replied. "Retire from intrigue and treachery. You have no choice."

"No choice!" Brutus laughed, a short bark like the sound of a hunting dog in the night. "Little brother, what shred of proof do you have?"

"The bay," Travis replied, searching within for the heat and rage that he had expected ever since learning of their betrayal. "A wide beach where we dug the pits and buried the mollusks to render the royal purple dye."

"You speak nonsense."

"White sand rising from the deep waters," Travis persisted, finding only an ancient weariness within himself, for the years of pain, for the memories that had dogged him all his life, for the evil that this man fed upon. "Curving out and around like two encircling arms. Almost meeting, but not quite. A natural harbor."

"You have been touched by the sun," Brutus said, uncertain now. "Perhaps the mine has addled your brain."

"A gathering place for the forces you and Titus and the other traitors were assembling," Travis continued. "Far from any town and spying eyes. A seagoing force, ready to attack the empire once the present civil wars had destroyed the legions. When the victor was rendered too weak to defend against an unexpected assault." Travis waited for another protest, and when none came, he pressed on. "Not all the emperor's generals are Christian, are they? Many would be delighted to see a return to the old ways, an end to this new religion and all it represents. You yourself care nothing for any gods, new or old. But it was as good a basis as any to fuel your rise in power." Travis pointed at the letter in the dirt. "This is but a portion of the news we will bear to the emperor's camp, if you do not return to Rome."

The hate blazing from Brutus' swollen features was a force as strong as the sun. "And you? What concern could a feebleminded country oaf like you have for the matters of gods and empires?"

"I have heard," Travis replied slowly, "the message of Christian faith."

"Faith!" The laugh was shrill with rage. "Listen to me, little brother, and I will share with you the secret of this world. Life and faith and allegiance are words empty of meaning. They always were, and always will be. All that matters is power and pleasure. Join with me, and I will show you what the words truly mean. Pleasures and wealth and power beyond your wildest dreams."

"There is nothing you can give me that interests me at all," Travis replied, "save the knowledge that I will never have to see you again."

The shoulders slumped, the lithe wrestler's body wilted in defeat. "What choice do I have?"

"None," Travis said. Taking a step toward the square's center. Another.

As Travis expected, the deflation was only pretense, a ruse to cover the hand dropping and grasping the knife hilt. In a sweeping motion Brutus unsheathed his knife and flung himself forward, his entire body behind the movement, extending his reach farther than Travis would have thought possible. Even though he had been ready, hoping for submission but half-expecting the attack, still Travis was almost caught by the razor-edge blade as it swept out and around and back. Brutus pounced a second time, moving with the speed of an enraged cat, missing by a hair's breadth. He stalked Travis as he continued his backwards scramble out farther and farther into the suddenly emptied square. On the border stood Raffa and Damon and Gaven and now a squad of legionnaires, six of them or seven, Travis had no time to count, gathered to one side, massed together as though conferring over the fight, staying well away.

Another pounce, the blade sweeping close enough to shred the cloth over his chest. Travis allowed himself to fall to one hand as he continued his retreat, recovering and tossing up a cloud of dust. Brutus responded with a cruel laugh. "Frightened, little brother? Do you see the hand of death holding the blade? You should."

Another step back, and with a sense of both triumph and relief Travis felt the uneven central stones beneath his feet. Righting himself from his backwards-leaning crouch, he unsheathed his own blade.

"Ah, finally, finally, you remembered what it was there hanging by your side." Brutus weaved, and with each movement sought to catch the sun's rays and reflect them back into Travis' eyes. "Pity it will prove so useless."

Travis said nothing, held his guard a notch too low, allowed his foot to stumble on one of the rounded dust-covered stones. Brutus leapt, plunged. But Travis had slipped away, again sliding on the uneven stones. Again moving backward another pace. "What, little brother, still suffering from the poison's effect?" The laugh was little more than a snarl. "Pity it did not finish you and that old man off as I intended."

Travis shook his head, a quick gesture to flick aside the gathering sweat, but it was enough. Brutus lunged again, this time the knife aimed high and straight for the heart. Suddenly Travis' weakness was gone, replaced by speed and strength, so much of both that Brutus was caught totally by surprise and off balance, overly committed to a thrust that had missed, his weight too far forward, unable to draw back. Travis dropped his knife and spun on one heel, grabbing Brutus' knife-wrist in one steel grip and the shoulder with another, swinging Brutus with him, around and across the central stones, tripping him and flinging him up and over the lip of the well.

Brutus screamed shrilly, the sound echoing up and out until it cut off abruptly with a resounding thud. Raffa and the others rushed across the plaza, gathered by the well, looked down into its gloomy depths.

A soft groan echoed up from below. "Lower me," Raffa urged. "Let me finish him off."

Travis looked across the well, his chest heaving, shook his head once.

"As long as he is alive, he will be a threat," Raffa insisted.

"And I am telling you to leave him," Travis said, straightening with effort. He looked at the legionnaires. "He is your charge, you see to him."

One soldier looked from the dark maw to Travis and back, said doubtfully, "We were ordered to arrest you if you survived."

"I would not," Raffa said softly, "advise you to try."

Travis stopped him with an upraised hand, asked the soldier, "Is my brother a magistrate now as well?"

"No."

"Then how do you come to follow his orders of arrest?" A fleeting look of bitterness was his reply. "These are strange times," Travis said in placation, "when a citizen can be taken on the whim of another."

"Strange indeed," the soldier agreed, his attention caught by another groan from the well. "Very well, you are free to go."

Travis moved away. Once clear of the central well, he motioned to Damon, and said, "Fetch the servant Hanno. Take him to a blacksmith and have him released from his fetters. Then bring him to the house of Nathaniel."

"I hear and obey, sire," Damon replied, and for the first time gave a centurion's salute before turning away.

As they walked back toward the city gate, Raffa grumbled, "First the slave of Fabian, and now Brutus himself you allow to slip through your clutches. Such vermin should be crushed."

Because it was Raffa, Travis sought to shrug off the fight's aftermath. "I have discovered different answers to the questions of life. Ones I never dreamed possible."

Raffa inspected him. "It is this Christian sect?"

"Not a sect," Travis replied. "A new world, a new life which beckons mightily."

The warrior mulled that over as they passed under the tall city portals and started down the paved thoroughfare. Great columns lined the thoroughfare, casting stark rails of light and shadow across their way. "Because it is you who speaks these words," Raffa finally said, "I would seek to know more."

"When I know the words," Travis replied, "I will share them with you."

CHAPTER XXIV

Their meal was a silent affair, quieted by the somber man seated at the far end. Lydia tried hard to hold to her own joy, yet was subdued by each glance in her father's direction. Hannibal had greeted their return with a moment's delight, then subsided—not into grief, but rather into a grave and determined silence.

Lydia's gentle gaze followed Hannibal as he rose from the table. He left the chamber not speaking a word, nor meeting anyone's eyes. When he was gone, she said to Travis, "I am so worried for him. If only he would recover."

"I am not sure," Travis replied, "that recovery is the proper word."

"What do you mean?"

He grasped her hands with his, unconcerned with the glances and the smiles from about the table. "He seems more resolute than afflicted."

"Perhaps." A trace of her impishness returned. Lydia lowered her voice, asked, "What did Pherenice say to you before we left the cloister?" She held tight to his hands when he tried to draw back. "Don't deny it. I saw her take you to one side. What did she say?"

"I told her about Inigo, the old priest in the mines. She has decided to issue an imperial decree in her own name to have him freed and brought to the cloister." Travis did not attempt to mask his pleasure at the memory. "He is a very good man."

"Then we shall both have reason to return from time to time. That is good." She paid no mind as the others rose and left the chamber, granting them privacy. "That was not all Pherenice told you."

"No."

"Tell me."

"She said she was glad I came." He studied the beautiful face before him, decided to tell her all. "She said it had wrenched her heart to hear you cry through the nights."

For an instant the joy and the love were overshadowed, like ripples of unseen winds marring the reflection upon a pool's surface. With visible effort Lydia gathered herself, whispered, "I missed you so."

"She asked me to remind you," Travis went on, "of Christ's example. How He retreated to the mountaintop to pray, then returned to service within the world."

She nodded slowly, her attention drawn to the empty doorway. She looked at him in mute appeal. "Speak with Father."

"What should I say?"